DEATH
AT THE
SCOTTISH
BROCH

DEATH
AT THE
SCOTTISH
BROCH

A MIA REID, ARCHAEOLOGIST, MYSTERY

ROSE KERR

LEVEL
BEST BOOKS

Author Photo Credit: Dawn Stafford

First edition

ISBN: 978-1-68512-802-9

Cover art by Level Best Designs

This book was professionally typeset on Reedsy.
Find out more at reedsy.com

For Gary

Praise for Death at the Scottish Broch

"*Death at the Scottish Broch* is an action-packed mystery that begins with danger on a Canadian university campus and propels the reader forward to an archaeological dig on the starkly beautiful Isle of Skye. The intrepid Mia Reid comes face to face with the death of a beloved colleague while she works tirelessly to unearth clues to his murder. With valuable artifacts, sparkling gems, intrigue, and the possibility of a newly rekindled romance, this is a series to watch!"—Paula Charles, author of Hometown Hardware Mysteries

"A well-written, and plotted story rich with interesting and entertaining facts about archaeology. *Death at the Scottish Broch* is brimming with intrigue and escapades that take you from Lakeview, Canada to Scotland and will have you hunting for clues along with Mia."—Christina Romeril, author of the Killer Chocolate Mysteries

"The latest addition to the venerable world of archaeological mysteries, Rose Kerr's *Death at the Scottish Broch* is sure to delight. Canadian academic Mia Reid heads to Scotland's storied Isle of Skye to uncover ancient secrets with an old friend and colleague. But the questions threaten to bury her before she's over her jetlag. Juggling admirable loyalty and responsibility to the university students now under her care, Mia works administrative magic to salvage the threatened excavation. And becomes entrenched in dangerous modern mysteries of the murderous kind. Old legends, international intrigue, mysteries of the heart, and seamless plotting kept me turning the pages."—Mary Feliz, author of the Maggie McDonald Mysteries

"The author did a great job in staging this whodunit with a well-written and fast-paced mystery that I could not put down until all was said and done. The drama had plenty of suspects and clues were sprinkled throughout for Mia to dig up and piece together. The narrative was visually descriptive, and I felt I was part of the non-stop action as Mia and her friends sought the identity of the perpetrators. There were several twists and turns, especially when I thought I knew who was behind the caper, and yet once the author changed directions it became clear that a better story and motive lay with another suspect. Overall, a terrific start to this new series."—Dru Ann Love, 2017 Raven Award, 2024 Macavity, Anthony, and Agatha Winner, Author Champion, Book Advocate

Chapter One

Mia pedaled her bike through Lakeview City's rush hour traffic. Motorists sped along the road, some dangerously close to the lane markers. Her thoughts were on the day ahead. Her last day before heading out to Scotland for a dig. This year had been a challenge. She loved working with students at the university, but the politics involved with academia didn't sit well with her.

Mia checked her side-view mirror and made the turn off University Avenue. She noticed a large black SUV following her. As she arrived at the Lakeview University building housing the Department of Archaeology, the SUV surged forward, cutting her off. She braked hard and flew over her bike. The vehicle stopped, and two men jumped out.

She struggled to stand as one of the men picked up her daypack. The other man grabbed Mia by the arm and pulled her to her feet.

"I'm fine. Let me go." Mia yanked her arm away from him. "My daypack, please." She held out her hand for the pack, but the man holding it ignored her.

"I'm sorry, miss. Our driver was following too closely. I hope you're not hurt."

Mia took off her helmet, adjusted her glasses, and rolled her neck from side to side. "Nothing's broken." She glanced at her hands and winced at the scrapes.

The man continued speaking, "Your bike's damaged. Let me give you money to repair it."

He pulled out a wallet, fat with cash. "Please, we don't want any trouble.

It'll cost this much to replace the wheel." He thrust three one-hundred-dollar bills into Mia's hands.

"It won't be that much. I can take care of repairing my bike." She glared at the man holding her daypack. "My pack, now."

The man holding her daypack nodded at his companion.

"Please miss. Take the money." He raised his hands and walked away. His companion gave Mia her daypack, and they hurried to their vehicle and left.

Mia raised her hand to her head. The sidewalk appeared to sway back and forth. She sat on the curb, taking stock of what had happened. Her bike's front tire was pushed in, and some of the spokes were broken. Her khaki pants were shredded at the knees, and her palms scraped. She dropped her head to her knees, and the wave of dizziness passed as quickly as it had come on. Mia heard footsteps running on the sidewalk.

Two students stopped to help her. "Wow, who was that?" The male student picked up Mia's bike.

The woman kneeled by Mia. "Professor Reid, can I give you a hand?"

Mia blinked her eyes. "Diana. Yes, I'd appreciate some help."

Diana held out her hand and helped Mia up. "Did you know them?"

"No. They cut me off. Then they stopped and gave me money to fix the tire. Jim, how many of the spokes are damaged?"

Jim glanced at the tire. "I'd say at least two-thirds are toast. Unless you have a spare tire, you won't be biking home tonight."

"I'll call the bike repair shop down the road. They might fix it today. Thanks for stopping, you two. I appreciate the help."

Jim hefted Mia's bike over his shoulder. "Nothing major today. We're just wrapping up before summer break. We'll help you get your bike in."

Mia limped her way into the building, Diana carried Mia's daypack, and Jim handled her bike. By the time they reached Mia's office, her hands were throbbing.

Jim leaned her bike against the wall. "I don't mind helping you get your bike to the shop."

"Thanks, Jim. I should be all right."

"Do you have disinfectant you can use on your hands? They must hurt."

Diana placed Mia's daypack on the visitor's chair.

"There's a first aid kit in my cupboard. Again, thank you both for your help. I appreciate it."

The students left, and Mia dropped in her desk chair. Ugh, not how she wanted to start her day. She grabbed her first aid kit and made her way to the bathroom.

Back at her desk, Mia turned on her computer. She called the bike shop and left a message. Opening her email account, she saw an urgent message from Ethan Carter. Mia was meeting him at the dig on the Isle of Skye in Scotland tomorrow evening.

She opened the email.

> *Mia, forgive the brevity of this message. I've made an amazing discovery! The broch we've been working on has given us treasure.*
>
> *I've found what I think is a ceremonial dagger and a ring. Both could belong to a person of wealth. I've attached photos.*
>
> *The local historical society is excited about the finds and is bringing in the press.*
>
> *And I'm not sure, but I think I'm being followed. If anything should happen to me, remember our undergrad years. Be careful.*
>
> *Can't wait to see you this week. We have much to talk about.*
>
> *Ethan*

Mia opened the attachment. The handle of the dagger appeared to be metal with a design, and it had a short, serrated blade. It could be a sgian-dubh, a small single-edged knife that was worn as part of traditional Highland dress. The ring appeared to have gemstones surrounding an enormous center stone.

Mia pursed her lips and enlarged the photo. She couldn't see all the details. Printing it might help to see them clearly.

Before she could hit print, her office line rang.

"Dr. Reid here."

"Please hold for Dr. Bateman."

She didn't have long to wait. "Could you come to my office in twenty minutes? I have a matter we need to discuss."

"I'll be there."

"See you shortly." Dr. Bateman hung up.

Mia puzzled for a moment. Why did the dean need to see her? She was cleared for the dig, and she'd completed her curriculum for fall semester classes. Frowning, she turned her attention to her email program and forwarded Ethan's message to her personal account. She hit print, then hurried to the printer room.

Mia grabbed the photo and returned to her office. She used a magnifying glass to look at the details. The photo was still too grainy. She put the glass away, picked up the photo and the copy of Ethan's email, and tucked them in her daypack.

She glanced at her torn pants. It wouldn't do to meet with Dr. Bateman looking like this. She had a second set of clothing in her closet for emergencies. Black dress pants, a white shirt, and a black blazer would have her looking professional.

Mia quickly changed her clothes and took a few minutes to deal with her long, wavy hair. She pulled it back and braided it. Her palms were still red and scraped from her fall. Her knees were sore, but fortunately, the skin wasn't broken. Checking the time, she took her daypack and laptop and locked them away in the cupboard behind her desk. She hurried out of her office and locked the door. She had minutes to make it to her meeting with Dr. Bateman.

Dr. Bateman's administrative assistant, Lottie Myers, looked up as Mia stopped at her desk.

"Dr. Bateman is expecting me."

"Just knock on the door before entering."

Mia complied with the request.

"Ah, Dr. Reid. Good, we can start." Dr. Bateman rose and walked around to the front of the desk.

Mia glanced at the man occupying one of the chairs. She hadn't expected to see Christopher Wilson at the meeting. She took the chair next to him.

Dr. Bateman put his glasses on and leaned against his desk. "I asked Dr. Wilson to be at this meeting. Let me get straight to the point. I've received word the department will have funds for one professor for the next academic year. You and Christopher are the two best candidates. A decision will be made next month with input from other members of this department." Dr. Bateman raised his hand as Christopher Wilson started to say something. "Please let me finish. I know this is irregular, but you're both strong candidates. Mia, I understand you're away on a dig in Scotland for part of the summer?"

"That's correct. I leave tonight."

"And Christopher, you're working locally?"

"Yes, I'm working on the Lakeview Islands."

Dr. Bateman nodded. "Right. I expect to see you both at the fundraiser tonight at the Lakeview Museum. Members of the committee will be in attendance and will speak to you both individually."

Mia adjusted her glasses. "Do you know when this will take place? I have to be at Pearson airport by nine-thirty."

"I'll make certain the committee members speak with you as soon as possible. I'll notify them of your timeline."

"Is this an interview with the committee?" Mia asked.

"No, it's an opportunity for them to speak with you informally." Dr. Bateman stood.

"Sir, I need to speak to you about a personal matter," Christopher Wilson said.

Mia rose from her chair. "I'll leave you to it. I have a few things to take care of this morning. Thank you for letting us know about the changes. I'll see you both this evening." Mia walked out of the dean's office.

Lottie looked up as Mia walked by her desk. "Is the meeting finished? I need to speak with Dr. Bateman."

"Dr. Wilson is still with him." Mia turned to close the door but stopped when she heard what Christopher was saying.

"Was that necessary?" Christopher asked Dr. Bateman.

"Yes, it was. You have the position, but I had to let her know about the process. I'll make certain the members of the committee talk with her tonight. Their questions will be tough ones, and she won't make the grade."

Lottie hurried to close the door. "Did you need something, Dr. Reid?"

Mia balled her hands into fists and felt her legs tremble. How dare they? The committee had made their decision. What was the point of talking with them tonight? Mia took a deep breath and let it out slowly. She gathered her thoughts, telling herself to calm down. She wasn't sure she was happy here. Maybe the decision would be made for her.

"Dr. Reid, was there anything else?" Lottie asked.

"No, thank you. I need to get back to my office."

Mia arrived at her office to find the door open. "I know I locked it before I left," she muttered.

Papers were strewn on the floor. She hurried to her desk; the computer was blinking with an alert message. One more wrong attempt would lock it down. She crouched by her cupboard where she had stored her laptop and daypack. The cupboard was intact. She glanced over her shoulder at the door. Was an intruder in the area waiting for her?

Grabbing her desk phone, she called security.

"Security, Mathews here."

"This is Dr. Reid. I was out of my office for a meeting, and when I returned, my door was open, and my office searched. Could someone come up here?"

"Not a problem. I'll send Lewis over. Your office number again?"

"I'm in the east wing, third floor, room twenty-one."

"Right, Lewis will be there shortly."

Mia hung up and carefully looked around the office. She didn't want to touch anything. Nothing appeared to be missing, but it would take a while to sort through the papers. Mia sighed. What else could go wrong today? She nudged her glasses up the bridge of her nose.

"Dr. Reid? I'm Lewis, from Security." A lean man with graying hair stood in the doorway.

"Lewis, thanks for getting here quickly."

"What happened?" Lewis's face was creased with age, but when he walked into the office, it was with a strong, confident stride.

Mia told him what she had found when she returned from her meeting. "And you're sure you locked the door?"

"Yes. I have artifacts in my cupboards I use for teaching. When I leave my office, I always lock it up."

"I heard you took a tumble on your bike this morning."

Mia frowned. "Who told you that?"

Lewis walked to the cupboards and crouched to look at the locks. "Diana and Jim were chatting about it when they walked by the desk. I asked them how you were. They said you seemed shaken up."

"Do you think this has something to do with my accident this morning?"

"Well, you tell me. What are you working on?" Lewis stood.

"Nothing. My classes are over. I leave for Scotland tonight to work on a dig."

"Is anything missing?"

"Not that I can see."

"And did they access your computer?"

"I locked my laptop in the cupboard, and it's fine. The desktop had a last-attempt warning. Whoever it was didn't have my password and didn't want to lock the computer down."

Lewis walked back to the office door. "These doors are so old it wouldn't take an expert to open them. There are a few scratches that look fresh."

"Is your department able to do anything while I'm away?"

"We can monitor the office. I'd suggest you change your password on your desktop, store any valuables the school might need, like the artifacts, in the department's lockup, and keep electronic copies of important documents."

"Thanks, Lewis. I'll get those things done today. I have most of my important documents saved on the cloud and on several external drives."

"Sounds good. Sorry to see the mess here, but it tells us something."

"What's that?"

"It tells us the intruder was careless and wanted you to know someone had been in your office."

Mia leaned back against her desk and watched him leave. She shook her head. Given what she'd learned from Dr. Bateman, she had to clean up her office and her computer. She prioritized the rest of her day. First on her list was connecting with Ethan about his finds. She composed an email.

Ethan, Exciting finds! I'm looking forward to seeing them and you. I'll be in Skye by suppertime tomorrow. One of my students is traveling with me. Stay safe. Mia

That done, she focused on getting her office sorted and organized. Mia had been working steadily for forty minutes when her cell phone rang.

"Mia Reid."

"Hi, this is Ben from Cycle World. You called about a damaged tire?"

Mia explained the situation.

"When can you bring it by?"

Mia glanced at her sturdy Timex watch. It was getting close to lunchtime. "I can be there in an hour or so."

"Perfect. See you then."

Mia texted Alex Bennett, her closest friend.

M: Have to take bike to shop. Want to meet for lunch at Noodles around noon?

A: I'll be there.

M: Chat then.

Mia filed the papers and transferred the digital files to her external drive. She opened her email program and emailed her travel arrangements to her travel folder. That completed, she turned her attention to the mess in the office. Forty-five minutes later, Mia unlocked the cupboard and took out her daypack. She tucked the photos Ethan had sent her in with her laptop and slung the pack over her shoulder. She picked up her bike and left.

Chapter Two

The clerk at Cycle World told Mia her bike would be ready by three that afternoon. Mia left the shop and walked toward the restaurant. She had plenty of time before meeting Alex. She stopped in front of a shop displaying dresses and shoes in the window. Alex was always telling her she should update her wardrobe. These dresses were pretty, and the colors were something she'd wear: subtle greens and blues. The sleeveless dresses worked for the summer, but were they practical? Did they suit her needs? Mia sighed. Maybe that was the problem. She didn't think about clothes as something other than a means to a need. She needed to wear clothing, so she made sure it was practical and useful. Being pretty wasn't high on her list of requirements. She certainly wouldn't need any of them this summer at the dig. Cargo pants, long-sleeve shirts, T-shirts, sweaters, and the occasional pair of shorts were all she'd need.

She glanced to the side and, in the store's window, noticed the reflection of a man watching her. He was on the other side of the street and looked like one of the men who had cut her off this morning. What was this guy doing? Was he following her? Suddenly, she didn't feel comfortable and remembered Ethan's warning that he was being followed. Could this have anything to do with Ethan's discovery?

Mia made a show of looking at her watch and hurried down the street. The restaurant was only a block away. She waited at the corner for the light to change and casually glanced behind her. The man had followed her to the corner.

The light changed, and Mia moved with the crowd of pedestrians. A horn blasted through the air. Someone was impatient. Mia crossed the street and stepped aside to see what was happening. A black SUV was blocking the intersection, and Mia saw the man who had been following her hurry to the vehicle. The SUV surged ahead, and Mia recognized the men in the front seat from her mishap of this morning. They appeared to be arguing about something.

Mia walked into Noodles and waited for the hostess.

"Dr. Reid, hi. Nice to see you again." The hostess picked up a menu.

"Hi, Trish. Could I get a booth for two?"

"Sure can. Follow me." The hostess took another menu and walked across the restaurant. "How's this?"

"Perfect. Alex will join me soon. Could I have a large water and a diet Pepsi?"

"Not a problem. I'll have your server bring it to you shortly."

Mia took her phone and checked her emails. Ethan had sent her a brief message.

> *Mia, I'll meet you at the B&B. Looking forward to catching up. I'm going to check on the site after dinner tonight. Be vigilant and safe travels.*
>
> *Ethan*

Mia heard footsteps coming toward her. She looked up and saw Alex trotting across the room.

"Hi there. Sorry, I'm late! Couldn't help it. Had to deal with a pompous politician this morning, and he wouldn't listen to anything any of us had to say." Alex grinned. Her green eyes crinkled at the corners as she slid into the booth across from Mia. Alex dropped her monstrous purse that held what she deemed essential for her day on the seat.

"Dare I ask which pompous politician?"

"Hmm, you know I can't tell. But he's not one of my favorite people." Alex was an educational psychologist and worked in the Ministry of Education offices.

The server arrived with Mia's drinks.

"Could I have a diet Pepsi and my usual lunch? Spaghetti Bolognese, regular garlic bread," Alex said.

"And Dr. Reid, for you?"

"I'll have the risotto and cheesy garlic bread."

Alex waited until the server had left. "What happened to your bike?"

Mia grimaced and filled her in on her eventful morning.

Alex's eyebrows rose as Mia spoke. "Wow, you've had a day. What are you going to do about work?"

Mia sighed. "I'm not sure I'm cut out for the academic world. I enjoy working in the field a lot."

Alex shrugged. "Something else might turn up this summer. You know Lakeview Museum would love to have you on staff."

"I know. I'm not sure where I want to focus my energies."

"You leave for Scotland tonight?" Alex changed the subject.

"I do. One of my students is coming along. Diana Scott's meeting me at Pearson airport. She's excited about the dig. And I heard from Ethan this morning. He's discovered a few things."

The server arrived with their meals, and Mia waited until she left. Then, she told Alex about Ethan's discovery.

"Wow, that sounds exciting! Does he know how old they are?"

"He didn't say."

Alex swallowed her spaghetti. "Remind me again, what's the place you're working on?"

Mia smiled. "You mean the broch?"

Alex nodded.

"It's a round tower made of stone. They're only found in Scotland. And this one is about two thousand years old!" Mia leaned forward. "It could have been used as a defense from raiders, as a lookout, or as a place for people or animals to stay." Mia took a drink. "Some have roofs, and some don't. This one doesn't. We're excited to see what we're going to find there!"

"Sounds like it's exactly what you enjoy working on."

"I do. And I want to say thanks again for keeping an eye on Gran and my condo. I appreciate you doing this."

"No worries. I enjoy spending time with your Gran. And I'll make sure your mail's taken care of." Alex took a drink of Pepsi. "What are you wearing to the fundraiser?"

"My one and only black dress. I'll jazz it up with jewelry and some nice shoes."

"Honestly, Mia! You need to invest in some decent clothes. You're not a grad student anymore."

"I know. I hate shopping, and I keep putting it off. I promise I'll go shopping when I get back." Mia paused for a moment. She wasn't sure if she should tell Alex about the man who had followed her.

"What are you thinking about?" Alex asked.

"It's probably nothing."

"Well, something's bothering you. What is it?"

"I was window shopping on my way here, and I thought one of the men who cut me off this morning was following me."

Alex sat back, her eyes wide. "I can't believe you were window shopping. Which store?"

"I don't know. I just remember the dresses in the window. They were sleeveless and had a wrap thing going on. Aren't you worried about the guy following me?"

"Did you get a good look at them this morning?"

"One of them. The one who kept giving me the money. The other guy was holding my daypack."

"Well, unless you plan on taking this to the police, I'm not sure what to suggest."

"I'm not going to the police. There's no point. Probably just a coincidence."

The talk moved on to generalities until the server arrived with their bill.

"Let me take care of this. You're helping me out with Gran." Mia paid the bill, and they walked out of the restaurant.

On the sidewalk, Alex gave Mia a hug. "You be careful. Keep in touch with me every day. A simple text is all I need. If you don't, you'll have Gran and me after you."

"I will. Promise. Thanks again for your help."

* * *

The rest of the afternoon sped by. Mia organized the delivery of a box of her belongings to her condo. After picking up her bike, she got home with no mishaps. A quick stop at the concierge desk to let them know about her travel plans and that Alex would check her mail and condo. She asked them to deliver the box from the university when it arrived.

An elevator ride to the fourteenth floor got her home. She hung her bike on the rack in the utility room.

The kitchen was a few short steps away. Mia glanced in it as she walked down the hall to her bedroom. She was grateful she'd cleaned up the kitchen before going to work. One less thing to do. Mia dropped her daypack on the chair in her bedroom and opened her walk-in closet. The closet was one of the reasons she'd bought the condo. It had a large wall of drawers, an island, several hanging rods, and there was a window looking out on the lake. The closet led to a sumptuous ensuite with a steam shower and a deep stand-alone tub. The clothes she needed for the dig were already in their packing cubes. While she checked her packing list, she made a quick call to her gran.

"Hi, Gran. Just calling to see how you're doing." Mia put her phone on the nightstand and set it to speaker. At eighty, Marie Tremblay, Mia's maternal grandmother, showed no signs of slowing down. She was active in many of Lakeview's arts and cultural groups and had only recently stepped down from the board of directors with the city's cultural center.

"Mia, good to hear from you. I'm just getting ready to go out. Will I see you at the fundraiser at the Lakeview Museum tonight?"

"Yes. I should be there in less than an hour. Why are you going tonight?"

"The Museum's board of directors wants me to sit on the board. They're sending a car for me in about an hour. I expect I'll have an escort most of the evening, but I would like to see you."

"That would be great. I'm leaving for Scotland tonight. I'll be working with Ethan Carter on a dig on the Isle of Skye."

"I remember." Gran chuckled. "Are you all packed?"

"Just a few things left to finish up. I have to be at the airport by nine-thirty. I'll be leaving from the fundraiser. It'll be great to work with Ethan again. It's been over a year since we saw each other." Mia added the packing cubes to her large backpack. Now she just needed her toiletries and a jacket.

"How are you getting to the airport?"

"There's a car picking me up at the fundraiser. I'm going to have to run and shower."

"See you soon. Love you."

"Love you too." Mia disconnected the call. She walked into the ensuite and turned on the jets in her shower. The quick shower refreshed her. She dried and straightened her hair.

Mia took her contacts out of their case and put them in. Some subtle makeup completed the look. She had to be professional and put together. After all, the committee might decide she was the better choice over Christopher Wilson. She snorted at that thought. Not likely. She just wanted to get this over with.

She pulled her black dress out of the closet and gave it a close look. The dress had been an expensive purchase six years ago. Made of lightweight wool, the dress hit just above the knees. A boatneck, three-quarter sleeves, and seams down the sides completed the design. She draped the dress over the chair in her bedroom and searched through her jewelry box. An art déco necklace and earrings would work with the dress.

A spritz of perfume, and then she zipped up her dress and added the jewelry. Slipping her feet into ballet flats, she grabbed her evening clutch and added cash, her ticket for the event, driver's license, university ID, lipstick, and phone. She closed her backpack, making sure her travel clothes and documents were packed at the top. Grabbing the pack, she stopped in front of the hallway mirror and gave herself an assessing look. She was happy with the results. Professional yet approachable. Mia's blue eyes appeared larger than normal with the application of mascara, liner, and shadow. "Hmm, I look good tonight. Alex is right. I need to update my wardrobe. A project

14

when I get back."

* * *

The Lakeview Museum had sold out the event tickets a few weeks ago. This summer fundraiser was an opportunity for the board to meet the public and encourage donations for their educational programs.

Mia saw her gran being escorted by an older gentleman. She thought the man looked familiar but couldn't place him. She raised her glass to her and smiled. Gran nodded in her direction, and the gentleman walked her to Mia.

"Gran, you look fabulous." Mia bent to kiss her on the cheek.

"Thank you, my dear. That necklace looks wonderful. And you are stunning. Charles Gordon, do you know my granddaughter, Dr. Mia Reid?"

"I do. My company's funding the dig she's working on this summer. Nice to see you again," Charles said.

"Are you on the museum's board?" Mia smiled, glad she could place him.

"Yes, and I'm doing my best to have your grandmother join our group. Her experience working with other boards would be invaluable to us."

Mia glanced at her Gran. Charles was laying it on thick. He'd better back off, or Gran would turn them down flat.

"I wonder, Charles, could you freshen my drink, please?" Gran asked.

"Of course."

Mia watched as he strode toward the bar. "Gran, be nice. You know they'd appreciate your help."

"Yes, I know, and I believe in what the museum is doing. I'll see what I can do to help. Now, tell me about this dig."

Mia took a sip of champagne. "I signed up for this one in January. Ethan suggested we work together this summer."

"And what's happening with your career at the university?" Gran put her hand under Mia's elbow as they walked around the exhibit featuring art made by Indigenous women from across Canada.

Mia frowned. "It's not going great." She explained what Dr. Bateman had told her and Christopher Wilson that morning. "I don't think I'm in line for the position."

"Anything I can do?" Gran asked.

Mia shook her head. "Thanks, but I doubt it. I know I can find work. Who knows, I may head to South America and work with Mom and Dad."

Gran chuckled. "I'm sure they'd love to have you with them. Try not to stress too much. Something will turn up."

Charles arrived with a fresh drink for Gran. "Here you go, Marie."

Gran smiled. "Thanks. I was just about to tell Mia something that may interest you as well. Have either of you heard rumblings about artifacts being sold at private auctions reaching astronomical prices?"

Mia shook her head. "No, I haven't."

Charles sighed. "I have. But I have no clue who's doing this."

Gran's lips closed together in a straight line. "I don't either. And I've been keeping my ear to the ground. The people involved aren't the antique dealers I worked with on Queen Street. People coming in from all over the world. And the auctions take place in private."

"How does this work?" Mia asked.

"Apparently, items are posted online and people apply for invitations to attend a special auction. I'm certain the artifacts are stolen property. Now, Mia, I need you to promise you'll be careful. The antiquities world is changing quickly, and I'm worried about you."

"I'm sorry to interrupt, but I have to take Marie to meet other board members." Charles took Marie's elbow.

"I'll touch base with you before I leave," Mia said to her grandmother.

Mia circulated in the crowd until Dr. Bateman arrived with several individuals who peppered her with questions about her background and experience. After being grilled for twenty minutes, they left her in peace. She checked her watch and saw she had enough time to grab a bite to eat before leaving for the airport.

After selecting some food from the buffet, she joined a couple of colleagues to talk about their summer plans. Mia noticed Dr. Bateman and Mr. Gordon having an animated discussion across the room. She wondered what that was all about. One of her colleagues asked her a question about the dig on the Isle of Skye. Mia answered her question, and then she excused herself to find Gran.

Mia found her, surrounded by some of her friends from the Arts Council.

"Gran, could I have a moment?"

"Mia, are you heading out?"

"Yes, I just wanted to say goodbye."

"How did the interview go with the committee?" Gran asked.

Mia shrugged. "Hard to tell. I answered their questions the best I could. I won't worry about it. This is out of my hands."

Gran smiled, "I have all the confidence in you. You'll keep in touch?"

"I will. A text or a phone call daily. Don't worry about me. Dad made sure I knew how to take care of myself in any situation. I've kept up with my martial arts training." Mia glanced around. "How are you getting home?"

"With Fran and Tom Esly. They live in the same building as I do. As a matter of fact, we're leaving in a few minutes."

"We'll talk soon." Mia hugged Gran and hurried to retrieve her things.

Chapter Three

Mia changed her clothes and removed her contacts before checking in at the international terminal at Pearson Airport. Diana was waiting for her to go through security. They picked up drinks and snacks while waiting to board their flight.

Once on the plane, Mia pulled out her eye mask and earbuds and took the blanket provided by the flight attendant. She hoped to sleep most of the flight. Diana, sitting next to her, mimicked her actions.

* * *

The flight to Glasgow was uneventful, and arrived slightly ahead of the scheduled time. Mia and Diana went through Immigration and then picked up their large backpacks from the luggage carousel. They breezed through Customs. They made a pit stop at the ladies' room. Mia washed her face, brushed her teeth, and tied her hair in a braid. She glanced at her watch. Just past noon in Scotland, and back home in Lakeview, it was after seven in the morning. Her stomach gurgled. She had to eat before leaving the airport.

Mia went out to wait for Diana and watched people go through the arrivals area. Two men walked by who looked exactly like the two men who'd run into her yesterday. What were the chances they were in Scotland at the same time as she was? Diana exited the washroom.

"That's strange. I thought I saw the two men who ran into me yesterday."

"Where?"

Mia pointed down the hall. "I'm sure it's just a coincidence. Or someone

18

who looked like them." Mia shrugged. "Anyway, I'd like to get some food before we leave. How about you?"

"Yes. I'm hungry. How long's the drive?"

"Depending on the traffic, about five or six hours. I wasn't sure we'd be able to make the ferry at Mallaig, so we're going to have to cross the bridge at Kyle of Lochalsh. There should be a coffee shop down here."

They found the coffee shop and placed their orders.

After eating their meal, Mia scanned her email but didn't see a new message or text from Ethan. She sent him a quick text letting him know she had arrived in Glasgow. And did the same with Alex and Gran. "Right then, let's find the car rental agency."

"Good day, miss. Do you have a reservation?" The rental agency clerk had a shock of red hair, freckles, and snapping blue eyes.

"Hi. Yes, I do." Mia pulled out her driver's license and credit card.

The clerk provided her with a form, and Mia filled in the required information.

"There you go, love. It's in slot eight in our car park. Have you driven in Scotland before?" The rental agency clerk held onto the car keys, almost as if he was afraid to give them to Mia.

Mia grinned. "I have. It'll take me a few minutes to remember the basics, but I'll be fine. I last visited the U.K. a year ago."

"Aye. Then it will work just grand for you." He handed her the keys and the information packet for the car.

Diana chuckled as they walked out of the airport. "I was afraid he wouldn't give you the keys."

"Driving on the left-hand side of the road can take some getting used to. And some people never get it."

Mia led the way to the car park. They found the car and dropped their backpacks in the trunk. Mia opened the car and sat for a few minutes, familiarizing herself with it. It was a small hatchback with a manual transmission.

"Okay, I need a few minutes to maneuver out of the airport and get on the right highway. Then I'll be fine." She entered the route to the car's GPS, and they started off.

The first part of the drive was on a highway that allowed them to move at a steady pace. Mia adjusted to driving on the left-hand side. There were parking areas along the road where drivers could pull over to check out the scenery or take a break. The two women chatted along the drive about what they expected from the summer. Diana hadn't been to Scotland before and had questions about the dig. Mia answered her questions with the information Ethan had given her.

She pulled into a parking area about two and a half hours into the drive. "I need a break from the road," she said as Diana looked around. The parking area was half full of cars and camper vans. On one side, a food truck was open. "I'm going to see if they have coffee at the truck."

"Sounds good. I could use something to eat."

They stepped out of the car and stretched. Mia's back was sore, and her head felt like it was full of cotton wool. Coffee would help with her head, and a break would help her back.

The woman at the food truck greeted them with a smile. At their request for coffee, she provided a variety of options. Mia chose a cappuccino and a sandwich. Diana selected an Americano with a pita sandwich. They walked back to the car and leaned against the hood to eat their food.

The scenery in front of them was spectacular. Dark, brooding mountains rose from the ground. They were in sharp contrast to the lush, green grass and blue river flowing in the distance. Diana reached into the car and pulled out her camera. She took several shots of the area and showed Mia the result.

"Wow, those are good. You got the mountains perfectly framed with the river running below them."

"Thanks. I love this camera. It's a good DSLR, and I picked it up secondhand. It takes excellent photos. I hope it'll work well on the dig."

"Oh, look over there, to the left." Mia pointed out the hairy cows that were native to Scotland. "They're called 'coos' here."

"I have to get a picture of those! And the sheep, where did they all come from?" Diana snapped photos. In the field across the road, sheep dotted the landscape.

After stretching a few more minutes, Mia glanced at her watch. "Ready to go?"

They threw their garbage in the bins and got in the car. "Not much farther to the bridge to cross to the Isle of Skye," Mia said.

As they drove, the mountains seemed to close in on the road. The vegetation was verdant, and the trees lining the road were in full leaf. Farther back from the road, pine trees stood tall and strong.

Approaching the village of Kyle of Lochalsh, Mia slowed the car, respecting the speed limit. The bridge to the Isle of Skye was a short crossing, less than two minutes.

Mia checked the GPS. It would be about an hour before they arrived at their B&B outside of Dunvegan. Mia noticed the arrows painted on the road directing drivers to stay in the correct lane. As they drove by villages, homes stood away from the road.

They left the main highway to get to the village of Dunvegan. Mia slowed down to maneuver the narrow, twisty roads. She had to pull off to the side when she met traffic coming toward them. They finally arrived at the B&B around six in the evening.

The B&B had beautifully landscaped grounds with flowers growing in beds and borders and a well-manicured lawn. Chairs and tables were scattered on the lawn. The B&B itself was a large three-story home, painted white with window boxes filled with pansies. There was a yellow door at the front of the house. Mia followed the driveway to the parking lot behind the B&B.

Mia stopped suddenly. There were two police cars, and uniformed officers were talking to several people.

Her heart pounded. "What's going on? Why are the police here?" They hurried out of the car.

At their arrival, two men dressed in civilian clothing turned toward them. With a start, Mia realized she recognized one of them. Luke Forbes. He and Mia had dated exclusively in grad school and lived together their last year at school.

Mia watched as Luke spoke to the man next to him and nodded in her direction. They walked toward her.

"Mia, it's Luke, Luke Forbes." Luke reached Mia and Diana and held out his hand to Mia.

"Luke, what are you doing here? I thought you were at the British Museum." Mia shook his hand.

"Dr. Mia Reid, I'd like to introduce you to Detective Inspector Anderson of Police Scotland."

DI Anderson leaned forward and shook Mia's hand. "Pleased to meet you."

"This is Diana Scott. One of my students from Lakeview University, in Lakeview City, Canada." Mia waited until they had finished with the introductions. "What's happened?"

"I'm afraid there's been a death at the dig," Anderson said.

Mia gasped and looked at Luke.

"Mia, I'm sorry. Ethan Carter's dead. The students found him at the site this morning. He suffered a blow to the head."

Mia's knees buckled. She leaned against the car and looked up at Luke. "That can't be. We were going to work together this summer. He was so excited about a find he'd made."

"I'm sorry, but it's true. We've been here since noon. It appears he returned to the dig last night after dinner. He either fell and hit his head, or someone hit him and left him there. When the students went to the dig this morning, they found him. They tried to revive him, but it was too late."

Mia's eyes filled with tears. "Oh no. Shelly's going to be devastated. Has anyone connected with her? She's Ethan's wife, and at their home in Chicago."

Anderson nodded. "I spoke with her earlier this afternoon. I'll let you check-in, and then I'd like to speak to you about Dr. Carter."

"Of course, I won't be long."

Mia and Diana grabbed their backpacks and walked into the B&B office. Mia struggled not to let the tears fall. How could Ethan be dead? He was one of the good guys. He loved his wife and little boy so much. She couldn't imagine how Shelly was going to deal with this. Henry, their son, had been sick with cancer, and now Ethan was gone. Mia bit back a sob.

A woman stood behind the desk. She had dark brown hair, green eyes, and wore a green sweater and brown pants.

"Good day, miss. I'm Bridget MacDonald. How can I be of assistance?"

"I'm Mia Reid, and this is Diana Scott. We have reservations."

"Of course. If I can have you sign in and a credit card, please?" Bridget turned a guest book toward Mia as she spoke.

Mia put her backpack on the floor and filled in the required information. She handed over her credit card and then looked around. It was a well-appointed office with all the technology needed to run a successful B&B. The wall behind the check-in desk had a large picture window overlooking the backyard. Bridget ran the credit card, then gave Mia a room key. "You're in room seven, a private room, as you requested. It's on the second floor. I'm afraid we don't have a lift."

Mia said, "That's not a problem. Thank you."

Diana filled in her information and waited for her key. She was sharing a room with the other female student.

Bridget waited until they'd finished. "Did you know Dr. Carter?"

Mia nodded her head, and tears fell on her cheeks. She choked back a sob. "We worked together almost every summer. His wife Shelly and their son Henry accompanied us most of the time."

"Oh, miss, I'm sorry to hear that. He was a nice man. Always with a smile on his face." Mrs. MacDonald came around the desk with a box of tissues. "Here, have a seat." Mia found herself gently pushed into a chair, wiping her face with a tissue.

"Thank you." Mia cleared her throat. "It's a shock. I was emailing him yesterday, and he was so excited."

Mrs. MacDonald nodded. "Yes, they found a sgian-dubh and a ring yesterday. The students were so excited by the find. And so was Dr. Carter. I heard him return from dinner last night. He wasn't in too long before he went out again. He told me he was going to the dig to check on something."

"His email had photos of the finds." Mia wiped her eyes. "We've worked together for so long. I can't believe he's really gone." Mia shook her head. "I'd better freshen up, the officer wants to speak to me."

"Aye. They've been here most of the day. That Detective Inspector and his friend showed up around noon."

"They're not from here?"

"No, miss. The constabulary in our village is usually good enough for us. But not in this case. DI Anderson arrived with Mr. Forbes in tow." Bridget sniffed. "At least they haven't put on airs. And have got right to work. They were fortunate I had space to give them a couple of rooms, as they expect to be here a few days."

"I'll be down soon. Diana, I'll let you know what's happening as soon as I can."

"Thanks, Professor. Will you be okay?"

"I will. I just need a few minutes."

They grabbed their backpacks and went to their rooms. Mia climbed to the top floor and unlocked her door. The room had a spacious window and overlooked the backyard. From this height, she could see the loch. Walls painted a soft blue made the room seem cozy and inviting. A double bed was covered in a blue and white quilt. Night tables bookended the bed. A navy wingback chair sat by the window and had a white afghan on it. Opposite the bed was a wooden chair and a desk. A free-standing armoire was next to the window. The room was complete with a small ensuite.

She placed her backpack on the floor and walked to the window to look outside. The uniformed police officers gathered around Anderson and Luke. Anderson appeared to be giving them instructions. Mia wondered if Ethan's body was still at the site. And what was Luke doing here? He hadn't given her any explanation. She shook her head and thought, *"I won't get answers sitting up here."*

She opened her backpack and took out her toiletries bag. A quick stop to use the facilities, and then she combed her hair and freshened her makeup. Mia changed out of her traveling clothes, grabbed a heavier sweater from her pack, and headed downstairs.

"Let's find out what happens next," Mia said as she met Diana, who was waiting by the front door.

Outside, a young man and woman greeted them.

"Professor Reid? Phil Brown, Professor Carter's grad student. I've been working with him for the last couple of years." Phil extended his hand.

Mia shook his hand and took stock of him. He appeared to be in his mid-twenties. He had short, black hair. His brown eyes were red-rimmed behind his glasses. His hands were rough and calloused. He was about six feet tall and lean, well under two hundred pounds.

"Phil. It's good to meet you. Ethan spoke of you often. He said you were excellent in the field. How are you doing?" Mia released his hand.

Phil cleared his throat. "Not great. I found him."

"I'm sorry to hear that. I still can't believe he's gone." Mia swallowed hard and blinked her eyes as they teared up.

The second student held out her hand. "I'm Rina Williams. I'm Professor Carter's other grad student."

"Rina, hello." Mia introduced Diana to the two students.

"What's going to happen? The police aren't saying anything," Phil said.

Mia sighed. "I don't know. I've never been involved in anything like this. Let me talk to the police, and we'll take it from there."

"Can we sit down, and you can tell me about the dig?" Diana asked.

"That's an excellent suggestion. I'll go talk to DI Anderson and see what I can learn."

Phil nodded. "Thanks. We'll be under the tree. There's a screened-in shelter from the midges there. Mrs. MacDonald has offered some cool drinks and some food as well. She's going to set it up soon."

"That's great. I'll get back to you as soon as I can." Midges were tiny, black, ferocious flies. Mia was glad the B&B had an outdoor area with a screened-in shelter.

She strode toward the police officers. Luke saw her coming and stepped away from the group.

"Are you ready to talk to us?"

"Yes. Can you tell me what happened?"

Luke led her to DI Anderson. "We'll answer your questions, I promise. Anderson is wrapping up with the officers."

Mia stood with Luke as Anderson finished giving the officers his orders.

They left, and Anderson turned to Mia. "Let's have a seat." He pointed to chairs near a fire pit.

Mia and Luke followed him. "How well did you know Dr. Carter?" Anderson asked.

"I've known him for the last twenty years. His wife, Shelly, and I were roommates at university. Ethan and I met as undergrads; he was in all my classes. We became good friends. I introduced Ethan to Shelly. Ethan works at the University of Chicago, and I'm with Lakeview University, but we met up frequently at conferences or worked together during school breaks. We spoke on the phone often."

"How would you describe his work ethic?"

Mia thought for a moment. "He was very thorough, methodical in the field. Respectful of the area. He spoke with the locals about the dig he was working on. Why are you asking?"

"Some artifacts are missing. The students mentioned two finds in recent days that were of great interest. One was a ring, the other a sgian-dubh. They're missing. Do you know anything about these?"

"Ethan sent me an email with photos of a ring and a sgian-dubh." Mia opened her email. "Here's the message. The photos are in the attachment." She gave her phone to Anderson.

"When did you receive this?" Luke asked.

"Yesterday morning. He was very excited about the find."

Luke nodded. "Where would he have stored these items?"

"There should be a secure locker at the dig. The artifacts would be there. If Ethan had any concerns, he would have stored them elsewhere. Maybe the B&B safe. Have you questioned the students and volunteers? They might know where they are."

"We have. None of them have seen either the ring or the sgian-dubh since yesterday afternoon." Anderson handed Mia her phone back and looked at Luke.

Luke nodded. "Mia, I don't work for the British Museum anymore. I'm working with Interpol in the AART department."

Mia narrowed her eyes. "What is AART?"

"Antiquities and Art Recovery Team. We recover stolen or missing artifacts and return them to the rightful owners. I've been with them for three years. I was in Glasgow for a conference when Anderson received the call about Ethan's death. He and I have been working together for the past month, tracking antiquities that have gone missing. He asked me to come along because Ethan's death could be tied to missing antiquities."

"Are you looking at Ethan's death as murder or an accident?"

"It's too early to tell yet. Our pathologists will examine the body for more information," Anderson said.

Mia frowned. "What aren't you telling me?"

Chapter Four

Luke cleared his throat. "Ethan sent me an email yesterday evening. I didn't see it until this morning. He said a couple had stopped by the dig on the weekend. The man was interested in what artifacts had been discovered. The woman walked around the dig, looking around. They didn't give their names, but last night, the woman was outside the pub waiting to talk to Ethan." Luke pushed his hair back. "She approached Ethan and said she'd heard they'd found a ring and wanted to buy it. He told her she was mistaken and that even if they had found something like that, it wouldn't be for sale. In his email, Ethan said she wouldn't stop pestering him about it. He finally told her to leave him alone and went into the pub to meet with the students. She followed him in."

"Where was the man?" Mia asked.

"He was seated at the bar in the pub. Ethan signed off by saying he was going to check on the dig."

Mia blew a breath out. "He sent me an email saying he was planning to go to the dig after dinner. Have you asked the students about this?"

"They confirmed Ethan spoke with a woman at the pub. He didn't tell them what they spoke about. And she joined the man at the bar. When Ethan left the students, he told them he was going to call Shelly. The students stayed at the pub until ten and didn't see him again last night. They said that wasn't unusual. The man and the woman left shortly after Ethan did."

Mia rubbed her forehead. "And Ethan went to the dig?"

Anderson answered. "Yes. His bed wasn't slept in at the B&B. We're still trying to find the missing pieces. Ethan may have tripped and fallen, or someone may have been at the dig and attacked him. We'll know more when the pathologists finish their report."

"Do you know what this man and woman looked like?"

"According to the students, the man was about six feet tall with short brown hair. He wore glasses and had a beard. He appeared to be in his forties. The woman had short black hair and was about five and a half feet tall. She seemed to be about the same age as the man. One student said they had a Canadian accent." Anderson closed his notebook.

Mia stood. "Where's Ethan's body now?"

"It's with the pathologists in Portree," Anderson said.

"Can I go to the dig and look around?" Mia asked.

"Yes, we'll go now. It's a short drive and we still have sunlight for a few hours," Luke said.

Mia picked up her sweater, checked her pockets for her phone and wallet. "Right, let's go. I'll let the students know I'll be back soon."

The drive to the dig took five minutes. When they arrived, Mia noticed the police presence protecting the scene. SOCO were wrapping things up and were packing their vehicle.

Anderson stopped the car and said, "Just wait a moment. I need to speak to the officers."

Mia and Luke stood by the car as he hurried to the SOCO team.

"When did you last speak to Ethan?" Luke asked.

"We chatted by email yesterday, but we had a video call about two weeks ago. He was getting ready to leave Chicago and had mixed feelings about leaving Shelly and Henry behind. Henry's six and has been ill with cancer. Ethan almost didn't come to the dig. Shelly insisted he come. Henry's last treatment was a few months ago, and he's been recovering well." Mia adjusted her glasses. "He's a strong kid, and Ethan wouldn't have come if he'd still been sick. Ethan mentioned he wanted to return home for a couple of weeks in the middle of the dig. I didn't have a problem with him doing that. Usually, Shelly and Henry showed up mid-dig to spend time with him. Henry loved playing at being an archaeologist." Mia's voice trembled.

Anderson waved them over.

Mia got her first look at the site. The broch was a round stone structure and was half buried in the ground. The roof was gone, and one wall had disintegrated. To get inside the broch, you had to step down and over part of the wall. The broch had been divided into four large squares, and Mia could see signs of work in the squares. On the far right-hand side of the site was a large tent. Mia stopped at the edge of the wall. "Can I see where they found Ethan?"

Anderson nodded. "I'll take you. Please follow in my footsteps."

Mia walked directly behind him. When they stopped, she crouched down and examined the square. The ground was disturbed, but there wasn't anything else to show there had been violence. She'd imagined rocks overturned and dirt thrown around. Instead, the square was a little messed up, but everything seemed as if it was waiting for them to return to work.

"And Phil Brown, Ethan's grad student, found him. Is that correct?"

"It is. The students drove over in the van. They stopped at the tent and saw the state it was in. Then, Phil looked out to the squares and noticed something on the ground. It was Dr. Carter."

Mia scanned the area. "Did you find a weapon?"

"No. It's possible he fell, but that's unlikely. There isn't a rock or brick he could have fallen on that would have caused the injury he had."

Mia stood looking at the square. Her thoughts flew from despair to anger. Who had done this to Ethan, and why? Had he found more than the ring and the sgian-dubh? Ugh, why hadn't he given her more information in his email? Mia sighed. She'd have to speak with Shelly. Ethan might have mentioned something to her about his plans for the previous evening.

There wasn't anything else to see here. Mia turned around and walked toward Luke.

"I want to check the tent."

Luke followed Mia. She pulled open the flap and gasped.

The tent was a mess. There were artifacts strewn about the tables, and some were on the floor. Containers were toppled. On the far wall was a series of filing cabinets, and someone had forced them open.

"Was it like this when you were here earlier today?"

"Yes. And I've been told this wasn't how they leave the tent at night."

"Of course not. I wonder if whoever did this found what they were looking for?" Mia turned toward the filing cabinets. "Did the students check to see what was missing?"

"They said the only items missing were the ring and the sgian-dubh."

"We'll have to sort through all this."

Anderson entered the tent. "We should head back."

Mia and Luke followed him to the car.

At the B&B, Mia looked around for the students. They were still sitting in the screened-in shelter, chatting quietly.

Mia took her glasses off and rubbed her face. She needed information from Ethan's students, and she had to be careful how she asked them.

"Dr. Reid, over here!" Phil called out.

"I'll be right there." Mia turned to Luke and Anderson. "I want to ask them a few questions about the dig. Is that a problem?"

"Not at all. They might remember something new," Anderson said.

Mia, Luke, and Anderson walked to the students.

Phil grabbed a couple of extra chairs and set them up around the table. Diana was sitting next to Rina.

Mia sat and cleared her throat. "We were at the dig, and I have some questions for you. I hope you're up to answering them."

The students nodded in agreement.

"Okay. Did you see anyone at the site this morning?"

"No, we didn't. When we found Dr. Carter, no one else was around." Phil answered.

"What happened in the tent?"

Rina winced. "We're not sure. I can assure you it wasn't in that condition when we left yesterday afternoon. We're organized. Everything has its place, and it's kept that way. Everything was in containers or locked up."

"Were you able to tell if anything's missing?"

Rina shook her head. "We go to the tent first thing in the morning and drop off our packs. Our lunches and drinks go in a cooler. We were shocked when we saw the mess in the tent. We looked around, and Phil suggested we look at the dig."

"And why's that?" Mia asked.

Phil answered, "I wondered if Dr. Carter had caught someone in the tent and chased them off. There might have been damage done to the dig, and if so, he'd be checking it out. I was worried about him. He wasn't at breakfast, and that wasn't normal."

"And what did you see?" Mia asked.

"I saw something in one of the squares and went to see what it was." Phil paused briefly. "It was Dr. Carter. When I touched his neck, he was cold, and I couldn't find a pulse. There was blood on his head."

Mia's eyes welled up. She looked up and blinked. "That must have been difficult."

The group was quiet for a moment. Mia cleared her throat. "And then you called the police?"

"Yes, I didn't let Rina come any closer. I wasn't sure what the procedure was, but I didn't think we should walk around. The police arrived quickly and took over."

Mia sighed. "Thanks for telling me how things rolled out. And you didn't check if there was anything missing?"

"The only things we noticed gone were the ring and the sgian-dubh. They weren't in the filing cabinets where we stored them. We didn't check for anything else," Rina said.

"I can understand that. We'll have to go through and see what's there and if anything else is missing. How do you keep inventory?"

Phil leaned forward. "We log everything in the site laptop and in a ledger. Dr. Carter liked to have the information backed up. He said it was good practice to have two locations to log the information."

"I do the same. It's something we learned when we first started out. Is the site laptop at the site, or did you bring it back at the end of every day?"

"It should be in Dr. Carter's room unless he took it with him when he went to the dig," Rina said.

Mia looked at Anderson and Luke. "Was it in Ethan's room?"

"There were two laptops. We left them there," Anderson said.

"When will we be able to go back to the dig?" Rina asked.

Anderson shifted in his chair. "Not until we're done with the crime scene."

"I'll need to speak with the sponsor and verify we're going to continue with the dig," Mia said.

At her words, the students' faces fell.

"But I just got here," Diana said.

"You mean there's a possibility the dig could be canceled?" Rina asked.

Mia raised a hand. "Like I said, I'll talk to the sponsor shortly. I haven't had time to do so yet. In the meantime, I suggest we not worry about things that are out of our control." Mia looked at her watch. "My next question is, where's a good place to eat?"

"There's a pub a short walk from here. The meals aren't fancy, but they're good. It's a friendly place, and the locals eat there, too," Phil said.

"That sounds perfect. I'm going to call Charles Gordon— he's the dig's sponsor— and let him know what's happening. I'll join you there shortly." Mia stood and pulled her phone out of her pocket. She overheard Rina inviting Luke and Anderson for dinner.

Mia waited for Mr. Gordon to answer the phone and explained the situation surrounding Ethan's death.

"Oh, no. Are there any leads?"

"Not yet. The police are waiting to hear from the pathologists to see if Ethan's death was accidental or not."

"How are the students handling it?"

"They're upset. They worked with Ethan before and were students of his."

"Do they want to continue with the dig?"

"Yes, but the dig is an active crime scene. We can't work until the police release it. And we need to know if you want us to continue."

Charles didn't waste any time. "We'll continue with the dig once the police release the scene. I'll arrange for Dr. Carter's remains to be returned to his family. You'll let me know when I can do that?"

"I will." Mia paused for a moment. Should she tell him about the artifacts that were missing? She'd better. "You need to be aware, two artifacts Ethan found, the ring and the sgian-dubh, are missing."

"What? Those two finds were significant. We need to know where they are." Charles's voice rose as he spoke.

"I understand. The police are aware they're missing. With the artifacts gone, and Ethan's death, I'd like to know if you can add a security team to the dig?

"I can. There will be someone there tomorrow. And let me know as soon as you learn anything about the missing artifacts." Charles abruptly hung up.

Mia held her phone out and stared at it.

Luke walked up to her. "Did you reach the sponsor?"

Mia turned around and dropped her phone in her pocket. "I did. He was sympathetic about Ethan's death but upset about the missing artifacts." Mia's eyes blurred, and she rubbed them.

"Are you okay?" Luke asked.

"My long day is catching up to me. I need a meal and some sleep."

"Let's get you to the pub. It's a short walk. Can you manage?"

"Yes."

Chapter Five

They started walking to the pub, the students well ahead of them.

"Mia, I owe you an apology for my behavior when I left you. I had every intention of staying in touch. I'm deeply sorry for how things turned out."

Mia glanced at Luke. "What happened? I was away on a dig for the summer, but I thought we'd planned to meet in September. Before I realized it, you were getting married."

Luke sighed. "It was a series of small mistakes leading to a big one. Jacqueline was waiting for me when I returned with my newly minted 'doctor' title. We had been close before I left for grad school. She assumed we'd pick up where we left off. I wish I'd been smart enough to realize she was more interested in the letters behind my name than me. We dated and then shortly after we were together, she came and told me she was pregnant."

Mia drew a sharp breath. "And was she?"

Luke shook his head. "No. She knew I'd do the right thing and marry her. It soon became apparent she wasn't pregnant. We stayed together for almost five years. I was determined to make it work, but she wasn't."

"I wish I'd known. I thought I'd misread our relationship that last year." Mia stopped outside the pub. "Are you divorced now?"

"I am. There are no obligations on my part towards her. But that's a story for later. Mia, I'm truly sorry for hurting you and not getting in touch with you."

"Well, at least I have a better understanding of what happened. And I've moved on. It's been almost ten years. But I'm very glad I didn't see you until now." Mia pulled the heavy wooden door to the pub and stepped in. "Because I don't know how I would've reacted."

Mia took in the dark walls, wooden floors, the setup of the tables and booths on the floor of the pub. The yeasty smell of beer and pub food permeated the air. The bar was along the far right-hand side, and the wood top gleamed, as did the brass rail. The pub was busy. She wondered how many tourists were in the pub as she heard accents from around the world. At the back, she saw Phil stand and wave his arms. "The students are at the back. It looks as if there's room at their table."

Mia and Luke made their way to the back, and Phil greeted them. "Glad you made it. This place is full tonight. We've saved you a couple of seats." Phil gestured to the end of the table.

Mia grabbed a chair, and Luke sat next to her. Diana and Rina were on the other side of the table enjoying some chips, or crisps as they were called in Scotland.

The waitress arrived with a tray of drinks.

"I hope you like beer. We ordered enough for all of us," Phil said.

Mia smiled. "Sounds good to me."

"What will you have for dinner?" The waitress asked, pulling out an order form.

Phil pointed to the menu on the table. "Take a look. I can tell you that everything we've had has been excellent."

Mia picked up the menu and glanced at it. The students gave the waitress their orders, and she waited patiently for Mia and Luke.

Mia looked up at her. "I'll take the shepherd's pie."

"And I'll order the fish and chips," Luke said.

"Won't be long with the food." The server turned toward the kitchen.

"I'd like to make a toast to Dr. Carter. He was one of the best profs I worked with, and I learned a lot from him. I'll miss him." Phil raised his glass.

The rest of the table did the same.

The pub's patrons noticed and fell silent. One of the locals called out, "To Dr. Carter, may he rest in peace." And everyone in the pub toasted Ethan.

"I want to say a few things. First, I spoke with Charles Gordon, the dig's sponsor." Mia heard the students draw a breath. "He's told me the dig will continue as soon as the police release the site."

Phil and Rina nodded. "That's great," Phil said. "We need the work."

"That's a relief," Diana said.

"I need to know if you're comfortable working at the dig. Do any of you have concerns?"

Rina frowned. "You mean like safety?"

"That's one concern," Mia said.

"I won't go there by myself. I wouldn't feel safe," Rina said.

"And that's reasonable. Mr. Gordon is arranging for a security team to start tomorrow." Mia took a drink of her beer. "As for being at the dig on your own, I want to be very clear. None of you are to work by yourselves. And no one is to go there after hours." Mia looked at each student around the table. "Is that understood?"

They all nodded their assent. "There wouldn't be any reason for any of us to go there by ourselves. Dr. Carter had the same rule. We all worked on the buddy system," Phil said.

"And that will continue with me in charge. I'd like to know more about the volunteers. Can you tell me about them?"

"We've had a few volunteers from the historical society. They're knowledgeable about Skye's history. They've worked on other digs and have experience." Rina reached for the chips on the table. "Sorry, I'm famished."

"Are they trained as archaeologists?" Luke asked.

"I doubt it. One of them is a retired university history professor," Phil said.

Mia nodded. "Having local people who are knowledgeable about the area is helpful. They can fill in gaps that we wouldn't be aware of. And local legends are often based in truth."

The server arrived with their meals. The discussion moved to more general subjects. When they finished their meals, Mia glanced at her watch.

"I just have one more thing to say before I head back to the B&B." The students stopped chatting and waited expectantly. "I'd like to meet tomorrow morning at nine. I'll ask if there's a room we can use. If you could bring your notes with you and we'll talk about what you've learned about the site. I'd appreciate photos and drawings as well. We may as well use the time we have to bring Diana and I up to date."

"That sounds like a good use of our time. We have our own notes. Dr. Carter had notes on the dig's laptop and I think on his own as well," Phil said.

"Anderson said the laptops were in Ethan's room. Do you know if they're password protected?" Mia asked.

"The site laptop isn't," Phil said.

"Great, I'll see if I can access Ethan's room tomorrow morning. Questions?"

"What's going to happen to Dr. Carter?" Phil asked.

Mia closed her eyes briefly. She couldn't wrap her mind around the fact that Ethan was gone. "Mr. Gordon will send his remains home to his family. But that can't happen until the pathologists' examination is complete. The process is a little different here than at home."

Mia waited a moment to see if there were more questions. "It's been a long day. I'm going to head back. I'll see you all in the morning."

Luke stood. "I'll walk back with you."

The temperature had dropped since they'd entered the pub, and Mia was grateful she'd worn her heavier sweater. She turned to Luke. "What made you leave the British Museum? I thought you enjoyed working there."

"I was happy there for several years. Then, I had a run-in with someone who was looking to move some stolen artifacts. It wasn't a museum staff member. It was one of the patrons who was asking. He thought because I was a newer employee, I'd be willing to help him. He got rather upset when I wouldn't."

Mia drew a quick breath. "You're kidding?"

"No, I'm not." Luke sighed. "And when I told Jacqueline about it, she insisted I do as he asked. She didn't believe there was anything wrong with his request. I reported it to my supervisor, and we contacted Interpol." Luke paused a second. "That was the last straw, as you would say. I didn't fit with Jacqueline's vision of a husband, and she started divorce proceedings shortly after that incident. Our marriage was done."

"Is that when you began working with Interpol?"

Luke nodded. "I worked closely with an agent from AART. When the agent repatriated the artifacts, he asked if I was interested in working for them. London is my home base, but I travel frequently and for extended periods."

"Do you like it?" Mia asked as they climbed the hill to the B&B.

"I do. I feel that what I'm doing is making a difference. Artifacts are being returned where they need to be."

They walked for a few minutes in silence.

"How about you? Is there anyone in your life now?" Luke asked.

"Not recently. I was involved with someone a few years ago. I thought we had a good relationship until he decided I wasn't his type anymore. Since then, I haven't taken the time to become romantically involved with anyone. My work with the university and travel have kept me busy."

"Can I interest you in a nightcap? Mrs. MacDonald told us we could make use of the bar in the sitting room."

"Thanks, but I'm going to pass. I'm exhausted, and I want to speak with Shelly before I turn in."

"Another time, then. Good night."

Mia unlocked her door and glanced around her room. The room came with a tea and coffee service. She wouldn't mind a cup of tea while she spoke with Shelly. She crossed the room and unpacked her things. A quick shower and then a call.

Twenty minutes later, she was in her pajamas. Tea had been brewed, and she was ready to talk to Shelly.

She called Shelly's cell phone and waited while it rang. Finally, someone answered.

"Shelly Carter's phone. How can I help you?" The voice wasn't Shelly's, and Mia wasn't sure who it was.

"Hello, this is Dr. Mia Reid. I'd like to speak with Shelly. Is she available?"

"Mia, it's Laura, Shelly's mother. I'm glad to hear your voice."

Mia sighed. Someone she knew. "I'm sorry this happened. How is she?"

Mia's voice broke.

"She's in shock. But I know she wants to speak with you. I'll tell her you're on the phone."

A few moments later, "Mia, is that you? Are you in Scotland?" Shelly's voice sounded weak.

"Yes, I'm here. I'm devastated. How are you?"

Shelly's voice cracked. "Not great. I never expected this. Have you seen him?"

"No. The police took him to the pathologists. When did you last speak to him?"

"Yesterday, he called after he'd had supper. He said the ring and the sgian-dubh had generated a lot of interest. He was worried about the security at the site, so he brought them to his room." Shelly sighed. "He mentioned a woman at the pub asking to buy artifacts. After she spoke to him, he was worried about the security at the dig. He planned to go back to the dig last night to make sure the rest of the artifacts were secured.

"Do you have any idea where he hid the ring and the sgian-dubh?" Mia asked.

"He said he'd hidden them in the same place your old Professor Jones used when he was in a location that wasn't secure."

Mia heard someone calling Shelly. "How's Henry?" she asked.

"I haven't told him yet. I'm not sure how. Mom and Dad are here, and we're going to tell him tomorrow morning. Mia, I have to go. Please, please, find out what happened to Ethan."

"I will. I promise."

Mia put her phone down and exhaled a breath she didn't realize she'd been holding. Shelly didn't sound good, and no wonder. Her world had been shattered. Mia leaned across the bed and grabbed a tissue. She wiped her eyes and blew her nose. She'd kept her emotions under control while talking to Shelly, but right now, she let the tears flow. It wasn't fair. Ethan wasn't supposed to die. He had so much to give to his family and friends. Not to mention his work. He was a leader at the university and well respected in the archaeology world. His death would cause ripples throughout the field. Mia shook her head and glanced at her watch. She needed to talk to someone. Gran was her go-to when things were tough. With the time difference, it was just before dinner in Lakeview. Hopefully, Gran would be home.

"Hello, Mia," Gran said.

Mia bit back a sob. "Oh, Gran, it's awful!"

"Mia, honey, take a breath. In and out."

Mia did as she was told.

"Okay, now what's awful? You need to tell me everything."

"It's Ethan, he's dead."

"Oh no! What happened?" Gran asked.

Slowly, speaking through tears, Mia filled Gran in on what had happened at the dig.

"And what's going to happen now?" Gran asked.

Mia wiped her eyes. "I'm not sure. We're waiting for the pathologists to provide a time and cause of death. I guess it depends on what they learn. The dig is a crime scene, so we can't work. And Shelly wants me to find out what happened to Ethan."

"How are you going to find that out?"

Mia lifted her chin. "I'm going to do what I do well. Dig around, ask questions, see who was in the area, and find out what they wanted."

Gran sighed. "I don't like that idea. Let the police figure out what happened to Ethan. It could have been an accident."

"I doubt it. Ethan made a couple of good finds. They're missing, but I may be able to find them. I'm going to check his room tomorrow morning. As for the police, well, I'm not sure what they're going to do. Oh, I forgot to tell you, Luke Forbes is here. He's working for Interpol with the AART."

"Well, that's an interesting turn of events. How are you two getting along?"

Mia took a sip of lukewarm tea. "It's okay. We've talked about what happened, and he's told me what he did and why." Mia gave her Gran an abbreviated version of Luke's explanation of his marriage and work history.

"I always liked him. He was a decent man. How are you feeling seeing him again?" Gran asked.

"I don't know. It was unexpected to see him, and the news he gave me wasn't good. As for a relationship, I'm not considering that as a possibility. How are things at home?"

They chatted a few minutes longer until Mia felt better. Her nerves weren't as raw, and she thought she might get some rest. Gran had always been able to calm her down.

Mia disconnected the call and then sent Alex a text.

M: Can we talk?

A: Sure, I'm walking home from work.

Mia made the call.

"How was the flight?" Alex asked.

"Okay, but I got some bad news when I arrived." Mia told Alex the events of the day.

"That's awful. Do the police have any idea who might have done this?"

"No. They aren't sure it was murder. They're waiting on the report from the pathologists."

"You said the artifacts were missing? Do you think Ethan hid them?" Alex asked.

"That's what Shelly said. Ethan told her if anything happened, I needed to remember what Professor Jones had taught us."

"And what's that?"

Mia sighed. "Different places to hide items when we were at digs that weren't secure. Maybe I'll remember them after a sleep. How come you're walking home?"

Alex chuckled. "I wondered when you'd ask. I had a couple of annoying meetings today and need to walk off the frustrations. The education minister isn't cooperating with our department. He's putting up roadblocks. Nothing like what you're going through, though."

They talked for a few more minutes, and Mia disconnected the call, promising to touch base with Alex the next day.

Mia set out her clothes for tomorrow and then turned on her e-reader. She settled into bed and hoped to get some sleep.

Chapter Six

Mia made her way to the breakfast room. She'd slept soundly and felt better than she had last night.

Mrs. MacDonald was putting out the food on the sideboard. The smell of freshly brewed coffee and homemade baked goods permeated the area. She closed the lid on the buffet dishes of eggs, bacon, and sausage, and checked on the bowls of fruit salad.

"Good morning, Miss. Did you sleep well?" Mrs. MacDonald asked.

Mia smiled. "I did. My bed's comfortable. And it's incredibly quiet here."

"I'm glad to hear that."

"Is there a room the students and I could use for a meeting this morning?"

"There's no one else here except your group and the police. You're welcome to use the breakfast room. I'll make certain to keep the coffee and pastries out for you."

"That would be nice. Thank you."

"Help yourself to breakfast. I set out enough so you can choose to have a full breakfast or something lighter."

Mrs. MacDonald went out to the kitchen and Mia helped herself to coffee and selected eggs, bacon, toast, and fruit. She carried her food to a table by the window overlooking the grounds.

Luke arrived a few minutes later.

"Good morning. May I join you?"

"Sure."

Luke left his phone on the table and headed to the buffet. He returned with a full plate.

Mia glanced at him and chuckled. "I see breakfast is still your favorite meal."

Luke poured some milk in his tea. "It is, and this spread is wonderful. Mrs. MacDonald doesn't stint on choices."

They ate their meals in companionable silence. Neither of them were early morning chatterers. Mia's thoughts kept returning to her conversation with Shelly. She remembered Professor Jones very well. Mia and Ethan had enjoyed working with him in the summers. He'd taught them to be resourceful in remote locations. They'd worked at digs that had the potential to be looted, and he'd shown them where to hide valuable artifacts that could be pocketed away.

Luke cleared his throat. "You look deep in thought. How did you sleep?"

"Reasonably well, considering everything that happened yesterday." She picked up her coffee cup. "I spoke with Shelly last night."

"I would expect that was a tough call. I know you two were close."

"We still are. And yes, it was difficult. She's upset by Ethan's death and wants me to find out as much as I can about the circumstances. She also mentioned that Ethan had told her if anything happened to him, she was to let me know to remember Professor Jones."

"That's cryptic enough. Do you know what it means?"

"I might. We worked with Professor Jones in remote locations. He made a point of showing us how to hide smaller antiquities so looters couldn't take them."

"And have you remembered something?" Luke put his teacup down.

Mia smiled. "I remember one occasion where he hid a dagger and a necklace that we'd found in Central America. It was a Mayan dig." Mia put her napkin by her plate. "I'd like to go through Ethan's room to see if he's hidden the ring and the sgian-dubh."

"Let me touch base with Anderson. He'll want to be there as well."

Mia watched as Luke made the call.

"Right. He'll be here in a few moments. He was just getting ready to come down for breakfast."

Mia stood as Anderson walked into the breakfast room.

"Good morning. You want to get into Dr. Carter's room?"

"Yes. I think I might know where the missing artifacts are."

"Let's go then."

Anderson led the way. Mia was surprised to discover the room was around the corner from hers. Anderson cut through the police tape and unlocked the door.

Mia walked into the room and glanced around. Ethan had been organized, but his room didn't reflect that. "Who made this mess?" Mia asked. "There's no way Ethan left his room like this."

"We searched the room. The team wasn't concerned with putting things back where they should have been."

Mia's lips pressed together in a straight line. "Fine. I'll ensure his things are packed up before they're sent back."

Anderson nodded. "We're still waiting on the postmortem results, and that will take a few more days."

"Mia, can you explain to Anderson what Professor Jones taught you and Ethan?" Luke asked.

"We were working in a remote area in Central America. We'd found a gold necklace and ring that had emeralds and rubies embedded in their design. There were looters in the area. One of the other digs had had some items stolen. Professor Jones was worried about the small artifacts that could easily fit in a pocket or be tucked in a backpack. He showed us a few simple hiding places." Mia walked into the bathroom and looked around.

She saw Ethan's toiletry bag and opened it. A bamboo travel toothbrush case was in it, and Ethan's toothbrush was in a glass by the sink. Mia took the holder out of the bag and shook it. There was a rattle. She opened it up and tipped it forward. A ring tumbled out into her hand. It had some dirt embedded amongst the stones, and it appeared to be the same ring Ethan had sent photos of.

She stepped out of the bathroom. "I think this is the ring they found."

"Where did you find it?" Luke asked.

Mia explained and said, "The toothbrush holder is the right size for the ring. But the sgian-dubh wouldn't fit in it."

45

Mia set the ring on the desk and looked around the room. "Did you check under the nightstands and lamps?"

Anderson nodded. "Feel free to check them again."

Mia shook her head. "If your team didn't find anything there, then he didn't put it there. Luke, could you help me move the mattress?"

They pulled the mattress off the bed. Setting it aside, Mia ran her hands around the bed frame. On the left-hand side of the frame, she found something taped to the underside. She dropped to the floor and pulled a cloth-covered item.

Mia walked to the desk and unraveled the cloth. Under the layers, the sgian-dubh appeared. Adorned with gemstones, the handle featured intricate designs carved on the metal. The blade was dirty, but Mia could see there was writing on it. There was no doubt, it was the same sgian-dubh that Ethan had sent photos of.

Luke drew a breath in. "That's a beautiful piece. And valuable." He picked up the ring and looked at it closely. "I'd say both pieces belonged to the same person."

"How can you tell?" Anderson asked.

"The markings on the ring and the sgian-dubh are the same. It means they were made by the same person for the same individual."

Mia looked at each piece carefully. "I'd like to clean them up and examine them. Do they need to be taken by the police?" she asked Anderson.

Anderson shook his head.

Mia picked up the artifacts. "I have a small plastic bag in my room. I'll put them in there. We'll take them to the dig when we have access and clean them." Mia glanced at her watch. "I need to get ready for my meeting with the students."

"What are you meeting with them for?" Anderson asked.

"I want them to give me an overview of what they've done at the dig. Including photos, drawings, notes. They should have all of that with them. It will give me, and Diana, good information so that when we return to the dig, we don't waste time. I'll need the site laptop, and if you have Ethan's laptop, I'll take it too. I'd like to compare his notes."

"I have both laptops in my room. I'll bring them downstairs," Anderson said.

"Would you mind if I sat in on the meeting?" Luke asked.

"Of course not. Is there a particular reason you want to?"

"Not really. But I would like to learn what the students know, especially with the people who've been at the dig, either visitors or volunteers."

Anderson spoke up. "I think that's a good plan. I'm off to Portree to meet with the pathologists."

Mia shrugged. "I don't have a problem with you coming to the meeting. We meet at nine, in the breakfast room."

"Are you going to tell the students you found the artifacts?" Luke asked.

"Yes. They need to know. I'll bring them with me to the meeting." Mia glanced around the room. "When do you think I can pack Ethan's things?"

"If you give us a few more days, you'll be able to put them in order then. I don't want anything to leave the room without my knowledge," Anderson said.

"Mrs. MacDonald might do that for you," Luke said.

Mia shook her head. "No. I can do this for Shelly. I need to get ready for the meeting with the students. Luke, I'll see you there."

In her room, Mia blew out a deep breath. It had been tougher than she'd let on to be in Ethan's room and seeing his things. It was a sharp reminder that he wasn't there anymore. Although it was too early for Shelly to see the message, Mia quickly sent her a note letting her know she'd found the missing artifacts. She knew Shelly would appreciate knowing that.

Taking a plastic bag from her large backpack, she placed the ring and the sgian-dubh in the bag. Then she took her laptop, a Moleskine notebook, and pen, adding them to her daypack with the ring and sgian-dubh. She tucked her phone in her cargo pants pocket. Ready for the meeting, she went downstairs to the breakfast room. She could hear the murmur of voices and the clink of cutlery on dishes as she approached the room.

She stopped in the doorway and watched the students for a moment. They were talking amongst themselves, and Diana appeared to fit in with them. Mia hadn't heard them come in last night, so she didn't know how long they'd stayed at the pub. She wasn't here to mother them, and by the looks of them this morning, they were all ready to work. That was good. It meant they took the dig seriously.

Phil noticed her in the doorway. "Professor, come in. Have you eaten yet?"

Mia set her things on the table next to them. "I did. It was an excellent breakfast. And please, call me Mia."

Diana put her coffee cup down. "How are you? Did you get some sleep?"

Mia nodded. "I'm good. And, I found the missing artifacts."

"Oh, that's amazing! Where did you find them?" Rina asked.

"I'll tell you about it when we start the meeting. I want to get another cup of coffee." Mia went to the sideboard and poured herself a fresh cup. Out of the corner of her eye, she saw Luke standing in the doorway. "I've invited Luke to join our meeting. He's interested in learning about the dig and any people that may have stopped by." Mia waved Luke in the room.

"Good morning, everyone. I hope you don't mind my being here."

Anderson arrived with the site laptop and with Ethan's. "Here you go. I'll leave them with you. The tech team looked at them yesterday and there didn't seem to be anything we need on them."

Mia smiled. "Thanks. They'll be helpful."

They took a few minutes to rearrange the tables and chairs.

"First of all, here's the ring and the sgian-dubh." Mia took the items out of the bag. "I'd like you to verify those are the artifacts you found at the dig."

Phil and Rina took an artifact each and examined them. Then they switched.

"Yes, these are the ring and the sgian-dubh we found on Monday morning. We didn't clean them properly because we were excited about the find." Phil handed the ring to Diana, who scrutinized it.

"Who found them?" Mia asked.

"I found the sgian-dubh," Phil said. "It was exciting. I didn't know what it was, but Professor Carter knew."

"I found the ring," Rina said. "It was amongst shards of pottery. I almost missed it because it was covered in dirt."

"We cleaned up the ring a bit," Phil said. "Professor Carter wanted to see if there were any markings on it."

"How valuable do you think these are?" Diana asked.

"I'm not sure. There are gemstones on both items, but the monetary value isn't necessarily the important thing. It shows that a person of some standing and wealth was at the broch. I don't know if we'll be able to identify who that person was, but it shows the broch was an important part of the local history."

"May I?" Luke asked, extending his hand toward the artifacts.

"Of course." Phil handed him the sgian-dubh.

Luke pulled a jeweler's loupe out of his pocket and made an examination of the sgian-dubh.

"What are you looking for?" Rina asked.

"Any identifying marks that could tell us what clan this belonged to. The sgian-dubh was a small dagger that fit into a man's stocking. They always kept it on the fighting arm side to have easy access to a weapon if they were attacked. Clans would use different symbols to embellish their weapons and to identify them."

Luke put the sgian-dubh down. "The gemstones are genuine and they're valuable. The markings are Celtic."

"Professor Carter would be so happy." Phil grinned and high-fived Rina's hand.

Mia smiled. "I want to get some more opinions on this find, but Luke has experience in this area. I think this is excellent news!"

"I'm acquainted with a few individuals who can verify the authenticity of this item. One of them lives in the area," Luke said.

"What about the ring?" Rina asked.

Luke brushed off some of the dust on the ring and checked it out with the loupe. "There's an inscription on the outside of the band. I'm thinking my expert will be able to read it once it's been cleaned."

"Where did you find these?" Diana asked.

Mia filled them in on the hiding places Ethan had used.

"Have you ever hidden artifacts that you discovered?" Phil asked.

"I have. It's a precaution when you're in a remote location, and the artifacts are small but valuable. It's easy for them to be taken."

"Have you heard anything about getting access to the dig?" Rina asked.

"Nothing yet. Why don't the two of you bring us up to speed?"

Phil opened his notebook, and he and Rina shared their information with Mia and Diana. Luke stayed in the vicinity, listening in.

Rina pulled out her notebook. "I've done drawings of the dig and the artifacts we've found. They show where we found the artifacts."

Mia took the notebook and looked through it carefully. "It seems as if the artifacts were clustered in two areas. Was anything found anywhere else?"

"No. And Professor Carter thought that was odd. Even the pottery shards were found in the same place the ring was found." Rina went to refill her coffee.

Mia passed the notebook back to Diana. "It could mean someone looted the site before. And they missed the ring because it was with the pottery."

"Could the pottery have held human remains?" Diana asked.

"Unlikely. They buried their dead in graves," Mia said.

Mia's phone pinged with a text. "Excuse me, I need to check this." She stepped away from the table. The text was from DI Anderson.

A: Dig will be cleared for you to resume work at noon today.

M: Thank you

"Good news. We can access the dig at noon today. Are you ready to go back?"

Mia watched the faces before her. She saw relief and sadness on the faces of the students.

Rina set her coffee cup down. "I think I'm just realizing now that Dr. Carter won't be back. We need to get back to the dig and get some work done."

Phil spoke up. "I'm glad we can go back, but I'm sad that Professor Carter's gone."

Mia glanced at her watch. "We have a couple of hours before we can go to work. Why don't you show me what you recorded in the site laptop?"

The students took turns explaining the finds, and how they had documented them. They provided a clear explanation of the method used, and

Mia was satisfied with the information she received.

Mrs. MacDonald came in to tidy up the breakfast server. "Did you want some more coffee?"

"I think we're good. We can return to work now that the dig has been cleared. We'll be out of your hair by noon," Mia said.

"Ah, not a problem. Will you be wanting box lunches?"

"Mrs. MacDonald's box lunches are a work of art," Rina said.

Mrs. MacDonald blushed. "Go on with you."

"We'd very much appreciate that. Thank you," Mia said.

"They'll be ready at the front desk at noon." Mrs. MacDonald stepped out of the breakfast room.

Mia sent a text to Charles Gordon advising him they had access to the site. She wasn't expecting an answer because of the time difference and was surprised when he called her.

"Dr. Reid here."

"I want to inform you security arrived at the site earlier this morning. They have it all in hand. Have the police determined the cause of death?"

"Not yet. I understand they're still waiting on a few reports."

"When you hear of anything, let me know."

"Of course. We'll be taking today to get the tent back together and to take an inventory of what we have."

"Sounds good. I'll be in touch soon." Mr. Gordon disconnected the call.

Mia stepped back into the breakfast room. Luke was putting his phone away.

"All right. Let's get ready to get to work. Don't forget your bug spray. We'll meet here at noon, grab our lunches, and head off to the dig. Phil, who has the keys to the van?" Mia asked.

"I do. I'll bring them with me when I come downstairs," Phil said.

Chapter Seven

They gathered in the lobby with their daypacks and picked up their lunches.

"Here are the keys to the van," Phil said as he handed them to Mia. "Dr. Carter added you to the van's drivers."

"Thanks. I may need directions. Can you sit in the front with me?" Mia picked up the keys.

They piled in the van, Luke grabbing a seat at the back. Phil rode shotgun in front with Mia.

"It's not far. Just over five minutes."

With Phil's help, Mia found the turnoff to the site. Two other vehicles were in the parking lot. "Who are these people?" Mia asked.

Phil peered through the windshield. "One of them is a volunteer. How did he hear the site was released?"

Mia shrugged. "Small community. Word travels fast."

A tall, white-haired man dressed in a plaid shirt and wearing a down vest walked up to the van. His corduroy pants had seen some wear. He carried a cap in one hand, and a daypack was slung over his shoulder.

Phil smiled. "Hello, Angus. Mia, this is Angus McCloud. He's one of the volunteers with the dig. He's a former history professor and has retired here. Angus, Dr. Mia Reid, a colleague of Dr. Carter's."

Angus extended his hand to Mia. "Hello. It's a pleasure to make your acquaintance. I'm so sorry about Professor Carter. He was a wonderful man."

Mia shook his hand. "Thanks. It's good to meet you."

"I hope it's fine that I came by. I was waiting to hear when the dig would open again and was in the pub when I heard the news. I'm happy to help where I can."

"From what I understand, you're a seasoned volunteer. We appreciate your help. Our only task today is to restore the tent." Mia grabbed her daypack. "I think the other vehicle belongs to the security team Mr. Gordon arranged for. I'm going to check in with them. Why don't you go to the tent? I'll be there shortly."

"If you don't mind, I'll accompany you," Luke said.

Mia and Luke approached the security men near their van.

"Hi, I'm Dr. Reid, and this is Luke Forbes. I understand Mr. Gordon contacted you?"

The shorter of the two men nodded. "Harry MacAllister, my partner Ken Smith. We'll be here until six, then a new team comes in. We'll keep a close eye on the dig. If anything happens, we'll report back to Mr. Gordon."

"Excellent. I'll give you my contact information. Please inform me if anything happens as well. I'm here and will deal with anything immediately." Mia reached into her daypack and pulled out a couple of business cards. "Is there anything you need from me?"

Harry took them and gave one to Ken. "If you can show us the perimeter we need to take care of, we'll set things up. And will you need crowd control?"

Mia looked around the dig. No one else had shown up other than Angus. "I'm not sure about the crowd control. Typically, we get people who are curious about what we're doing coming by. With Dr. Carter's death and the artifacts that have been discovered, we may see more people than normal. So, yes, we'll need a perimeter set up."

Harry nodded. "We can set up some fencing to keep people from coming onto the property. We'll take care of that today."

Mia and Luke walked into the tent. The students and Angus were chatting quietly between themselves. Angus's eyes were wide as he looked around the tent.

"Who would do this?" Angus asked.

Mia set her pack down on the ground. "No idea. The students found it like this before they discovered Ethan. Has anyone been asking about the dig in the village?"

"Of course, there's been talk about the dig. Most people are interested in what you might find," Angus said.

"The ring and the sgian-dubh raised interest," Phil said, heading toward the table.

"True. But none of the locals would cause this type of damage." Angus gazed around the tent. "Nobody from the village would do this. The broch's been here for centuries, and it's always been treated with respect." He put his daypack down on the ground.

Mia cleared her throat. "We should get started."

Luke stood next to Mia. "What's first?"

"Let's check the artifacts here to see if any are missing. Once we've sorted things out in the tent, we'll continue working on the squares. Rina, did you bring the site laptop?"

"I did. I'll set it up, and we can start checking the inventory with our catalogue on the laptop." Rina pulled the laptop out of her bag and cleared a space on the table for it.

"Great. Diana, I'd like you to start with the filing cabinets. Check the contents and make sure they're included in the inventory. Phil, if you could start with the artifacts that are strewn about the tent. I think you would do a great job of identifying them."

Mia glanced at Angus. "Could you help Rina with the inventory for now?"

"Glad to help." Angus picked up his daypack and walked around the table.

"And what are we going to do?" Luke asked.

"I want to see how they work together. Can you lend a hand where needed?"

"Of course, it's been a while since I've been in the field. I may be a bit rusty."

Standing to the side, they watched the team start on their tasks. Mia was confident Ethan had trained the students well, but she wanted to see first-hand how they worked together.

It quickly became clear that the students were well-versed in their tasks.

Rina reviewed the laptop log. "Professor, sorry, Mia. Could you come here?" Rina asked.

Mia approached the table. "What's up?"

"The logs are current and up to date. Do you want us to verify the artifacts are still here by going through each of them?"

Mia nodded. "How are the logs set up?"

"We list the artifacts in the order we found them and then cross-reference them with their respective storage locations. That gives us a lot of information to work with. The initial log lists the location, description, and necessary follow-up for each item. The second log is where they're stored."

"Ethan taught you well," Mia said.

Rina grinned. "He was a stickler for details. He wouldn't let us get away with 'dagger' when it wasn't a dagger. We had to identify and describe the object as accurately as possible."

"The details are crucial when uncovering smaller artifacts, especially those used daily. It shows us how the people who lived here used the site." Mia leaned over to study the current page. "This shows the different pottery shards that were found. How do you identify who found the artifacts?"

Rina pointed to the last column. "We use our initials. The log's first page has a legend explaining abbreviations, including people's initials."

"Right, let's go through each container."

"As long as no one removed items from the plastic bags, we should be able to return everything to its original state," Rina said.

Phil walked to the table. "I've got a group of artifacts that all seem to belong together. Could I see one of the logs, and I'll start putting them in the correct containers?"

Rina reached for a binder. "This should help. They're hard copies of what's on the computer."

"Perfect. I'll start going through this." Phil took the binder.

"I can give you a hand," Luke said

"Appreciate it. There's a lot here."

"Thanks, Luke. Rina, can you manage here?" Mia asked.

"Yep, it's going to work out well."

"Angus, would you mind giving me a hand in this section?"

"Not a problem."

Mia and Angus settled in a section on the right-hand side of the tent. They began sorting through the bags of artifacts that were scattered about.

"How long have you been doing volunteer work with digs?"

Angus kneeled on the ground as he sorted through the bags. "I started about twenty years ago. I was teaching in Edinburgh and had summers off. There was a dig a short distance away, and they needed volunteers. I enjoyed being able to see some of the history I taught laid out in front of me. It brought it to life. I've been doing this every summer break since then. I've retired from teaching now and I do a lot of work with the local historical society. There's been much interest in this dig. From across Scotland, not just locally."

"Why's that?"

Angus pushed his cap back on his head. "Bonnie Prince Charlie went through Skye in the summer of 1745. He had gold coins with him to cover expenses."

Mia smiled. "Do people think there'll be a treasure?"

"Perhaps. He hid in the area, and the great Flora MacDonald helped him with his escape plans. Legend has it he paid handsomely for help. People wonder if he left any of that wealth behind."

They worked side by side. Angus told Mia some of the folklore of the area. He talked about the clans in Skye that had helped Bonnie Prince Charlie and how he had been disguised as a woman servant, Betty Burke.

"He wasn't much of a lady's servant. Standing six feet tall, he clumped along when he walked. He didn't understand he had to keep his steps smaller and to take care when raising his skirts. Instead of walking behind Flora MacDonald, he walked ahead of her." Angus laughed softly. "Then he dressed as a manservant. Much better casting than a woman's servant."

They'd been working steadily for an hour and a half when Mia called for a break.

"Let's grab a bite to eat and talk about what we've found."

They gathered around the table. Mia informed the students about the security team's round-the-clock presence at the dig. She also told them they were setting up a perimeter around the dig.

Rina frowned. "I thought part of what we did was talk to people about what we're doing. How are we going to do that if there's a perimeter?"

Mia swallowed her sandwich. "The perimeter isn't a solid fence. People will still see what we're doing. But it's going to provide a barrier. We'll find a way to meet the objective of talking to people about the finds."

"What about having a bulletin board with some information and photos?" Angus asked.

"That would work. We'd need to come up with appropriate descriptions."

"I've been to sites where the bulletin board explains the dig and the purpose behind it. Sometimes there's an opportunity for the public to go through some of the artifacts and ask questions," Luke said.

"I'm going to send a message to Mr. Gordon and ask if he has any ideas on how we can deal with this." Mia added a reminder on her phone.

"What exactly was a broch used for?" Diana asked.

"I'd like to answer that," Angus said.

Mia nodded, "Go ahead."

"People built the brochs in the Iron Age, over two thousand years ago. They're circular dry-stone towers and may have served as a defensive measure against raiders or for observation." Angus took a drink of water. "Many brochs were occupied. And it likely housed a wealthy farmer family or the head of a tribe."

"That's too cool." Diana grinned. "This is why I love archaeology. Someone walked along here thousands of years ago. And we're finding evidence they were here."

"The artifacts we're finding should also give us information on what they did. Their tools were more advanced than North America's during that time. The tools unearthed provide evidence that the people who live here engaged in farming, fishing, and hunting. They were also warriors when needed," Angus said.

After they finished their lunch, Mia turned to the students. "Why don't you take a few minutes and stretch your legs? I'd just ask that you stay away from the squares. We still need to examine them, and we can do that tomorrow."

"Sounds good. I need to walk around a bit." Phil stood up. "Anyone want to join me?"

The two other students joined him outside the tent. Mia watched as they stood looking toward the grid and then walked toward the parking lot.

"It's difficult for them to come back," Angus said.

"I asked them if they wanted to continue, and they all did. I think they feel it would be a dishonor to Ethan if they didn't stay. But I don't want them to be afraid to work here."

"Mr. Gordon's security team should help alleviate those fears." Luke tossed his garbage away. "There isn't much more that can be done. The police are looking into everything."

"I didn't expect we'd be able to work today."

Luke glanced in Mia's direction. "According to Anderson, it's unlikely the students would have any connection to Ethan's death. And the police scrutinized the site." Luke's phone rang. "Excuse me, I need to take this."

Mia watched as he stepped out of the tent and took the call. He spoke briefly with whoever was on the other end and then looked at Mia, his expression dark.

Luke hung up the call. "That was Anderson. The pathologists' report shows that Ethan's cause of death was a blow to the back of the head. The police are treating this as a murder."

Chapter Eight

"Are they certain?" Mia asked.

"Yes. The type of wound indicates that someone struck him from behind. Anderson mentioned returning to search for potential weapons in the area. They also found drugs in his system."

"What type of drugs? Ethan didn't take drugs except for over-the-counter medications."

Luke shrugged. "I don't know. I'm simply delivering the message."

"I'd better call the students back to the tent." Mia walked closer to the parking lot and called out, "Hey! I need you guys back here."

Diana turned in her direction and waved. They started walking back to the tent.

Mia waited until they were close. "I need to speak with you in the tent."

"Is everything okay?" Phil asked.

"We'll talk in the tent."

They gathered around the table.

Mia drew a deep breath. "Luke heard from DI Anderson. Someone murdered Ethan. The police are on their way back here and will be doing another examination of the site."

"What makes them believe he was murdered?" Rina asked.

"The type of wound on his head, and he had drugs in his system," Luke said.

Rina's face paled. "Then that means someone was here when he came over on Monday evening. Were they waiting for him?"

"They don't know." Luke rubbed his face. "Do you remember if he said he'd be meeting anyone?"

Mia observed the students. Rina shook her head. Phil appeared to be thinking about something. "Phil, has something occurred to you?"

"I'm wondering how he would have had drugs in his system. He didn't use drugs."

"I know. Do you think someone may have slipped something in his food or drink?" Mia asked.

"There was a lot of celebrating because of the ring and the sgian-dubh. People were coming to our table with drinks for us. It wouldn't have been hard to slip something in one of his drinks." Phil frowned. "But wouldn't he have looked drunk or slurred his words?"

"I think it would depend on what he was given," Mia said.

"That woman who was looking to buy artifacts and the guy she was with were at the pub when we were there. And I remember they came over with drinks for us," Phil said.

"That's right! The woman gave him a shot of whiskey. I remember he downed it quickly." Rina's eyes shone with tears. "I wonder if that's what happened."

"You need to tell Anderson about this," Luke said.

Phil nodded. "Not a problem."

They didn't have long to wait. Anderson and his team pulled into the parking lot less than ten minutes later.

Luke walked toward Anderson and called out, "Could you come here?"

Anderson nodded and gave instructions to his team, then headed toward Mia's group.

"Did you need something?" Anderson asked.

"Phil and Rina may have additional information for you." Mia turned to Phil. "Why don't you go ahead?"

Phil and Rina told Anderson what they'd remembered from their celebrations on Monday evening. Anderson asked Phil if he could describe the woman.

"She was slender, with short dark hair, and pale skin. She wore black jeans and sneakers."

Mia interrupted them. "That sounds like the woman Ethan described to Shelly. That's how Shelly described her to me."

"Why didn't you mention this earlier?" Anderson asked.

"I thought Shelly had told you."

"Phil and Rina, I'd like you to work with a sketch artist today. I'll have one of the officers drive you to the police station. You can work with the artist there."

Anderson stepped out of the tent and returned shortly with an officer. "Officer MacLeod will take you to the station. And he'll bring you back to the B&B when you're done."

Mia rolled her shoulders. "Can we continue to work the tent? We've been here all afternoon, and we've made some headway."

"Yes. We did a thorough search and have the fingerprints we found on file. Most are from the students and Dr. Carter. The volunteers need to be fingerprinted for elimination purposes. Do you have a list of their names?" Anderson asked.

Mia glanced at her watch. It was just past three. "Angus is here, but I don't know who else volunteered. Angus might know."

"Right, I'll go speak with him now," Anderson said.

Mia led him to Angus who was at the table checking information in one of the binders.

"Angus, DI Anderson would like a word with you," Mia said.

Angus looked up. "Ah, of course. How can I be of assistance?"

Anderson pulled a chair up by Angus. "I need a list of the volunteers for the dig. And anything you can tell me about them."

Mia sat by Angus.

"I have a list here on my phone. Do you want me to send it to you?"

"That would be helpful."

Angus found the list and sent it. "What else do you need?"

"How well do you know them? Have you worked with them before?"

"Three of them were students of mine at uni. They studied history and are teachers in the area. They're interested in the history of Skye and are quite knowledgeable about the broch. Two of them have worked on digs in Skye for the last three summers. The third one just moved back to the island last year, and this is her first dig." Angus took a breath.

Anderson nodded. "Do you think any of them might be swayed by someone looking to buy artifacts?"

"You mean stealing the artifacts?" Angus's eyebrows puckered together. "No one here would steal artifacts, and they certainly wouldn't sell them." His lips pressed together in a straight line. "Now look here, are you accusing us of stealing artifacts?"

"Of course not. But someone was asking Dr. Carter about buying artifacts; he returned to the dig and was killed. One could reasonably concur that the person inquiring is the one responsible for his death," Anderson said.

"We've had a few days where we had up to fifty people stopping by to look around and ask questions. I know Dr. Carter had asked if one of the volunteers could take care of dealing with the visitors. We sat down to make a list of the questions people might ask. We put that list together and were going to use it this week."

"I'd like to see that list," Mia said. "We can use it to put information together to hand out to people."

Angus nodded. "I'd be pleased to give it to you."

"No one else comes to mind that might have wanted to purchase the artifacts?" Anderson asked.

Angus shook his head. "I can ask around. The other volunteers aren't coming in until next week."

"That's fine. I'll arrange for someone to talk to the volunteers. Thank you for your time. If you think of anything else, please contact me." Anderson gave Angus his business card. "I'm staying at the B&B until we settle this matter." Anderson stood.

Luke walked up to Mia. "Learn anything new?"

Mia shook her head. "Just the list of the volunteers. Did you learn anything?"

"There have been a few people stopping by to see where Ethan died. Ghoulish, but people will do that."

Mia shuddered. "Have the security people been moving them along?"

"Yes, they're imposing figures, and don't let people dawdle about."

"Good. I'm not sure I like the idea of having visitors at the site. I know people are curious about what we're doing, especially if they're from the area. But I don't like people gawking at where Ethan died."

"How are you going to handle working that square?"

Mia took off her glasses and rubbed her face. "Honestly, I don't know. I could close that one off. Our focus should be on the location the sgian-dubh was found. I have a feeling we'll find more artifacts if we work there."

"It might be easier for the students as well. How are you holding up?" Luke asked.

"I'm not sure. When I'm busy, I'm fine. But then I turn around to tell Ethan something and realize he isn't there." Mia blinked away the tears. "It's challenging." Mia cleared her throat. "I'm going to keep working on storing the artifacts we have."

"I'll lend a hand. Anderson doesn't need me."

They worked steadily until just past five o'clock. Mia looked around. The tent was reorganized. Artifacts returned to their correct bins and checked off the lists. Diana had photographed every artifact and was uploading the photos to the site's cloud account.

"I think we can call it a day. We've done a lot of work, and we'll be ready to work outside tomorrow," Mia said.

Angus looked up from the container he was putting away. "Did the police say we'd have access?"

"Anderson told me they'd finished with the square. We'll be able to continue our work."

Diana smiled. "That's great. I'm looking forward to it."

"Angus, you're welcome to join us at the pub for dinner tonight. We should be there in about an hour," Mia said.

"Thanks for the offer, but I need to get myself home. I'll be back tomorrow morning if that's all right."

Mia gave Luke the keys to the van, "I'll meet you at the van. I want to speak with the security guards before we leave."

Mia walked to Harry. "I wanted to let you know we're done for the day."

"We have a change of shift coming up shortly. If anything happens, we're to contact Mr. Gordon and then you."

"All right. Have a good evening."

Mia started the van.

"Do most digs need security?" Diana asked.

"It depends on the dig. Usually when there's treasure hunters in the area, it's important to have security. And who's funding the dig. Not every funding agency can afford security round the clock."

"That's right. Usually, government-funded digs don't have the resources to bring in security. A lot of digs in third world countries don't have the finances to pay for it, and many of the artifacts can get looted," Luke said.

Diana piped up. "When I was in Belize last year, we had enforcers from the local militia. They worked the different digs throughout Belize, and nobody came near the digs they worked on."

Mia smiled. "Local militia sounds like mercenaries. Were they?" She looked in the rear-view mirror.

Diana shrugged. "Not sure, but they were armed. Machetes and machine guns. I was only there for two weeks. This was a dig I'd found on my own. My parents weren't exactly thrilled when I told them about the security team."

Luke chuckled. "I imagine you had a grand time."

"It was amazing! We were working on one of the temples! We found some fantastic artifacts, and the company we were working for did a lot of work to promote the finds."

Mia pulled into the parking lot of the B&B. "Sounds like it was a good two weeks. What artifacts did you find?"

"A lot of pottery, and we found a statue of a jaguar. The temple was used to purify their dead. It was creepy because of the drawings on the walls of the temple. But the jaguar statue was incredible."

"I heard about that find. It made big headlines. What happened to the jaguar?" Mia pressed the fob to lock the van.

Diana grinned. "Way above my pay grade. But it made for a great story at home and at school." Diana's phone buzzed with a text. "I just got a text from Rina. She and Phil are done with the police and are at the pub. They'll hold a table for us. I'm going to change my clothes and meet them. Did you want to join us?"

"Sure. Luke, how about you?"

"Sounds good to me."

"Diana, will you be all right getting to the pub? I need to make a few calls before heading out for dinner."

"I will. It's not far. I can manage on my own."

Mia climbed the stairs to her room and closed her door, drawing in a deep sigh. That had been a tougher day than she expected. She wanted to talk to Alex and Shelly. Toeing off her boots, she padded to the chair and called Shelly.

"Hi. I wanted to touch base with you and make sure you'd received my message about finding the sgian-dubh and the ring."

"Yes, I did. That's great news. Where did you find them?"

Mia explained to Shelly where she'd found the artifacts.

"I'm glad Ethan remembered Professor Jones's hiding places." Shelly sighed. "I spoke with DI Anderson, and he told me Ethan was murdered and had drugs in his system. Do you have any other information?"

"Two of the students went to the police station to work with a sketch artist. They saw the woman who spoke to Ethan outside the pub. The students believe someone spiked one of Ethan's drinks."

"Yeah, Ethan wouldn't have taken anything. He hated even taking something for a headache." Shelly sighed. "Who else is working at the dig?"

"Do you remember Luke Forbes from grad school?"

"I do. Ethan enjoyed working with him, and the two of you were quite the item at school. We thought you two were a good match."

"Well, he's here, and he's working for Interpol."

"What? How is he involved with them?"

Mia filled Shelly in on what Luke was doing. "Shel, I have to go. It's dinner time here. I'll keep in touch, and let you know if I learn anything else."

They hung up the call a few minutes later.

Mia pulled her backpack out of the armoire. She reached in and clicked on a latch that opened a separate hidden compartment. Mia tucked the plastic bags holding the ring and the sgian-dubh into the compartment and closed it securely, then placed her backpack in the armoire.

Mia jumped in the shower and then changed her clothes. Before leaving her room, she sent Alex a quick text.

M: Got out to the dig today, police are saying Ethan was murdered. Heading out for supper in a few. Call later?

A: That's awful. Going to a meeting shortly. I can call when walking home.

M: Sounds good.

Chapter Nine

Mia hurried downstairs and saw Luke sitting in the breakfast room.

"I hope I didn't keep you waiting."

"Not at all. Diana headed off a little while ago, and I told her I'd escort you to the pub."

They walked out and started down the lane.

"Did you get your calls done?" Luke asked.

Mia looked up at him; she'd forgotten how much he paid attention to detail. "I spoke with Shelly. She's pleased we found the sgian-dubh and the ring. She said Anderson called her with the pathologists' report."

"He would have. Anderson is a thorough investigator. He won't leave anything to chance."

"How long have you worked with him?"

"I met him a couple of years ago. It was one of my first cases, and while he initially doubted the necessity of Interpol's involvement, he eventually embraced the idea of collaborating with us." Luke paused as they stood, waiting to cross the road. "Once he got on board, his cooperation has been unmatched by any other police officer I've worked with."

"Why's that?"

"He's from this area and is a huge history buff. If he wasn't working this case, he'd be volunteering at the dig." Luke opened the door to the pub.

Mia's mouth salivated when she smelled the pub's food. She was hungrier than she'd thought.

Mia saw Phil waving in their direction. They were at the same table they'd had last night.

"Back there." She pointed to Luke.

They walked to the table and joined them. "How was the police station?" Mia asked.

Rina put her glass of beer down. "It was different. Nothing I've experienced before. In my mind, I assumed the sketch artist would use a charcoal pencil and a sketchbook. No way. They had computer software that created the face of the person we were describing."

Mia raised an eyebrow. "How did they make out?"

"We did well. We both described the same features. The police gave us copies." Phil opened the photo app on his phone and turned it to face Mia and Luke. "This is the woman that was at the dig. And we're pretty sure she's the one who approached Professor Carter about buying artifacts."

"May I?" Mia asked as she reached for his phone.

"It's remarkable. It looks exactly like a photo. And you're certain this is what she looks like?" Mia asked.

Rina nodded. "We even got them to include the nose ring. Although that might be gone if she's trying to hide."

"Yes, and changing her hairstyle would be something else she could do. But she can't change the shape of her eyes," Luke said. "Did you share this with Diana?"

Diana nodded. "I have it in my photos. I've memorized her face. If I see her, I'll point her out."

"Make sure you don't approach her. She could be dangerous," Mia said.

The server arrived to take their order. That done, Luke asked the server, "Have you seen this woman?"

The server peered at the photo on the phone. "I couldn't say for certain. She looks familiar, but we see a lot of folks come through. Why are you looking for her?"

"We're curious if she's been around in the last few days." Luke took the phone from the server.

"If I spot her, should I mention you're looking for her?" the server asked.

"That would be grand. Thanks." Luke smiled at the server.

Mia waited until she'd left to place their order. "Really? Is that a good idea?"

Luke shrugged. "Who knows? Maybe she'll be back, and if someone tells her I want to speak to her, she may think I'm interested in selling her artifacts."

"She might learn you're with the police. If she does, she'll know you won't sell her anything." Mia's eyes narrowed. "I don't think that's a great plan."

"Mia, it'll be fine. I think she needs to know someone's looking for her. It might stop her from coming around to the dig," Rina said.

"It might, or it might encourage her to access it when we aren't there."

"Don't forget, the security guards will deal with her." Phil pointed out.

"That reminds me, I need to touch base with Mr. Gordon." Mia pulled out her phone and added a reminder. "I'll speak with him after I've eaten."

The server arrived with their meals. Mia and Luke dug into their food. Fish and chips for Mia, and steak and kidney pie for Luke.

The students discussed what they'd seen in the tent. Phil made sure Diana was up to date on the work.

Mia noticed Luke looked toward the door of the pub every time someone came in. What or who was he looking for? Was Anderson supposed to meet them? Did Luke think the woman who'd approached Ethan would show up here again? With a start, she realized Luke had purposely taken a seat where he could see the door, and his back was against a wall. That reminded her of stories her father had told her about when he and her mother were working digs in Central America. He'd made sure to sit in the same position to keep an eye on who was coming in and out of the restaurants or bars. Her eyes went to the door as it opened once more, and she jumped when she recognized Dr. Bateman walking into the pub.

"What is he doing here?" she muttered under her breath.

Luke leaned forward. "What did you say?"

Mia nodded in Dr. Bateman's direction. "He's the dean of my department at the university. He knows I'm working here, and yet he didn't mention he'd be here." Mia frowned as Dr. Bateman took a seat at a table. Mia pushed her seat back and rose.

Luke grabbed her arm. "Maybe just wait a minute and see what happens. We can observe the situation before doing anything."

Mia sat down and watched as Dr. Bateman spoke with the server and shortly after a pitcher of beer and a glass of whiskey were on the table. The server left two additional glasses next to the beer. Dr. Bateman pulled his phone out of his pocket and appeared to answer a phone call.

The students laughed at Phil's remark. Mia had missed it. "Sorry, what was that?" she asked.

Phil chuckled. "I gave a poor imitation of a Viking marauder. Just in case we run into one on this dig."

Mia smiled. "Hmm, don't think that will happen. At least not in this century."

"What's the plan for tomorrow?" Phil asked.

Mia pushed her plate away and took a drink of beer. "We'll be able to get back to digging. Are you all okay with working in the squares?" Mia watched them as she asked the question.

"I'm not sure I'm ready. Could I keep working in the tent?" Rina didn't meet Mia's eyes.

"We could use someone with experience in the tent. I think the idea of the bulletin board with information on the dig and what we've found is a good one. Rina, could you work on that?" Mia asked.

"Yes. I'd need to print photos and get some documents put together."

"Any place nearby to print?" Mia asked.

"There's a print shop in the village," Phil said.

"Okay. Rina, if you'll take the lead on that project I'd appreciate it. The rest of us will work in the squares."

"I'll have to use the site laptop to write the documents. Will that be a problem?" Rina asked.

"It shouldn't be." Mia's phone dinged with a text. "Excuse me. I need to check this."

It was a message from Charles Gordon.

Please contact me with an update.

"I need to make a phone call. I'm going to head back to the B&B. Let's meet in the breakfast room before going to the dig. We should plan on being there by eight."

Luke stood with Mia. "I'll walk back with you."

"Thanks. See you all later."

Mia sent a text to Charles Gordon.

Will call in about fifteen minutes.

Mia and Luke got up. "I'm going to see Dr. Bateman and find out what he's doing here."

"I'll be right beside you."

"Dr. Bateman, hello. I wasn't expecting to see you here."

Dr. Bateman looked up, and his eyes widened. "Dr. Reid. I didn't realize you were staying in the village."

"There's a B&B just up the road. It's close to the dig. I didn't think you were able to get away this summer."

Dr. Bateman cleared his throat. "I had a holiday planned for a tour around Scotland. Charles Gordon asked if I'd stop in and see how the dig was going. You know I'm considered an expert in Scottish history and the find of the sgian-dubh and ring will no doubt bring people looking for more treasure. Charles thought I'd be able to provide some assistance. A shame about your colleague, Dr. Carter."

Mia focused on Dr. Bateman. "Yes. His death is a loss to the archaeology community and to me personally. The police have advised me his death is being investigated as a murder. I'll be working closely with them to have his killer brought to justice."

"I don't believe I know your friend." Dr. Bateman stood and reached his hand toward Luke. "Dr. Bateman, dean of the school of archaeology at Lakeview University."

"Luke Forbes, AART agent with Interpol."

Mia noticed Dr. Bateman's eyes narrowed as he looked at Luke.

"And what is AART?"

Mia's attention wandered as Luke explained his position with Interpol.

"Well, it seems as if there's a lot of interest in your dig," Dr. Bateman said.

"The artifacts Ethan found are of interest to many people. Especially the locals. We'll be putting together a bulletin board with information on the artifacts we've found. Do you plan on coming to the site?" Mia could be blunt when required to.

"Yes. I plan on being there tomorrow morning, sometime before noon. Can you give me directions?"

"I'll send the coordinates to you by text. If you have any questions, don't hesitate to contact me."

"Excellent. Now, if you'll excuse me, I have colleagues that I'm meeting with shortly, and I'd like to prepare." Dr. Bateman sat and reached for his whiskey.

"Of course. See you in the morning."

Mia and Luke left the pub and started toward the B&B.

Two men passed by them, hustling toward the pub. Mia turned around to look at them and frowned. They looked like the two men who'd run into her at the university. And were they the same men she'd seen at the airport? Why would they be here?

Luke called her name. "Mia, everything all right?"

She looked back at him. "Yes, sorry. Just thought I recognized those two men. Did you say something?"

"I wondered when you last did field work?"

"Last summer. Ethan and I were in Peru. Shelly and Henry joined us for a month. Then Ethan and I went back to our respective universities for the academic year. Henry got sick in September. Ethan and Shelly were beside themselves."

"I'm sorry to hear that. Henry's doing better?"

"He's better, but not strong enough to have come out with Ethan. Ethan planned to return home to Chicago next month for a few weeks. Shelly's had a very rough year, and it just got tougher." Mia's lips pressed together.

"Are you going back to the university in the fall?"

Mia updated him on the recent events. "I don't know that I'm cut out for academia. There's a lot of politics, and I don't enjoy them. I like working with the students and seeing them light up with excitement."

"What are your options?"

"I could do some field work. There are opportunities in Lakeview. Or I could work with one of the museums."

"Where are your parents?"

Mia smiled. Luke remembered her parents well. They'd all worked together one summer. "I think they're still in South America. And yes, I could work with them, but I'd rather not. Something will turn up. I'm not too worried. I have funds put away. And my grandfather provided for me as well."

"Right, the trust fund. How's your grandmother?"

"She's great. Still actively involved in the arts scene in Lakeview. I saw her at the Lakeview Museum fundraiser before I left. She's the one who told me about the smuggling ring operating in Lakeview."

"How did she learn about it?"

"She has a lot of connections with people involved in the antique markets and the antiquities trade. Once she retired from her small antique shop, she dedicated her time to serving on the board of directors for several organizations. Some people she knows were in the market for high-quality artifacts and didn't care how they found them."

"Did she think your university or the museum might have been involved with the smuggling ring?"

"She didn't say. I can't think of anyone from the university or museum who would do something illegal."

Luke shook his head. "You'd be surprised. The patron who approached me is wealthy and has connections in a big industry. When I learned what he wanted, I was shocked."

They entered the B&B, and Luke motioned to the sitting room. "Do you want to join me in a nightcap?"

"I do, but I need to connect with Mr. Gordon and provide him with an update for today. I'll run up to my room to call. It shouldn't take more than ten minutes."

"Excellent. I'll meet you back here."

Once in her room, Mia took a minute to refresh her mind about the day's events. She decided to let Charles Gordon know about everything, including

DEATH AT THE SCOTTISH BROCH

that Phil and Rina had gone to the police station to work with a sketch artist. And that she'd met Dr. Bateman. She wanted answers about why he was here.

She placed the call to Mr. Gordon.

Mia provided him with a detailed report. When she mentioned the volunteers, he asked, "Do they have a decent amount of experience?"

"The one I've met has been working digs in the summer for twenty years. Angus is happy to help where he's needed, and he has a wealth of knowledge about the area."

"And are the police any closer to identifying Dr. Carter's killer?"

"The sketch will help, but they aren't sure the woman killed him."

"How was the security team?"

"They were excellent. We all felt safe with them at the site. I was told there would be someone there twenty-four hours a day."

"Yes. I should've had them in place initially, but I didn't expect any problems. Where are you keeping the ring and the sgian-dubh?"

Mia froze for a moment. They were supposed to be in the safe at the B&B. Instead, they were in the secret compartment in her luggage. She didn't want to share that information with Mr. Gordon and have him think she was irresponsible. "Uh, they're in the safe here at the B&B. We could have stored them at the police station, but I was worried they'd go missing."

"That's probably the best location. Anything else to report?"

"Yes. I met Dr. Bateman at the pub this evening. I didn't realize you knew him or that he'd be here with the purpose of helping at the dig."

"That's my doing. When I heard Dr. Carter had died, I thought you might need some experienced help, and Dr. Bateman was available. He didn't mind leaving for his holiday early."

"I wish you had told me about this first. We're a solid team, and introducing someone else, especially someone with limited field experience, may set us back a bit."

"I am sponsoring the dig. And thought it would ease your workload. Dr. Bateman won't be there more than a week. You may find his expertise helpful. I'd like him to examine the sgian-dubh and the ring."

"I'll arrange for him to examine them. Is there anything else?"

"Nothing else. Have a good evening." Gordon ended the call.

Mia put her phone down and toed off her shoes. She took off her sweater and put it in the dresser. Opening the armoire, she pulled her backpack out and opened the compartment at the bottom. Taking the artifacts out, she wondered whether they'd be more secure in the B&B safe or if she left them here in the compartment. Mia didn't want anyone else to get hurt over the artifacts. *"Ugh! Probably safer in my backpack. The safe would be a logical place for potential thieves to break into."* She tucked them back in the compartment and put her sneakers and heavier jacket on top of the compartment. Satisfied, she put the backpack in the armoire, put on a pair of shoes, and went downstairs to join Luke.

Chapter Ten

Luke was sitting in one of the wing chairs by the window. When Mia walked in, he stood, "What would you like to drink?"

"I'll have a whiskey, no ice."

Luke grinned. "Glad to see you still know how to drink it. Did you want some water?"

"On the side." Mia watched as he poured two fingers of whiskey in the glass and then added room-temperature water into a smaller glass. He brought the drinks to the table between the two chairs.

"Cheers." Mia and Luke touched glasses.

"Oh, my, that's good."

"It is." Luke put his glass down. "What did Mr. Gordon have to say?"

Mia filled him in on her conversation. "It appears Dr. Bateman is here at Mr. Gordon's request. I'll have to work around him and make sure he's happy with what he's doing."

"It might not be as bad as you think. He might prove to be helpful."

Mia rolled her eyes and changed the subject. "Can you talk about your work, some of your cases?"

"I've been working on cases in Great Britain. I've not gone on the continent yet. Although there is the possibility of that happening soon."

"Would you work in North America?"

"I might. We go where we're needed. One of our agents worked in New York City for a few years. She helped bring down a large smuggling ring that crossed the United States."

"Did she work alone?"

"No, she worked with the local police and the FBI."

"What exactly do you do?" Mia sipped her whiskey.

"It depends on the situation. Sometimes, we're working with law enforcement; in others, it's with the country's government, or we could work with the agency that's had something stolen. Our responsibility is to ensure that the artifacts are returned to their rightful owners."

"Wouldn't the artifacts automatically go back to the country of origin?"

"In theory, yes. We work hard to find the owners or the heirs, but sometimes they can't be located. If someone steals an item from a country's museum or from a dig, we repatriate it to that country."

"Nothing's as simple as you think." Mia put her glass down.

"If only. There's usually something that's challenged with the items. From my perspective, there was only one case where it was cut and dried. That's because it grabbed attention in the antiquities world."

"Are you in any danger when you do this type of work?"

"It depends." Luke shrugged when Mia rolled her eyes. "Well, it's true. If a cartel or smuggling ring is involved, then yes, it can be dangerous. If it involves a museum and an honest mistake was made, then it's not so dangerous. Unless you count board members who don't want to give up the artifacts, and they tie us up in red tape." Luke sipped his whiskey. "I've had a few hairy moments when dealing with smugglers. This cartel that you've brought up from Canada sounds as if it's going to be trouble."

Mia sighed. "It wasn't me. It was Gran. And I'm concerned that she even knows about it. She should be enjoying her time as a volunteer and not worry about these kinds of things."

"If I remember correctly, your Gran was quick to note if anything was off. And I doubt she'd be foolish enough to try to take on a cartel or smuggling ring."

"You're right. She has the chief of police on speed dial. She'd call him up if she discovered anything." Mia yawned and tried to cover it up. "Sorry, I assumed I'd be over the jet lag. I should get to bed. Tomorrow's a full day at the dig."

"I'll be there. Can you set me up with tools to work?"

"Sure, but won't you be busy with Anderson?"

"I'll be watching anyone who comes to the dig. Ethan's death leads me to suspect someone is here to steal artifacts. Until my superiors tell me differently, I'll be around. Consider me additional hands to do the grunt work."

Mia chuckled. "You might be sorry. How long since you worked in the field?"

"Too long."

"Not a problem. We can set you up. Wear comfortable clothes. And long sleeves to protect you from the midges."

Everyone was in good spirits the next morning. Breakfast had been a lively meal with the students joking with Luke when they learned he was joining them at the dig. On the drive over, Phil teased him about his clean work clothes. "You know those are going to be trashed by the end of the day?"

"I'm aware. I'm sure I'll be able to find more clothes if I need them. My jeans will work just fine for today. And Mrs. McDonald has graciously offered to wash anything that I need done."

"All right, guys. Let's leave off ragging on Luke. We should be thankful to have someone of his experience and expertise with us." Mia rolled her eyes when she said this, and everyone, including Luke, burst into laughter.

Mia pulled the van into the parking lot. "You guys head to the tent. I want to get an update from security about last night."

The students hustled to the tent, and Mia walked toward the security team. Hearing a footstep, she turned and saw Luke behind her. At her raised eyebrow, he said, "It's a good idea for me to listen in as well. Security needs to know who I am and why I'm here."

"No problem with that. But let me start the conversation."

They stopped a few feet away from the security team and Mia waited until they had finished speaking.

"Morning. How did things go last night?"

MacAllister, the same security guard from the previous day, answered. "The overnight team said it was a quiet night. No one even drove by. An electronic report was sent to Mr. Gordon, with a copy to you."

"Thanks." Mia nodded at Luke. "This is Dr. Luke Forbes, and he's working with Interpol."

Luke shook hands with the team leader and gave them his contact information. He briefly explained his role at the dig.

"Great, we're here for the day. Some of us will be in the tent, and the others will be in the squares. Oh, and Dr. Bateman is supposed to come by later this morning. Could you direct him to the tent when he arrives?"

MacAllister made a note. "Not a problem."

At the tent, Mia and the team spent a few minutes preparing their tools and stowing their lunches.

Phil held out some tools and gloves to Luke. "We guessed at the size for the gloves. There are other sizes in the locker. The tools are extras that we have."

"Thanks." Luke put the gloves on. "Great fit. I appreciate this."

"All right. Let's get to work. Rina, are you going to organize the bulletin board?" Mia asked.

"Yes. I wrote up some descriptions of what we're doing and what we've found to date. Can I include the information on the ring and the sgian-dubh?"

"Of course, but add a note that we keep the more valuable artifacts in a different location. Just don't tell anyone where they're located."

"Is Angus going to be helping me with this project?" Rina asked.

"He said he'd like to. And from what I recall, he mentioned something about putting the bulletin board together. I hope he has something, otherwise we're going to have to build it ourselves." Mia glanced around the tent. "There's not a lot here we could use."

Phil picked up his water bottle. "He mentioned he has a large sandwich board that he can put up. And he has sandbags that will help keep it in place."

"Sounds great. Okay. Time to start our day. I'll let you figure out where you want to work, and I'll work alongside whoever might need help. Luke will assist where needed."

Luke put his gloves in his back pocket and pulled on a baseball cap.

Each person grabbed their equipment, and they walked to the squares. The broch's circular wall had crumbled in some spots, but enough structure remained to provide shelter from the wind.

In short order, everyone was busy with their tasks. Mia watched the students for a few minutes and, satisfied they knew what they were doing, turned her attention to her section of the square. The work was physical and repetitive. Scrape away a layer of dirt, ensure there wasn't an artifact in the dirt. Brush dirt away from rocks and stones in the ground. Around her, the students talked about what their plans were for the treasure they'd find.

Her thoughts wandered to the ring and the sgian-dubh. Who could they have belonged to? The ring had gemstones in it, and the center one was large and red. Could it be a ruby? If so, where did it come from? The ring had markings on its band. It wasn't crudely made. An artisan had worked on it and spent considerable effort. She made a mental note to examine it closely tonight. The sgian-dubh would need closer examination as well. She was curious about the design on the blade. Both the handle and the ring had the same jewels and the same design on the metal. That's why she thought they'd belonged to the same person. In her mind, that person might have been of royal blood. After hearing about Bonnie Prince Charlie from Angus, she wondered if they could have belonged to him. She had remembered to bring them in her daypack for Dr. Bateman to examine whenever he showed up today.

A shout from Diana drew her attention. "Dr. Reid, Mia, come here!"

Mia hurried to Diana's side. "Did you find something?"

Diana was brushing dirt away from a flat, circular object. "I think it's a coin. Can you see?"

Mia leaned closer. The object looked like a coin. The color was a dull yellow. "Here, let's get a few photos first." Mia put her brush next to the coin. "Phil, get the camera."

Phil hurried over with the camera and gave it to Diana. She snapped several photos and took a moment to check their quality. "They look good. Can you check them?" she asked Mia.

"They're good photos. It's definitely a coin." Mia leaned forward with the camera and focused on the top of the coin. She snapped a couple more photos. "Can you make out the lettering on it?" she asked Luke.

Luke took the camera and said, "Yes. I can see it clearly. Well done, Diana."

Diana grinned. "Whoo! My first big find!" She looked at Mia. "It's a big find, isn't it?"

Mia smiled. "Yes. You did well with this one. Now let's get it out."

Diana worked to remove the coin from the dirt.

Phil crowded by Diana to check out the coin. "Wow, this is in amazing condition!" Phil's voice rose.

"I agree." Mia opened a small bag. "Once everyone's seen it, we'll pop it in here. Diana, don't forget to label it with the date and your initials."

Luke pulled out his loupe and examined the coin. "Well done, Diana. The markings show circa 1740s. It may very well tie in with Bonnie Prince Charlie's travels across Skye."

Phil glanced around. "I wonder if there's going to be more?"

Chapter Eleven

Diana and Mia took the coin and hustled to the tent.

"Do you have something for us?" Angus asked.

"Diana, you do the honors."

"Check it out." Diana placed the baggie with the coin on the table.

"Oh, that's a beauty!" Rina leaned forward to get a better look.

"Diana uncovered it. She did great work getting it out of the ground." Mia pointed to the coin. "There's a date, and some other marks that I can't make out."

Angus picked up the bag. "We can clean it up. Once we remove the dirt and grime, it will show up."

Rina opened the site computer. "I'll log it in, and then we can start cleaning it. Did you find anything else this morning?"

"More pottery shards, nothing else like this."

Rina finished with the computer and then logged the information in the ledger. She glanced at Angus. "I'm done with it. You can take it away."

Angus grinned. "This will be a pleasure to clean."

"I'd like to watch you clean it," Diana said.

"Follow me then."

Mia and Diana followed him to the cleaning station. The table had several large tubs used to clean artifacts. The tubs would be filled with water. They used a drying rack at the far end of the table to place the cleaned artifacts to dry.

Angus picked up the five-gallon jug of water and poured water into one tub. He grabbed two toothbrushes and a soft towel. He used a toothbrush to brush away any dirt. When he was satisfied most of the dirt had been removed, he put the coin in the water and taking the other toothbrush, started brushing away the remaining dirt. He kept at it until he was happy with the results. The soft towel gently sopped up the excess water on the coin and then he laid the coin down on the drying rack.

"Ah, lovely," Angus said.

Mia leaned forward and saw the letters and designs on the coin clearly. The coin had fleurs de lis stamped on it, and Mia could easily see the letters FR.

"Pretty, isn't it?" Angus asked.

"It sure is!" Diana's voice rose. "I'm so happy I found it!"

"Yes. This dig is full of surprises. Ethan would be happy." Mia's eyes filled with tears. She took off her glasses and brushed at her eyes. "Sorry, I don't mean to be all emotional here."

Angus peered at her. "It's all right, lass. He was a good friend, wasn't he?"

"He was." Mia drew a deep breath. "Okay, let's get back to work. I'll leave you to this. Rina, if you want some time out in the squares, you're welcome to join us."

"Thanks. I'm going to finish up in here today. I'll be out there tomorrow."

Mia and Diana joined the others in the squares and settled into work. Luke was working nearby, and he asked, "Everything okay?"

Mia nodded. "All good. Rina and Angus were happy with the coin." She wasn't going to share with him that she'd gotten weepy thinking about Ethan. She still couldn't solve the mystery of who attacked him. As she swept dirt away, she tried to get a picture in her mind of Ethan's last night. From what she understood, it was a clear night. Even though the site wasn't lit, the moon had been full, and he would've had a flashlight with him. Had he interrupted someone in the tent? Or had he seen the disarray in the tent and gone out to check the dig?

"Oh wow!" Phil called out. "Come and see!"

Luke hurried to Phil's side. "Mia, come here!"

"What did you find?" Mia asked as she strode to Phil's section of the square.

"Look! There are at least a dozen coins and what seems like small colored rocks." Phil pointed to a section that had been unearthed. A mound of what appeared to be gold coins and small rocks were in the section. There was also a small pouch next to the coins.

"Phil, that's amazing! Well done." Mia bent forward, her hands at her side, not wanting to disturb the find. "Diana, do you have the camera?"

Diana got busy taking photos. "What are the small rocks?"

Luke glanced at Mia. "They might be loose gemstones. It's possible the pouch was used to carry the gold coins and gemstones."

Mia nodded. "I agree. Let's get the photos done. Then we can examine the items thoroughly."

Phil worked carefully to dislodge the coins and gemstones, transferring them into small baggies to keep them safe. "What are these worth?" he asked.

"Hard to tell. Luke, do you know?" Mia asked.

"Not right off. It's something that we'll need to evaluate. We'll check age, what the composition of the coins are, and for the gemstones we'll need to determine the cut, weight, and stone. You did well, Phil. I'm happy you didn't toss the gemstones away."

"When I saw the colors, I didn't think they were rocks."

"Let's check the area to make sure we haven't missed any." Mia brushed away some dirt and then ran her bare hands over the surface. She felt something roll underneath her hand, she stopped and picked up a dark green stone. "One more for the bag."

"Is that an emerald?" Diana asked.

"Possibly. We'll need to have it examined to be certain." Mia shrugged. "We need to figure out where these can be kept. I'm not comfortable leaving them here."

"The B&B has a safe. They should be secure there," Phil said.

"I may have another location." Mia dusted off the dirt on her hands. "Phil, let's bring these in to be catalogued. I'll make certain to speak with the security guards to make them aware we've found artifacts with potentially high monetary value."

Phil and Mia hurried to the tent.

Phil put the baggies on the table. "Take a look."

Rina gasped. "Wow! That is a find."

Angus trotted up to the table. "Oh my! This is grand. Perhaps the rumors are true."

Mia frowned. "What rumors?"

"They say Bonnie Prince Charlie took shelter in the broch when he was trying to escape. I didn't think much of it with just the one gold coin. But this amount would've been something he would have had with him."

"I don't want this getting out. It could make our lives difficult. Especially if people think there's more treasure to be found."

Angus nodded. "I understand. I won't share this information with anyone. But, this is a small village, and it won't take long for people to hear about it. There's always been rumors about a lost treasure at the broch."

"Rina, could you and Phil log these in the system. I'll try to get in touch with Mr. Gordon although he may have his phone turned off."

"Sure thing. How do you want us to log the gemstones?"

Mia frowned. "Hmm, list the number of gemstones, their size, and their color. Right now, we aren't positive they're gems."

"I'll do that. Angus, could you give us a hand?"

Mia stepped to the far side of the tent and her call to Mr. Gordon.

"Mia, what can I do for you?" he asked.

Mia filled him in on the find and the security issues with it.

"That's a good point. I suppose the safe at the dig isn't secure enough?"

Mia glanced at the small safe that was tucked by the filing cabinet. "No. Someone could pick it up and walk away with it. It's fine for documents, but not for something like this."

"Can you send me photos of the coins and the gemstones?"

"I will as soon as they're logged in. Rina, Phil, and Angus are doing that now."

"Excellent. Now, what does the security team suggest about increasing security?"

"I haven't spoken with them yet. I'm concerned about trespassers showing up. We might need to increase the number of guards. At other digs I've been involved with we also installed security lighting for overnight use."

"Those are good suggestions. I'll contact them and request they bring in more guards and that they install security lighting. I'll tell them to go ahead with the generator and lights for the evening hours." Mr. Gordon paused, "This doesn't fix the problem of where to put these finds."

"There's a safe at the B&B, and we can use it. I'll touch base with the police to see if they can suggest anything."

"Is there a bank in the area?"

"I'm not sure. A safe deposit box would be good to use."

"Try all three options, and I'll trust you to go with the one that works best. I've changed my plans and will be joining you in Skye earlier than expected. I should be there later this evening. My pilot is getting ready to take off. Send me the photos, and I'll speak to the security team now."

"Will do." Mia disconnected the call and considered her options. She could take the gemstones and the coins to the bank or place them in the B&B safe. They would also be safe in the hidden compartment where the ring and the sgian-dubh were. She was confident that would work. In the meantime, if anyone asked where they were kept, she'd say for security reasons, she couldn't divulge the location. She nodded to herself. Decision made. They'd stay in her hidden compartment.

Returning to the table, she found Rina and Angus logging the items in the system.

"These are great. I can't believe there are ten different gems. And eighteen gold pieces." Rina's face was lit up.

"They weren't that much deeper in the ground than the first gold piece we found." Mia picked up a gemstone. It was a dull gray. "I wonder if this is a diamond?"

"It might be. It isn't overly large, but it will be a stunning stone when it's cleaned up." Angus drew closer to see the gemstone Mia had in her hand. "May I?" he asked.

"Of course." Mia handed him the gemstone.

Angus scraped away some of the dirt. What fell away revealed the stone was cut in a pear shape. "This shows excellent craftsmanship." He picked up one of the gold coins. "If word gets out, the locals are going to be quite excited."

"Yes. There are changes coming to our security. Lights are going up for the evening shifts and I'm looking into a secure place to keep these items. But before that, I'm going to photograph them and send the photos to Mr. Gordon."

Rina cleaned up a section of the table, and Mia set up the coins and gemstones for the photos. She took photos of both sides of the coins and different angles of the gemstones. Checking the photos for clarity, she sent them to Mr. Gordon with a brief explanation of the photos.

"I'd better get these in the safe for now. Rina, can you give me a hand?"

Rina and Mia returned the coins and the gemstones in the correctly labeled baggies. Rina helped Mia carry them to the safe. Mia entered the combination and deposited the baggies. Once the safe was locked, she sighed. "That feels better, secure for now. How's the information for the signage going?"

"I finished the descriptions of what our daily tasks are, why we're working here, and I'm almost done with the history of the broch. Angus has been helpful with that. I'd like you to review them before we go to print."

"Not a problem. And what are we using to display the information?"

Angus interrupted. "I brought a large sandwich board I had at home. There's a plexiglass covering that will protect the documents and photos from the elements."

"That's excellent. You've covered everything. Let me know when you want me to review what you've written."

"Probably after lunch. I want to follow up on a few things first," Rina said.

"I'll leave you to it then." Mia went back to the squares.

Luke looked up as she approached. "All good?"

"Yes. The coins and gemstones are secure in the safe. I need to decide what to do with them before we leave today."

Luke stood and dusted his legs off. "Why don't we take a walk?"

Mia followed him away from the dig and realized he was leading them away from the security guards as well. "What's up?"

Luke stopped just short of the perimeter. "I'm getting strange vibes from the security guards. Nothing I can pinpoint. Just a feeling that they're not what they should be."

"Like what?"

"Did you notice their weapons? Those are not tasers, they're Glocks. They appear to be ex-military."

Mia casually looked at the closest security guard. She noticed the gun in his shoulder holster, and the earpiece in his ear. She blew out a breath. "Okay, I don't know anything about security guards except the ones I've encountered at work and in my travels. Are you saying these guys may be a problem?"

"They might be overqualified for what we need."

"Mr. Gordon hired them, or his office did. Do you want me to make him aware of our concerns? To be honest, after what we found this morning, I'm more comfortable with these guys around than not having anyone here."

"Where have you decided to keep this morning's finds?"

Mia glanced around and lowered her voice. "Right now, they're in the safe. I'll be taking them back to the B&B and tucking them in a special compartment I have. It's where I have the sgian-dubh and the ring. I'll show you where it is later today. I told Mr. Gordon I was going to keep them in the B&B safe or at a bank."

"Do you not trust him?"

"I'm not sure who he'd give the information to. I don't know him that well. And he told me this morning that he's flying to Skye today." Mia took her glasses off and rubbed her face.

"Did he say why he's coming?"

"No. He'd planned on visiting later, but with the artifacts we've found, I think he wants to see them sooner rather than later. Right now, the artifacts are safe. When we leave today, I'll secure them in my room."

Chapter Twelve

"Mia, could you come here?" Diana called out.

Mia raised her hand. "I'll be right there." She looked at Luke. "Are we okay here?"

"Yes, I'll keep a close eye on this security team."

Mia and Luke walked to Diana's side. "Did you find something?" Mia asked.

"It looks like a pot of some kind, but I'm having trouble getting it out. I think it's intact."

Mia knelt next to Diana. "Let's see if we can get some leeway here." Mia took out a dental pick and dug away at the packed dirt. "You can see how deeply embedded this is. We'll have to be gentle. This is a great example of a pot that was used to store grains."

Phil grabbed the camera and photographed their progress.

Diana pulled out her pick and started working on the other side. Together they unearthed enough of the pot that Diana was able to extract it from the ground. "Oh wow! Look at it!"

Mia smiled. "There isn't any damage that I can see. Here, use my brush, and we'll see if there's any designs."

Diana took Mia's brush and gently cleaned the pot. As she did, the paintings along the sides of the pot appeared. The pot had Celtic designs carved into it.

"Great find, Diana," Phil said as the pot's designs came through.

Diana set the pot down on the ground, and they examined it carefully. Rina and Angus hurried to see the discovery.

"Any more gems?" Angus called out.

Mia winced and looked around. There wasn't anyone to hear except for the security guards. "Angus, please, we have to be careful."

"Aye, sorry, miss. Just got excited."

Luke pointed at the pot Diana had found. "It's an excellent example of everyday use."

"Would it have been used to store food?" Rina asked.

"I think so. If you look closely, it appears that chafes of wheat are painted along the sides."

Phil had finished taking photos and was checking them for quality. "The photos are good. Are we going to catalogue this too?"

"Yes. And then I think a lunch break is in order." Mia glanced at her watch. It was already past one o'clock. She wondered where Dr. Bateman was. He'd said he would be at the site around noon. She sent him a quick text, but didn't get a response.

Diana carried the pot to the tent, and she and Rina entered the information in the log. The rest of the team cleaned up and took their lunches out. Mrs. MacDonald had provided thick sandwiches, fresh fruit, and cookies, or biscuits, as they were called in Scotland. Mia read the information Rina had put together for the bulletin board.

The tent fell silent as they ate their food. Angus had brought his meal as well. When they had finished, Rina asked, "Where are you going to store the coins and the gemstones?"

"The B&B has a safe, and I'm going to ask Mrs. MacDonald if we can store them there. If it's a problem, I'll look into taking them to a bank. Although, if there isn't a branch here, I'd have to go to Portree for that." Mia tucked her lunch containers in her daypack and took a drink of water. "Please don't mention where we're storing the finds. The security guards are bumping up their security, and I'd rather we didn't have too many people stopping by the dig searching for more treasure."

"Dr. Carter would be thrilled with these finds. He kept saying he thought this was going to be a great summer," Phil said.

Mia smiled. "He'd be so excited."

There was a shout from one of the security guards, and Mia and Luke ran out of the tent. What they saw shocked them. Six people, carrying shovels, were running toward the dig. One of the guards yelled, "Stop right now!"

When the six people didn't stop, he raised his gun in the air and fired.

People screamed, and Mia ducked. "Oh no! We'll not have that," Mia said.

The six people stopped in their tracks. One of the security guards was on the phone; the other had the six sitting on the ground. He was fastening their hands together with what looked like zip ties.

Mia strode toward the guard, her steps urgent. "What's going on? Who are you? And what do you want?"

"We're here for the treasure. It belongs to us!" One of the men called out.

"What treasure?" Mia seemed puzzled. How had people heard about this morning's finds already?

"It's all over the news! You've found Bonnie Prince Charlie's cache of gold and jewels." One of the women said.

Mia turned to look at the group in the tent. "Did anyone post pictures on social media?"

"Mia, we know better. There's no way we'd do that." Phil shook his head.

"If it wasn't any of us, then the only other person could be Charles Gordon. Why would he do that?"

"Maybe he needs to drum up interest in the dig?" Luke suggested.

Mia frowned. "He better not. We don't need treasure hunters. These people didn't even wait until we were done for the day."

They could hear police sirens coming toward them. The two police cars stopped at the edge of the perimeter, and two officers jumped out of the vehicle.

They spoke with the security guards, and then one of them approached Mia. "What would you like to do with them, miss?"

"You mean I have a choice?"

"You do. Do you want them arrested for trespassing? Or do you want to let them go?"

"For Pete's sake. Let me go talk to them before anything happens."

Mia jogged across to where the security guards were watching the six men and women. She stopped a few feet away. "How did you hear about the treasure that was found this morning?"

One of the men said, "It was on the news on the telly. And then it was all over the Internet. Pictures and everything. It said there were gold coins and gems. And that you expect to find more! We just wanted some for ourselves."

Mia rubbed her face. The only person who could have done this was Charles Gordon. She was going to have to speak to him about maintaining confidentiality. "Right then. You realize this is an archaeological dig. What we find here is given to the historical society in the area. The items we find don't belong to us. And they wouldn't belong to you either if you found them."

The six people, two women and four men, looked at each other sheepishly. "We weren't thinking clearly. We thought we'd get Bonnie Prince Charlie's treasure," one of the women said.

Mia shook her head. "I'm willing to not press charges if you promise you won't come back and dig up our site. If you want to volunteer with the dig, you'll have to pass a screening test. And then we'll keep a close eye on you while you're here."

One of the men scoffed. "I'm not going to volunteer. I've got better things to do."

Harry, the security guard, stood in front of the group and started taking photos.

"What are you doing?" one of the women asked.

"Taking your photos. They'll be distributed to our security team. If any of you show up here again, you'll be arrested." Harry glared at the woman.

"You can't do that. It's invading our privacy!" the other woman exclaimed.

"You gave that up when you trespassed on our site," Mia said.

The officers moved the group out of the dig. One of the officers stopped in front of Mia. "You'll need to increase security. Whoever leaked this news to the media has got people quite excited about your finds."

Mia sighed. "Darn it. I'll talk to Mr. Gordon and see if he can shed light on this. And we have twenty-four-hour security at the site. No one will be able to come in without being seen." Mia watched the people being led away. "Thanks for your help, Officer. We'll be in touch if we need any more assistance."

The officer touched his cap and left.

"Okay, let's get back to work. I have a call to make, and I'll join you shortly." Mia walked up to Harry. "Are you going to contact Mr. Gordon?"

"I have to report what happened. I'll be including it in my report at the end of shift."

"Fine. I'm calling him now. The only way this got out is through him or his office. He needs to understand the damage that could have happened." Mia strode away toward the team's van. She opened the door and sat in the driver's seat.

Mia took a moment to compose herself. She had to deal with Mr. Gordon's lack of judgement on releasing this information to the media. And approach it as a breach of security. That was the only way he'd understand.

She made the call and waited to be put through.

"Mia, is there a problem?" he asked.

"Yes." Mia told him what had happened and elaborated on the seriousness of his actions. "You realize this has compromised the security at the dig. I'm not sure the team we have in place will be able to handle any other attempts at treasure hunting."

Mr. Gordon was quiet for a moment. Then he cleared his throat. "I don't understand what the fuss is about. This is giving the dig some additional publicity, which it needs. Ethan Carter's death was a black mark against the dig. This is great news and shows there's something worth pursuing."

Mia's voice sharpened. "Do not use Ethan's death as a publicity stunt. The police believe that someone murdered him. Maybe treasure hunters, probably more organized than the six that showed up here today. I'm giving you notice. You will be more circumspect about what you release to the media about this dig, and you will advise me before you release anything else. Am I clear?"

"Do you realize who you're talking to? I'm the one paying you." Charles Gordon snapped back.

"I know that. I'm the one on the ground here. You're putting every one of us in danger if you continue to do this. And I will not have any student placed in jeopardy. Do you understand? I will not continue this dig if you don't start paying attention to basic security matters." Mia bit the words out one at a time.

There was silence from Mr. Gordon. Mia was determined not to break it. She'd worked with tough patrons before, but he was reckless.

"All right. I understand what you're saying. No more leaks to the media. I don't want to jeopardize anyone on the team. I'll speak with the security people and ask them what they recommend. They're on the ground and should be able to come up with a plan. I'll see you either tonight or tomorrow morning."

Mia's shoulders dropped several inches. She hadn't known what he was going to come back with. This was a reasonable plan. "Let me know when you want to meet."

"Looking forward to it." Mr. Gordon disconnected the call.

"Ugh! What an idiot!" Mia banged her hands on the steering wheel. She let out a sigh and looked up. "Ethan, what did you get me into? This guy's reckless."

Mia gazed out the windshield of the van. She could see the students working. They didn't seem fazed by the trespassers. Luke was alongside them, and she could see him sharing a laugh with Phil. For the moment, they were all safe.

"Back to work. This isn't going to solve anything." Mia shrugged her shoulders and walked back to the dig.

Harry stopped her before she got to the squares. "Did you speak with Mr. Gordon?"

"I did. I explained what happened, and he admitted he'd leaked the photos of this morning's find to the media. He mentioned he was going to speak with you about security measures. Can you explain to him the repercussions of his actions?"

"Yes. I've worked for him before, and you have to make certain he understands some of the security issues. He tends to think of the grand picture and forgets about the day-to-day grind. I'll make certain he knows this will cost more in security. We'll bring more guards beginning with tonight's shift. You'll also see the lights being set up in the next hour, along with the generator to fuel them."

"Thanks. He'll be in Skye later today and will probably stop in tonight or tomorrow."

Mia and the students worked steadily through the afternoon. A few minutes before four o'clock, DI Anderson showed up.

"Dr. Reid, I heard there was some trouble earlier."

Mia stood and stretched. "Yes. It was taken care of. The police officers arrived quickly and helped diffuse the situation."

"Hopefully, that will send a message to anyone who might think of digging for treasure."

"I spoke with Mr. Gordon, and he's the one who leaked the information to the press. He didn't realize what he was doing and thought it would generate positive publicity for the dig. He now understands the position he put us in."

"Is security going to be increased?" Anderson asked.

"Yes. You can see the lights being put up around the perimeter, and there's going to be some close to the tent and the dig as well. I've been told there will be additional guards on each shift."

"Excellent. If I could speak with you privately for a moment?"

Mia followed him to the parking lot. "What's this about?"

"I'm going to ask you again if you know anyone who would have wanted Dr. Carter dead?"

Mia shook her head. "No. Ethan didn't rock the boat. He did his work, went home to his family, and he was kind. He was the one that people would turn to if they needed help, and he gave it quickly and easily. When I met him, he was known as the nice guy, the one who would help a fellow student without any questions. And he was like that all his life."

Anderson ran his hand through his short, blond hair. "Well, someone had it in for him."

"Maybe the students he brought with him can remember something that happened that last night."

"I'll be speaking with them again." Anderson looked over to the dig. "Where's Rina?"

"She's working in the tent today with Angus."

"Right then. Is it possible to gather them all together?"

"Sure thing." Mia walked back to the dig and called everyone close.

"I have a few questions about the dinner at the pub on Monday night. Did you notice anyone hanging around who shouldn't have been?" Anderson asked.

Phil and Rina shook their heads. "We had a lot of people congratulating us on the find. People were buying us beer," Phil said.

"There were a couple of people that handed us beer directly. And I remember someone gave Dr. Carter a whiskey, no ice or water. He enjoyed a glass of whiskey." Rina frowned as she spoke. "I can't remember exactly who, but it was a man, and I think I remember a tattoo on his wrist."

"What do you remember about the tattoo?" Anderson asked.

"It was a Celtic cross design, but there was color in the middle of the cross. I'd never seen one of those before."

"Could you draw it?"

"I'll try. Phil, did you see it?" Rina asked.

"Now that you mention it, I did. I was sitting next to you and thought it was a cool design."

She pulled out her small sketch pad and started drawing. Phil watched and added a few elements she'd missed. In a short time, they both agreed on what the tattoo looked like. Rina ripped the page out and drew the complete design on a fresh page. "This is it, right?" she asked Phil.

"Yes. The only thing that's different is the middle of the cross was red."

Rina handed the page to Anderson.

"Thanks, we'll get this reprinted and we'll do a canvas around the village and the pubs. We'll see if we can identify the tattoo."

"Are there tattoo shops in the area?" Luke asked.

"Not here, but there are some in Portree."

"It didn't look like a new tattoo," Phil said. "There weren't any fresh marks

96

on his skin."

Anderson left a few minutes later, and Mia glanced at her watch. It was almost time to wrap up the day's work.

"Time to stop for the day. Phil and Diana, could you tidy up the squares? Rina and Angus, can you clean up the tent?"

Mia sighed. Today felt like it had been two days long. From the highs of the finds to the lows of Mr. Gordon letting the information out to the media. She sat on a nearby rock and watched the students go about closing for the day. The information about the tattoo was new, and while Mia trusted the police would search for that person, she doubted they'd be successful in finding them. Why would that person stay around the area?

"Ready to head to the B&B?" Luke asked, jolting her from her thoughts.

Mia looked up at him. "Yes. It's been a day. I think we need to celebrate our finds. And it isn't a secret anymore since Mr. Gordon leaked the news."

"That's true. Not a wise decision on his part. The students have finished closing up."

"I'll go get the coins and gemstones. I'm bringing them back to the B&B."

"Are they going in the safe?"

Mia shook her head. "I have a better location. I'll show you when we get back."

They strolled to the tent. The students had completed their tasks. Rina had emailed Angus the information to be printed for the bulletin board. The students grabbed their things and started walking to the van. Mia opened the safe, and took the coins and gemstones out, and tucked them into her daypack.

The drive to the B&B was quiet. When Mia pulled into the driveway, she turned to the students. "I don't want what Mr. Gordon did to put a damper on our successful day. You all did great. We deserve to celebrate this evening."

"We will. I know I'm still processing everything that happened today. For our first full day back, it was awesome." Phil looked at the other students. "And you're right. We need to celebrate."

Chapter Thirteen

They hustled out of the van. "Let's get cleaned up and meet for dinner. Does forty minutes work for everyone?" Mia asked.

At their nods, Mia locked the van, and they walked to the B&B. Luke pulled her aside. "Where are you putting the coins and gems?"

"In my backpack's compartment."

"Are you going to talk to Mrs. MacDonald about the B&B's safe?"

"No. That way, she doesn't have any idea where the items are. And she can't let it slip."

"Smart. We'll be the only ones to know."

Luke followed her upstairs to her room.

She took her backpack out of the armoire and set it on the bed. Luke moved closer.

"Where did you have this done?"

"Dad worked with a friend to have this included in our backpacks. Mom has one, too. It's come in handy a few times." Mia removed the items covering the compartment. "There's a button to the left side." She pressed on the button and the compartment snapped open. Using a small flashlight Mia revealed the compartment. "Do you see how it works?"

"Ingenious. I've seen lots of hidden compartments, but not one like this."

Mia slipped the baggies with the coins and gemstones in the compartment, then added the ring and sgian-dubh and closed it with a click. "Now it's secured." She replaced the items on top of the compartment and tucked her backpack in the armoire.

"How mad are you with Mr. Gordon for telling the media about the finds?"

Mia sat on the desk chair and started untying her boots. "I'm not happy. I can't believe he'd be that irresponsible to leak the photos. And I'd like to know what happened to Dr. Bateman. He was supposed to be at the site today." Mia pulled her boots off and curled up her toes.

"Maybe he had something else he needed to do. You still do that with your feet."

"It feels good. Those poor toes have been in heavy boots all day. They deserve to stretch." Mia stood. "As for Dr. Bateman, I don't even know where he's staying. We might see him at the pub." Mia pulled her hair out of her braid. "Do you think we're going to get treasure hunters at the dig?"

"Yes. The news is everywhere, and the first group of people won't be the last. I hope the security team can deal with them." Luke checked the time. "I'm going to get cleaned up. We can talk some more later. I'll wait for you downstairs, and we can walk to the pub together."

"Thanks. I need to touch base with Alex and Gran. I'll see you shortly."

Mia sent a text to Alex and Gran telling them she was fine and about the finds for the day. A check of her watch told her she had to hurry to be on time for dinner with the students. She didn't want them to deal with questions from members of the public on their own.

Luke was chatting with Diana and Rina in the lobby when Mia came downstairs. "There she is. Phil's waiting for us outside. We thought it better to go down as a group."

"Good idea. I hope I didn't keep you all waiting too long."

Rina shook her head. "Diana and I just got down here."

They left the B&B and walked to the pub. When they entered the pub, Mia stepped in first. As they made their way to a table, there were congratulations from almost everyone they walked by.

They found a table and sat around it. The pub owner, Devon MacLeod and his wife, arrived with a pitcher of beer and appetizers. "Your food and drink are on the house. We're so happy to learn of your finds today! Can you tell us about them?"

Mia drew a breath. She really didn't want to give too much away, but the damage had already been done by Mr. Gordon. "I can tell you some things,

DEATH AT THE SCOTTISH BROCH

but we don't have a lot of information yet."

"That would be wonderful lass," Devon said. He pursed his lips, and a piercing whistle rang out. "All right, everyone, Dr. Reid here is going to tell us what they found today. So listen up."

Mia took a drink of beer before standing. "There isn't much I can tell you that hasn't already been reported in the news. But what I'd like to share is how exciting it was to find the coins and the gemstones." Mia provided the pub's patrons with a description of their discoveries. She kept the information factual and explained their methodology clearly. The patrons erupted in a loud cheer when she described the coins and gemstones. Mia smiled. Ethan would have loved this. She finished by telling the patrons about the process they'd use to clean up the coins and the stones.

"Are they in a safe place?" one patron asked.

"Yes, they're in a secure location."

"What happens next?" another patron asked.

"Once they're free from dirt, we'll have them evaluated, and they will be part of the artifacts that stay with the local museum."

"Does it prove Bonnie Prince Charlie was here?" a woman asked.

Mia looked at her carefully. She had a North American accent. Could she be the woman who had approached Ethan? "Well, no, they aren't marked with his initials. But it's been well documented in history that Bonnie Prince Charlie was here. It does tell us that someone of wealth was in the area. Or it could also have been stolen property. We'll check the coins to see if we can learn more from them."

Devon stood next to Mia. "Thank you, Dr. Reid. We'll let you get some supper. Folks, let them eat and drink, and maybe you can ask them questions later."

Mia smiled. "Thanks for your interest, everyone. We're putting a bulletin board near the dig with information on what we're doing. If you need more information, you might find it there. And if you're interested in volunteering, let us know. We can always use extra hands."

Mia returned to her seat and took a drink of her beer. Her throat was dry, and the beer tasted good.

"Well done, Mia." Diana reached for her beer. "You handled that like a pro. I hope one day I can do something like that."

Mia chuckled. "I wasn't expecting it, so I didn't have time to get nervous. Did I cover everything I should have?"

Luke nodded. "You gave just enough information, but nothing that hadn't been talked about earlier."

"I noticed you didn't say anything about the security," Phil said.

"I did that on purpose. Most of the people here will have seen them and know they're in the area. If any of them visit the site when we aren't there, they'll see it's under control."

"What did you think of that last woman who asked about Bonnie Prince Charlie?" Rina asked.

"She had a North American accent. Could she have been the woman who talked to Ethan?"

Phil shrugged. "She might be. But I can't be sure. Rina, what do you think?"

"There's a resemblance, but her hair color is different. The woman we saw that night had black hair. This woman's hair is brown."

"Hair color can be changed," Luke said. "Did you notice her eye color?"

Rina shook her head. "Nope, too far away. And eye color can be changed with colored contacts."

Their food arrived shortly, and they all dug in.

"Is there anything we need to look for tomorrow?" Phil asked.

"Hmm, I'm not sure. Like what?" Mia asked.

"Can we just start working the square in the morning, or do we need to check in with the police or the security team?"

"Unless there's a problem, I think we can start as soon as we get there. I'd like to have a normal day at the dig. Mr. Gordon, the dig's sponsor, may show up at some point. But it won't affect the work we're doing."

They sat at the table, talking quietly. The news came on the television, and the pub fell silent. The reporter showed photos of the coins and gemstones while describing the dig. When the camera cut to the dig, Mia was shocked to see there was a crowd of people. Security was present, and no one was trying to cross the perimeter.

"This isn't good," Mia mumbled under her breath. "I was hoping we wouldn't have the media in our faces."

The next photo that came up was Ethan's, and the reporter told the listening audience he'd been killed at the dig. "Is this dig cursed?" was the caption under the photos of Ethan and the coins and gemstones.

"Ugh! I can't believe they'd do this." Mia's face scrunched up, and her eyes teared up.

"It might blow over by tomorrow," Luke said.

Mia's phone rang a few minutes later. "Mr. Gordon, I'm going to take this outside. Hold on just a moment."

Luke stood. "I'll go out with you. I'd rather you weren't alone out there."

"I've spoken with the security team and they've planned to bring in additional personnel. There should be a team of six tonight and six tomorrow. They'll rotate and ensure the dig and tent are covered. I expect them to have at least one person in the tent during the day." Mr. Gordon sounded out of breath as if he were walking and talking at the same time.

"That's good. Are you here in Skye? You sound out of breath."

"I am. We landed an hour ago and I'm on my way to the cottage I've rented. Dr. Bateman is meeting me there. He and I have a few things to discuss tonight. What are your plans in the morning?"

"We'll be at the dig by eight. I think it would be beneficial if I spoke to the media tomorrow. A one-and-done deal. I can answer questions about what we're doing and what we've found. I don't want to let it go too long."

"That's an excellent suggestion. Are you comfortable doing that?"

"I am. I won't discuss Ethan's death, and I'll ask DI Anderson to be present. If he wants to comment on Ethan's death, that's up to him."

"Good. I'll be at the dig at eight in the morning. I'd like an opportunity to speak with the media as well. I'll wait until you've said your piece, and then I'll provide my perspective on things. I'll make sure everyone understands the significance of the finds."

"Do you want to see the artifacts we've uncovered?"

"Yes, please ensure they're available for Dr. Bateman and I to examine. I'll see you in the morning."

Mr. Gordon disconnected the call, leaving Mia surprised at the turn of events.

She looked at Luke, who was standing close by. "Well, he's here and plans on speaking to the media tomorrow morning."

"It may be for the best. He can take the heat and let you do your work."

"I don't know. He wants me to bring the coins and gems in so he can see them. I'm going to make certain there are security guards in the tent."

"Come on. Let's go back in, have another drink, and try to relax." Luke took Mia's arm and led her back into the pub.

They stayed for another hour. Luke walked back to the B&B with her.

"What are you going to do if the media ask about Ethan?"

"I'll direct those questions to the police. I'm not answering anything about his death. Luke, I'm tired, and it feels like tomorrow will be a challenge. I'd better get some sleep. I'll see you at breakfast." Mia hurried up the stairs.

Mia went through her bedtime routine, including the yoga routine that helped ground her when life got stressful. She settled into bed and whispered, "Ethan, I sure hope you're watching out for us."

At breakfast the next morning, Mia outlined the day's workload. "Mr. Gordon and Dr. Bateman are going to be at the dig this morning. We'll be speaking with the media. Mr. Gordon's asked me to bring the coins and gemstones in for he and Dr. Bateman to examine. Once they're done with them, Rina, I'd like you to clean them up. There will be two security guards while the artifacts are in the tent. I want to make certain no one from the press or public are in when you're cleaning them up."

"Sounds good to me."

"Luke, are you going to be working the square today?" Mia asked.

"I want to be with you when you address the media. Apart from that, I plan on being on the ground, working."

"Phil and Diana, we'll continue working the square as we were doing yesterday. There will be an increased security presence at the dig and that should help us maintain crowd control. The last thing we need is to be concerned with people trying their hand at treasure hunting. Any questions?"

The students shook their heads.

"All right then, just one more thing. If you see the people who tried to buy the artifacts from Ethan, please let me know immediately. We're not sure they're still in the area, but we need to keep a lookout for them. Let's get to the site."

Everyone picked up their lunches and bags for the day and, in short order, they were at the dig.

Chapter Fourteen

Arriving at the dig, Mia's heart sank as she saw the number of news vans in the lot. There were several cars that didn't belong to reporters. The security guards had set up a second perimeter to keep people away.

"Looks like it's a bigger crowd than I expected. Let's go straight to the tent. I'm hoping Mr. Gordon is here. Luke, if you could come with me, I'd appreciate it."

"No problem. I'm going to touch base with Anderson to apprise him of the situation." Luke pulled his phone out and made the call as they hurried to the tent.

Arriving at the tent, Mia was relieved to see a security guard standing by the entrance. "Morning. It seems our find has brought everyone out."

The guard, Davies, replied, "The news vans arrived late last night, and they camped out here. People started arriving at six this morning. They seem to think they'll be able to dig for treasure."

Mia shook her head. "I was afraid this would happen. I'm going to make a statement shortly. Is Mr. Gordon here?"

"He's in the tent with another gentleman."

Mia turned to the students. "Okay, we'll stick with our game plan. If the crowds become too much or are unruly, I'll ask the guards to disperse them. If that doesn't work, we'll contact the police."

"I've spoken with Anderson. He's on his way here as we speak. He asked if you'd wait until he arrived to talk to the crowd," Luke said.

"I will. It'll give me time to put my thoughts together and touch base with

Mr. Gordon."

Mia pulled open the tent flap and stepped into the tent. Mr. Gordon was sitting on one of the chairs, drinking from a to-go cup. Dr. Bateman was leaning against the table with his cup of coffee.

"Good morning, gentlemen."

"Dr. Reid." Mr. Gordon raised his cup.

"The detective working Ethan's murder will be joining us to speak with the people that are gathered here. We'll wait until he arrives before addressing the crowd. Have you checked in with security?" Mia asked.

"I spoke with the team lead when I arrived a few minutes ago. Apparently, the media camped out last night, waiting for us to show up."

Dr. Bateman finished his coffee and dropped his cup into the garbage. "Mia, I do apologize for not coming in yesterday. I'm afraid jet lag caught up with me."

"Not a problem." Mia eyed him critically. He appeared to be well rested. "I've brought the coins and the gemstones for you to look at. However, I'm going to insist on an additional security guard in the tent while we have them in the open. I'm concerned with the crowd of people here."

"I think that's a wise decision. Can we look at them now?" Mr. Gordon asked.

Luke interrupted, "DI Anderson just pulled into the parking lot. I think it would be best if we dealt with the press immediately. That way, you can take your time to look at the artifacts.

Anderson stepped into the tent. "Morning, Dr. Reid, I understand you're going to address the media. What do you plan on saying?"

Mia briefly outlined her plan with Anderson. "That sounds good. I'll be available to answer any questions."

"I'd appreciate that. Mr. Gordon, are you all set?

Yes, let's get this done. I'll let you speak first, and then I'll add my comments when you're finished."

"Perfect. Let's go."

Mia led them to an area just short of the parking lot, and they all assembled behind her. Mia approached one of the reporters. "My name is Dr. Mia

Reid. I have a statement to make."

The reporter turned to the crowd. "We're going to get a statement. Follow me."

Mia waited until the crowd had quieted. "Good morning. I'm Dr. Mia Reid, and I'm in charge of this dig. My friend and colleague, Dr. Ethan Carter, was killed here Monday evening. He was a skilled archaeologist, and the police are investigating his death. We've been able to begin work on the site again and are doing so out of respect for him. You've probably heard we found some treasure. Dr. Carter found a sgian-dubh and a ring. We've also found some gold coins and gemstones." Mia paused as the crowd started buzzing. She held up her hand and waited until everyone settled down. "None of these items are stored on site. They're in a secured location." Mia raised her voice. "Archaeology isn't about finding treasure. It's learning about the past and the people who were here. Artifacts provide insights into the residents of this place. Potshards, instruments, and weapons all give us information." Mia took a drink of water. "If you're interested in working with us as volunteers, we'll take your contact information and any experience you have. And then we'll be in touch with you. We're setting up a bulletin board with details on the dig and why we're doing this." Mia scanned the crowd. The news reporters were taping her. Some were making notes. "We've implemented security measures and erected a perimeter fence around the dig. This is for everyone's safety and security. The security team ensures the site is guarded around the clock. We don't leave any items of monetary value in the tent. Anyone caught trespassing on this property will be arrested." Mia noticed Mr. Gordon stepping up next to her. "Mr. Charles Gordon is our dig's sponsor, and he has a few words to say."

Mr. Gordon stepped up by Mia. He smoothed his hair back and adjusted his glasses. "I want to clarify a few points Dr. Reid made. The site is a private dig, and we have employed a top-notch security firm. They will not hesitate to stop anyone from accessing the dig. They will use force if necessary. The police are investigating Dr. Carter's death, and if you have any information on his death, please notify the police."

Mr. Gordon moved aside and wiped his brow. Mia frowned. What was wrong with him? "DI Anderson has been investigating Dr. Carter's death since he arrived here on Tuesday. Did you want to add anything?" Mia asked.

Anderson nodded. "Thank you, Dr. Reid. If anyone has information on what may have happened here on Monday evening, I encourage you to speak with me or one of the local officers. Dr. Carter's death is being investigated as a murder, and we aim to find his killer or killers and bring them to justice." A gasp went through the crowd as Anderson said his last sentence.

Mia wondered if people hadn't been aware that Ethan had been murdered. Well, now they knew, and hopefully, someone would have information to bring forward.

"If there are questions, I'll answer them now." Mia looked at the crowd.

"Is it true you've found Bonnie Prince Charlie's treasure?" one of the reporters called out.

It always went back to treasure. "As I said earlier, we've found some gold coins, gemstones, a sgian-dubh, and a ring. Unfortunately, there's nothing indicating who the owner or owners were. The dates on the coins match the dates of Bonnie Prince Charlie's time on Skye."

"What else have you found?" This came from a different reporter.

Mia provided a summary of what they had discovered in terms of daily use implements and weapons.

"How old is the site?" One of the locals asked.

"Brochs date back to the Iron Age. This one appears to have come from that era."

Mia glanced at the crowd, and it seemed their questions had been answered. "My team and I are going to return to work. Again, if you'd like to volunteer, please let us know. Thank you for listening and for your interest." Mia turned and faced the students. "Let's go."

In the tent, they picked up their tools. "Mia, that was a great speech," Rina said.

"I hope the message gets through that we won't tolerate treasure hunters."

Anderson said, "I'd like to speak with you all for a moment."

"Sure, what did you need?" Mia asked.

Anderson addressed the group, "I want all of you to keep a sharp eye out for anyone who might be suspicious. We have the sketch we compiled with Phil and Rina's help. Examine it closely, and if you see anyone that resembles that person, let us know immediately." Anderson handed out copies of the sketch to each of them. "I'll share this with the security team as well."

"Did any of you see anyone in the crowd that stood out?" Mia asked.

They all shook their heads.

"I'll be away in Portree today. The local officers will be available if the need arises," Anderson said.

Mia waited until he left. "All right, I'll let you guys get to work. Mr. Gordon, Dr. Bateman, I'll get the artifacts for you to look at. Let me see if MacAllister can send an additional guard."

Mia spoke with the guard outside the tent, and he contacted MacAllister on the radio. A few moments later, another guard appeared.

Mia led him to the table and opened her daypack. She pulled out the baggies with the artifacts.

A cloth covered the table, and a strong magnifying lamp had been clamped to the table.

Mia gently put the baggies on the table, and Mr. Gordon gasped.

"What are the stones on the dagger and the ring?"

"We think the center stone is a ruby, and the smaller stones are diamond and emeralds. They're repeated on the sgian-dubh."

Dr. Bateman leaned forward. "May I?" he asked as he reached for the baggies.

"Of course." Mia turned on the lamp and stepped slightly away from the table.

Dr. Bateman opened the baggie with the ring and the sgian-dubh. He held the ring under the magnifying lamp and then pulled a loupe out of his pocket. He conducted a thorough exam of the ring.

Mia noticed Mr. Gordon watching Dr. Bateman and realized his hands were clenching and unclenching. There was a sheen of perspiration on his forehead. She wondered if he was coming down with something.

"What do you think? What kind of value would it have?" Mr. Gordon asked.

Dr. Bateman put the ring down. "It's difficult to assess a monetary value on a such a cursory examination. But there's no doubt in my mind that it dates to the time of Bonnie Prince Charlie. The markings on the ring indicate it was designed for a man of great wealth. Possibly of royal blood. If the markings on the sgian-dubh are the same, then I would think the value will be increased substantially."

Dr. Bateman tucked the ring back in the baggie and then examined the sgian-dubh. "I haven't had the opportunity to examine one of these too often. But it's an excellent piece of workmanship. The stones are the same as the ring, and so are the markings. I'd say Dr. Carter made an excellent find. It's a pity he isn't here to reap the rewards."

Mia blinked her eyes rapidly. Ethan would still get credit for the find. She'd see to that.

"What about the gemstones and coins?" Mr. Gordon motioned to that bag.

Dr. Bateman put the sgian-dubh away with a sigh. "A beautiful piece." He opened the bag with the coins, and they tumbled out. One rolled off the table, and Mia scrambled to pick it up.

"Careful. We don't want to lose any." She wiped dirt from the coin, added it to the collection, and carefully counted them. "We found eighteen coins. Each one was photographed and logged in." She glared at Dr. Bateman. Her hands were shaking, and her temper was frayed. She didn't like the way he was handling their finds.

"Not to worry. We won't lose them." Dr. Bateman examined each coin quickly. "The dates on them are consistent with the time frame for Bonnie Prince Charlie. I believe this would help cement that he was here."

He picked up the gemstones. "These need to be cleaned in order for me to determine their value. I could take them to the cottage and get them cleaned up there."

"I'm afraid not. None of the artifacts will leave my possession while I'm responsible for them. We can clean them here, and then the historical society will take them."

"Perhaps not," Mr. Gordon said.

"What do you mean?" Mia asked.

"I'm in discussion with the Scottish government to take these items out and tour them around Great Britain and other parts of the world. We haven't arrived on mutually agreeable terms, but I'm convinced we will." Mr. Gordon ran his hand through his hair. "It's a simple matter of money. That will enable me to take them out of the country and tour them. They are beautiful items."

Mia could feel her heart beating faster. "Why would you risk taking them out? They should stay here. It's a great piece of history for the island."

"Yes, yes. But how many people will be able to see this? Not that many. Don't worry. This will work."

Dr. Bateman continued his examination of the gemstones. Mia watched with a sense of helplessness. It didn't make sense to her that Mr. Gordon would take the artifacts on a tour. She knew that was done, but nothing he'd talked about earlier had indicated he was interested in doing this. And with the talk of smuggling, it just seemed safer to her that the artifacts would stay in one location. She shook her head. Not something she should worry about, at least not now.

"You say you can clean them here?" Dr. Bateman asked.

"Yes. We're set up to do so."

Dr. Bateman put the gemstones back in the bag and zipped it closed. Mia picked it up and checked them carefully.

"Charles, I do believe Dr. Reid has some trust issues. She's counting the stones."

"It's easy for a stone to roll off the table, and we could lose it. I believe in making certain all our finds are accounted for." Mia didn't apologize for checking on the artifacts. "I'm responsible for each item here."

"Not to worry. Your attention to detail is exemplary." Mr. Gordon nodded at Dr. Bateman. "Are you ready to leave? I have several meetings lined up today, and I'll need you with me."

"I am. Dr. Reid, I'll be back tomorrow. I can lend a hand if necessary."

No way was he getting his hands on the gemstones. Mia just didn't trust him. "I'll see you tomorrow."

She watched as they left the tent and headed to the parking lot.

"Do you still need me here, miss?" the security guard asked.

"No, you can go back. I'm going to have one of the students clean the ring and the sgian-dubh. I'll lock the other artifacts in the safe."

Rina, Angus, and Luke came into the tent.

"Did you want us to clean the ring and the sgian-dubh?" Rina asked.

"Yes, please. I've left them here on the table. I'm going to work in the square while you clean them up." Mia started to leave.

"How did it go?" Luke asked.

"I'm not sure. They were happy with the artifacts. Mr. Gordon is talking about taking them out of the country on a tour." Mia told Luke about the conversation she'd had with Mr. Gordon.

"It does happen. He may have to pay a fair amount of money to do that. And if that's the case, then he'll be looking to make money on those tours."

"Are you staying in the tent?"

"I think I will. I'd like a closer look at the symbols on the ring and the sgian-dubh."

"I'll see you later then."

Mia stepped out of the tent and glanced at the crowd remaining outside the perimeter. She noted several reporters with cameras trained on the square. Locals watched with interest as the students scooped the dirt, brushed it away, and then passed it through the sieve.

She joined them in the square and set to work next to them. The work was tedious and repetitive. But Mia found a sense of peace as she worked.

A few hours later, Mia called for a break. They headed to the tent.

"No coins or gems this morning." Phil opened his thermos and poured a cup of coffee.

Mia chuckled, "We won't get big finds all the time. A lot of what we do can be tedious."

"Mia, did you want to see what we uncovered?" Rina asked.

"Of course. How did you make out?" Mia and the students hurried to the table.

Rina, Angus, and Luke had the ring, sgian-dubh, and gemstones laid out on some cloths. After cleaning and polishing, the ring and sgian-dubh gleamed. Mia picked up the ring. The design on the band was clear. Celtic symbols signifying family and honor encircled the band. Smaller gems circled the larger red stone. Some gems were green, blue, and white. Mia wasn't sure if they were emeralds, sapphires, and diamonds. "This is a beautiful ring. It cleaned up well. I'm surprised at the workmanship on it."

"The symbols on the ring and the sgian-dubh match. It suggests that someone crafted them for the same person. The sgian-dubh has the same gemstones in it." Luke picked up the sgian-dubh and pointed to the stones in the handle.

"Wouldn't the stones make it difficult to hold?" Phil asked.

"I don't think so. The stones are flush with the metal." Angus pointed to the stones. "And the handle is quite smooth."

"What's the symbols on the blade?" Diana asked.

"It looks like they're the same ones as the ring. All of them mean family and honor." Angus pointed to the ring.

Phil picked up the sgian-dubh. "This was so cool to find. And now to see it cleaned up, it's incredible." The light shone on the gemstones. "It feels like I found buried treasure." He chuckled at the thought.

Mia grinned. "Well, it is treasure. I'm not sure of the monetary value, but historically, this piece is invaluable." Mia reached for the sgian-dubh. "May I?" she asked Phil.

"Sure." Phil handed the item to her.

"We can tell the stones are valuable because of their brilliance. Even after being covered in dirt for centuries, they look stunning after being cleaned. The workmanship and attention to detail are clearly seen, and that means whoever commissioned this piece expected superior work."

"Do you think it could be Bonnie Prince Charlie?" Diana asked.

Luke cleared his throat. "If I may..."

Mia nodded, "Go ahead."

"It fits with the time frame of when he was in the area. We know he was here during the summer of 1745. Could someone who wasn't happy with his presence here have left these items behind, or stolen them? Not all the clansmen welcomed his presence in the area. And there was a significant reward for his arrest." Luke took the sgian-dubh. "It's also possible these items were given in payment for his safe passage. The sgian-dubh was worn as part of the traditional Highland dress. And we know he was given traditional Highland dress as part of his disguise."

"Well done, Dr. Forbes. You've studied some history," Angus said.

Luke flushed. "I've been doing some research in the evenings."

No one spoke up, and Mia glanced at her watch. "Let's get some work done. We'll focus on the squares. We'll break for lunch at mid-day and evaluate our morning."

Chapter Fifteen

When they wrapped up work that afternoon, Mia was pleased with their accomplishments. They'd worked through another layer on the squares. Despite not finding items that could be described as treasure, they had discovered more pieces that revealed information about the people who had lived in and around the broch.

Mia considered that information as valuable as the gemstones and gold they'd found earlier.

They gathered in the tent for a short debrief on the day's work.

Diana asked, "Mia, is what we're finding typical?"

"Yes. Well, except for the gemstones and gold. Even the ring and the sgian-dubh wouldn't be out of place. But the artifacts depicting the daily life, the cooking pots, the utensils, and bowls, those are all valuable information. You can see that they took time to decorate the pots and bowls. They painted designs on them. People have made their lives better since the beginning of time. And decorating items shows that."

"The designs on the pots and bowls are similar to what's been found in other digs in Scotland," Angus added.

"Did you work on a lot of other digs?" Rina asked.

"Aye. I've been doing this as a volunteer for about twenty years. Most of the time, I work for a month in the summer, and I usually stay within Scotland. It's my area of expertise."

"Have you been on a dig that's found gemstones and gold?" Phil asked.

Angus grinned. "A few. Certainly not a huge cache of jewels or gold, but enough to bring in the press. Although not at the level of interest that this dig has."

"Let's finish entering the artifacts we've found today and tidy up the area." Mia picked up her notebook and headed toward the site laptop.

Everyone made sure the work was complete and the tent cleaned up. Phil and Diana covered the squares to protect them from any weather that might come in and to keep them closed from prying eyes. Angus and Rina finished putting the artifacts in their proper storage containers, and Luke emptied the water buckets. Mia compared the site laptop spreadsheet with the information in her notebook. She finished the day's log with a few notes about the day and what had happened. She'd take the time to add more detail in her room.

Once she had completed that task, she headed out to the security team.

She saw they were still out in full force. The perimeter was keeping people away from the dig. She approached the team leader. "Hi. We're done for the day. We've closed everything up with the squares, and we're taking any valuables away as well."

"Thanks. Our replacements come on in a couple of hours, and they'll be working through the night. The lights will be operational as soon as it's dusk. And there will be one person outside the tent all night."

"That's great. Were there any problems today that I should know about?"

"A few people took photos of the site, but no one attempted to climb over the perimeter."

"Are you monitoring the people who are showing up?"

"Yes. There are security cameras on the lights, and they record continuously. The company's main server stores the video from the security cameras and saves it for two weeks. If anything happens, we'll be able to see who did it."

"I didn't realize that was happening. Are we being recorded where we're working?"

"Not in the tent. But the dig and parking area are under surveillance."

"Right. See you in the morning." Mia turned on her heel and headed to the tent. She wanted to let the team know about the surveillance. It made sense to have it, but she didn't want them unaware of it.

"Can I have your attention before we head back?" Mia called out.

Everyone stopped and focused on her. She briefly related what she had learned from the security guard. Mia observed the team as she briefed them.

No one appeared to be annoyed or alarmed.

"When did they start recording?" Phil asked.

"This morning."

Rina nodded. "I don't have a problem with the surveillance. I think it's a good idea."

Mia looked at the group. "Let's call it a day and head back to the B&B. You've all worked hard today. Great work."

At the B&B, Mia headed up to her room. She glanced in the mirror and groaned. A shower first to clean off the day's work. Working in the field was fun, but it sure was dusty. Mia peeled off her clothes and set them aside. The B&B website indicated laundry facilities were available for guests. Mia would need to use them before the end of the week.

Showered and dressed in clean clothes, Mia took a few minutes to send a text to her gran and Alex, telling them she had finished her day.

Both returned messages immediately, with happy face and heart emojis.

Mia applied some makeup and combed her hair. She pulled a jean jacket out of the armoire and her small crossbody bag and hurried downstairs to see if anyone was still around to go for dinner.

The students and Luke had gathered in the breakfast room.

"Mia, we thought we'd go to the local pizza place for a change of pace. Are you up for it?" Phil asked.

"Sure, I love pizza!"

As they headed out the door, Mrs. MacDonald followed them out.

"I'm meeting my sister for dinner and bingo. I'll be out until nine. Enjoy your evening." Mrs. MacDonald locked the door behind her.

"Do we walk or drive to the pizza place?" Mia asked.

"It's not that far, around a fifteen-minute walk," Rina said.

They headed down the road, with Mia and Luke bringing up the rear.

"Did you learn any more about who could have killed Ethan?" Mia asked.

"No, Anderson hasn't discussed it with me. He was going over the pathologists' report today. He spoke with Shelly again. But I'm not sure what they discussed."

"I need to touch base with her tonight. I want to keep her informed as much as I can. How long are you going to be working here?"

"My superior contacted me when I got back to the B&B. I've been told I'm to stay here and monitor the situation. They think Ethan's death is a result of looters at the dig."

"Why do they think that?"

"The woman who approached him about selling artifacts. The description matches a woman who was in France doing the same thing. And artifacts disappeared at that dig."

"I wonder if it's the same woman?"

"Possibly. They're aware that you've found gemstones and gold coins. That may bring looters out."

Mia lowered her voice. "But those are well-hidden and secured. No one knows where they are, well, except you and I."

"True. But looters may attempt to access the dig and find their own treasure. I think Mr. Gordon was smart to install the cameras. We may see someone trying to get in tonight."

Mia sighed. "I'd like the rest of this dig to go smoothly. Not that I'm unhappy you're here. It's been great to reconnect with you."

"It's been good to see you again. I've missed talking to you."

Mia fell silent; she wasn't quite sure what to make of Luke's last comment. *He missed talking to me. Really, he's the one who left, and she'd never heard from him again.* Men. She'd never be able to figure them out.

Phil turned toward them. "It's just around the corner. We've eaten here before, and it's pretty good."

Mia smiled. "Great. I've worked up an appetite."

They walked into the pizzeria. The smell of warm dough, melting cheese, spicy meat, and beer greeted them at the door. Mia glanced around the restaurant as Phil requested a table for the group.

A red and white checkered tablecloth covered the tables. The chairs were captain chairs that allowed the patrons to sit back and relax. Mia saw pitchers of beer and sangria on occupied tables.

"If you'll follow me, please," the hostess said.

As Mia walked on the cobblestoned floor, she could feel the unevenness under her feet.

"I wouldn't want to be wearing high heels here."

Rina chuckled. "Definitely not. I'd fall flat on my face!"

They sat around the table, and the hostess handed out the menus. Mia found the extent of offerings surprising. It wasn't just pizza; this was a full Italian restaurant. There were several tables with people in various stages of eating. Mia noticed their group was piquing the interest of one table in particular. The four people sitting at the table were finishing up their meal and getting ready to leave. There were three men, two of whom were wearing ball caps low on their heads. Mia couldn't see their faces. The woman with them looked to be in her early forties and had short, dark brown hair. The woman looked directly at Mia and then motioned to the men to hurry up. She left the restaurant without waiting to see if they were following her.

"Can I start you off with drinks?" the hostess asked.

"Is everyone good with beer?" Phil asked.

"Make it two pitchers," Luke said.

"I'll be back with your drinks shortly, and Ben will be your server tonight." The hostess left them to figure out their dinner.

After some discussion, they decided on three different pizzas and a few salads. The waitstaff delivered the pitchers of beer and took their meal orders.

Mia watched as the students talked casually between themselves. They were a smart, fun group that worked well together. Phil was the most experienced, and Mia liked the way he handled himself. He shared his knowledge without being preachy. Rina was quiet and almost as knowledgeable. Mia had been Diana's advisor last year, and they had a good working relationship. When she glanced at Luke, she was startled to find him staring at her.

"What's wrong?" she asked.

Luke smiled. "Not a thing. I was just thinking how well you've done since I was with you. And you're still doing a lot of work in the field."

"I can't imagine not being in the field. You liked it too. I'm surprised at the change in careers."

"That wasn't my original plan. I fully intended to spend my life with you and be a field archaeologist. These last few days working with you and the students has reminded me of that."

"I'm sure your back is reminding you of how tough it can be."

Luke rolled his eyes. "My back, my legs, and my shoulders. I can't believe how physically tough the work is. I'd completely forgotten about that."

"To be fair, we were a lot younger when we first worked together. And I need to stretch a lot more than I used to."

"Are you two complaining that you're too old to work in the field?" Phil asked.

"Phil! Don't say that!" Rina's eyes widened.

Mia shook her head. "Archaeology can be tough on your body. Especially if you haven't been in the field for a while. Luke hasn't worked a dig in well over eight years. I've had to add more exercise to my daily routine. Otherwise, I wouldn't be fit enough to work in the field when I'm not teaching. Ethan found it challenging to stay in shape with all the work he did at the university."

Phil put his glass down. "He used to bike to work as often as possible. And in the winter, he switched to cross-country skiing after work. He'd added weight training, too. I saw him several times at the gym this last semester. I know he found last summer's dig tough."

Mia smiled. "Both of us started lifting weights. We'd check in with each other before we'd go to the gym and then report back at the end of our session. We were accountable to each other. And last summer was tough. We were in Central America working with my parents. The heat and humidity were debilitating. We had to drink gallons of water to stay hydrated. And we worked early in the morning and then knocked off for the rest of the day. There was no air conditioning. We were living in tents."

Their meals arrived, and the pizzas were passed around. They devoured the meal and talked about their courses and plans for the coming year.

Their waiter arrived to take dessert orders. Mia groaned. "Not for me. This was an excellent meal. Just a cappuccino."

The students ordered dessert, and Luke added his cappuccino order.

"What's on the plan for tomorrow?" Rina asked.

"More of what we did today." Mia glanced at her watch. "I'm going to head back to the B&B. I need to make a few calls and wrap up my notes from today. Just a reminder, we'll be leaving the B&B at eight in the morning. We need to keep working steadily. By keeping up the pace, we'll be back on track by Saturday afternoon. You'll be able to take Saturday afternoon and all day Sunday off." Mia stood. "I'll see you in the morning."

Luke picked up his jacket. "I'll head back with you."

Chapter Sixteen

As they started walking to the B&B, Luke asked, "How are you doing? I'm sure it's difficult for you to find yourself without Ethan for the dig."

"It's been challenging. We were good friends. He was the brother I never had. When Henry got sick, we spent a lot of time talking about what-ifs. And the worst-case scenario." Mia cleared her throat. "We even talked about what would happen if either one of us died. And he made it clear he wanted me to keep an eye on Shelly and Henry. Not that I wouldn't anyway. Shelly and I go back even longer than Ethan and I do. I'm going to spend some time with her when I'm done here at the dig."

"I remember how close you and Shelly were. There were many times I felt like an intruder when we were dating."

Mia stopped walking and gaped at him. "I never knew that. I'm sorry."

"Water under the bridge. The three of you were a formidable team. You were all close, and you and Ethan worked well together at school. I should have made more of an effort. I can well imagine what Ethan thought of me when I stopped communicating with you."

Mia snorted. "It's a good thing neither one of us worked in Great Britain right after our breakup. Ethan was furious with you."

"I know. He contacted me about a month after Jacqueline and I got married and told me in no uncertain terms what he thought of me. I had a lot of explaining to do, and I'm not sure he ever forgave me."

"He didn't say anything to me about that." Mia glanced at Luke. "Did the two of you speak again?"

"That was our last communication. I hate it ended like it did."

"Well, we didn't talk about you very much. I'm the one who told him you were married, and I remember his expression. He was angry. Shelly told him to butt out and mind his own business. But I guess he didn't. You know that what you did hurt me a lot? It took a long time for me to trust anyone again."

"I'm truly sorry about that."

"Like you said, water under the bridge. I'm glad we've reconnected and that you're okay."

They turned the corner to the B&B and stopped.

"What happened?" Mia asked as she spotted the police car in the driveway.

Both Mia and Luke hurried to the back of the B&B, where they found Mrs. MacDonald and another woman standing in the driveway, speaking with a police officer.

"Mrs. MacDonald, what happened?" Mia asked.

"Oh, my dear. I'm afraid we've had a break-in. My sister and I came home from bingo and discovered that someone had broken into the house and ransacked the office. I called the police immediately. They're going through the B&B now. I'm afraid someone has gone through your rooms as well. This has never happened. We live in a quiet village, and I know everyone here."

The woman standing next to her put her arm around Mrs. MacDonald's shoulders. "It will be fine, love. Just wait. I'm sure nothing's been taken. We'll call the insurer and have the door fixed. I'll be staying with you overnight to be sure."

Mrs. MacDonald nodded. "Thanks, Mary. I appreciate that. Oh, where are my manners? Dr. Reid and Dr. Forbes, this is my sister, Mary McCloud."

"Good to meet you. I hope nothing was taken from the office." Mia glanced at the mess.

"I don't think so. It looks like someone tossed a lot of the paperwork. And then searched through my file cabinets and opened the safe. Fortunately, I didn't have anything much in there. About a hundred pounds, that's all."

"Do you normally go out in the evening?" Luke asked.

"Are you thinking it's someone local then?"

"Just wondering if your habits are well known."

"We like to go to bingo on Thursday evenings. It's our night out." Mrs. McCloud's hands shook as she held her keys.

The police officer had been taking notes. "Did you tell anyone you were going to bingo?" she asked.

"Well, anyone who knows us knows our bingo night. We go to the pub for dinner and then to the bingo hall. I don't understand why someone would break-in tonight." Mrs. MacDonald wrung her hands.

Mia glanced at Luke. "Do you think it might be someone looking for what we found at the dig?"

"That's a strong possibility. Especially if our rooms were tossed as well."

"If that's the case, then I'm very sorry, Mrs. MacDonald. We told the reporters that we had stored the artifacts in a safe place. But we didn't intend to have them think it was in your safe. I'll make certain you're compensated for any damages."

"That's not necessary, Dr. Reid. While I appreciate the thought, I have insurance, and that's what it's for. May I ask you where the artifacts are stored?"

Mia paused. Luke nudged her.

"I have a compartment in my luggage where I can store items safely. It's a trick of the trade I learned from my parents. I hope it worked." Mia looked at the police officer. "Can I go check my room?"

"Yes, but one of us has to be with you."

"Not a problem. I'll go check right now."

"I'll accompany you. Mrs. MacDonald, do you mind waiting here?" the officer asked.

"No problem. I'm going to sit on the porch. Mary, are you coming?"

The two sisters held each other up as they headed to the porch. Mia shook her head. "I feel awful about this. Luke, can you come with me?"

Mia hurried up the stairs to her room with Luke, and the officer close behind her. The door to her room was open. The linens were pulled off the bed, and the mattress flipped on its side. They had thrown her clothes out of the armoire, then opened her large backpack and strewn the contents on the floor. Her laptop was on the desk but had been untouched.

"Can I go in and check on my things?" Mia asked.

"Yes, ma'am. We've already lifted fingerprints."

Mia walked to the backpack and picked it up. She reached in and felt for the compartment. A click and it opened. She reached and sighed. The ring, sgian-dubh, gemstones, and gold coins were all there. She pulled out the bags with the artifacts and laid them on the desk.

"All accounted for," she said.

The officer's eyes widened at the cache of artifacts Mia had placed on the desk. "Ma'am you had that in your backpack?"

"I have a secret compartment. Let me show you." Mia pulled the backpack under the light and showed the officer where the compartment was and how to open it. "My father had this put in for me to use when I'm working in a location that isn't secure. I didn't want to take a chance on leaving these at the dig."

"That's a grand place to keep things. I suppose it could also be used for smuggling?" the officer asked.

Mia grimaced. "I suppose it could. I'm glad I had this, and it kept everything safe."

"Are you going to keep them here?" Luke asked.

"I don't know what I should do. They're safe now. No one found them." Mia turned to the officer. "Do you know if Mrs. MacDonald's security camera caught anyone?"

"We haven't checked the feed yet. There's just the two of us here tonight. My partner was going to check after he'd done a search of the house."

Mia tucked the artifacts back in the compartment and put the backpack in the armoire. The three of them returned downstairs.

The officer stepped out to the porch and called Mrs. MacDonald in.

"Could you run the camera feed, ma'am?"

Mrs. MacDonald stepped behind the front desk and took a moment to take in the mess. Papers littered the floor, someone had swept off the surface of the desk, and the desk chair was on its side. She shook her head and glanced at the officer. "Right then. It should be on the cloud. I'll need to get to my account."

"Go ahead, ma'am."

Mrs. MacDonald glared at the officer. "Gillian, stop using ma'am when you speak to me. I've known you since you were in nappies!"

"I'm sorry. It doesn't feel right to call you Bridget when I'm wearing my uniform."

Mrs. MacDonald sighed. "No, dear, I apologize. I'm a bit rattled tonight. I've never had a break-in, and it's upsetting." Mrs. MacDonald shook her head. "Now I need to remember that bloody password. Let me think."

The office was quiet for a moment and then Mrs. MacDonald leaned over the keyboard and tapped in several keys. "Thank goodness. That worked." Mia watched as Mrs. MacDonald scrolled to find that evening's camera feed. "Here it is." She clicked on the time stamp. "When should I start it from?"

"What time did you leave for bingo?" the officer asked.

"That would have been around six." Mrs. MacDonald rewound the feed to around that time. "There we are. Mary and I are leaving just after six, right after you all left for dinner. I'm locking up the door."

The officer stepped over some papers. "If you'll let me. I'll move this along." Mrs. MacDonald stepped away from the computer, and the officer fast-forwarded the recording.

"There we are. Someone showed up thirty minutes after you left. Do you recognize them?" the officer enlarged the screen.

On the screen were two figures dressed in blue jeans and a sweatshirt. When their gaze shifted toward the camera, Mia noted they were wearing ski masks that concealed their facial features.

Mrs. MacDonald groaned. "Now, how am I supposed to recognize them? They've got everything covered up!"

"Can you enlarge where their hands are showing?" Luke asked.

The officer did so. "Do you see anything?" she asked.

"There appears to be a tattoo on this person's wrist. Is it possible to isolate it?"

The officer tried to isolate and enlarge it, but it distorted the image of the tattoo.

"Mrs. MacDonald, could you send me the link to the video? I may be able to clean up the image on my laptop." Luke pulled out a business card and gave it to Mrs. MacDonald.

In a few minutes, his phone pinged with a new message. "Thanks. I'll just grab my laptop."

Mia viewed the video feed again and realized that the two people were of different sizes. "Could one of them be a man and the other a woman?" she asked the officer.

"Yes. There's a difference in their height and body type."

Luke returned with his laptop and set it up in the breakfast room. Mia joined him at the table. He did some editing and got a better picture of the two people.

Luke mumbled, "Clearer. Let's check that tattoo."

When the tattoo came into view, Mia gasped. "That looks like the tattoo Phil and Rina drew."

"That it does. It would certainly narrow things down." Luke took a screenshot. "I'm going to send this to Anderson. This might be a link to Ethan's death."

Mia glanced up and saw the officer approaching them.

"Were you able to improve the photo?" she asked.

"Yes." Luke turned his laptop toward her. "You can see the detail on the tattoo. It's like the one the students saw on someone who gave Dr. Carter a drink."

"Could you forward it to me?" the officer rattled off her email address. "I'll send it to our team here in the village, and from there, it'll go across the Police Scotland network."

"I've already sent it to DI Anderson. He's told me he'll get it out on the network. Do you recognize it?"

The officer shook her head. "I don't, but that doesn't mean someone else won't. We'll put it out to the public as well. It'll also go to the tattoo shops. Someone might recognize it and come forward.

The officer received a text and raised her eyebrows. "We're off. It appears we're having a busy shift tonight." She walked back to Mrs. MacDonald. "I'll make certain to send you the police report for your insurance. Are you going to be all right?"

Mrs. MacDonald nodded. "Thanks, Gillian. I'll be fine. Mary's staying with me tonight, and we'll do some cleanup before going to bed."

The officer nodded and headed out the door where her partner was waiting for her.

Mia drew a deep breath. "I don't like this one bit."

"I agree. A break-in has never happened before, and now we're here, and there's one. I'm glad you had the artifacts stored where you did. I wonder if they decided to try breaking into the bank for the artifacts?"

"Is that what you think happened?"

Luke shrugged. "Possibly." He glanced in Mrs. MacDonald's direction. "I'm going to give her a hand with the cleaning up."

Mia stood. "I will, too. I'll deal with this room." Mia gazed around the breakfast room. The drawers of the sideboard were pulled out, and their contents spilled over the floor. "It looks like there's some cleaning up to do everywhere."

"Let's see where Mrs. MacDonald can use our help."

They pitched in with Mrs. MacDonald and her sister in setting the breakfast room, office, and kitchen to rights. It was close to eleven when the students returned from the pub, and then they needed an explanation about what happened.

"Are the artifacts all right?" Phil asked.

Mia nodded. "They're safe. And thanks to you and Rina for describing the tattoo, we might be able to identify one of them."

"Is there anything we can do to help?" Rina asked.

Mrs. MacDonald came out of the kitchen and overheard Rina. "Ah, thank you, but no. The only thing we haven't been able to get to are your rooms. I'm afraid the beds will need fresh linens. I can get to them in a few minutes."

Mia held up her hand. "Please don't. We can take care of our rooms ourselves. You've had a bad fright, and most of the cleanup is done. The bedrooms aren't a priority tonight. We can put the mattresses back on the beds and have a good sleep." Mia's phone pinged with a text. She frowned. "Oh, for Pete's sake. That was Harry, the head security guard. Someone tried to get into the tent at the dig. I need to call him."

The room fell silent as Mia placed her call. After speaking with the security guard for a few minutes, she hung up.

"Did they catch the person?" Phil asked.

Mia shook her head. "Apparently, it happened when the guards were switching stations. The one who was going to the tent stopped for a smoke break. He was walking around the tent when he noticed two people, dressed in black, who were approaching the tent. It's possible it was the same two who were here tonight. Security has reported it to the local police and to Mr. Gordon." Mia ran her hand through her hair. "I need to touch base with him before I go to bed. Are we good here? Do you have any questions?"

The students shrugged. "Are we still leaving at eight in the morning?" Phil asked.

"Yes. We still need to get our work done. I'm confident the security team will monitor the dig carefully."

Mrs. MacDonald piped up from her office. "Breakfast will be ready at the usual time. Six-thirty. And I'll make your box lunches. I want to get back to my normal routine, and my sister is going to stay with me for a few days to help me out. I'm very sorry this happened."

"Thank you. But this wasn't your fault. In all honesty, it's probably ours and what we found at the dig." Mia's shoulders slumped. "I'm going to make a statement to the press tomorrow and clarify that we don't keep anything we find here or at the dig."

"But you already said that." Rina pointed out.

"I did. But it warrants repeating. If there's nothing else, I'll go make my call to Mr. Gordon. I'll see you in the morning."

"Wait, here's some fresh linens for your beds." Mrs. MacDonald hurried to the linen cupboard and handed linens to the group.

"Mia, I'll give you a hand setting your bed to rights." Luke walked up with her. "Are you concerned about what Mr. Gordon will say about the break-in?"

"No. Nothing was taken. But I do have to let him know about this." Mia stopped at her room. "Ugh, this is a mess. Is your room as bad?"

"No. It appears they knew which room was yours." Luke walked in and headed toward the mattress on the floor.

Mia walked to the other side, and together, they put the mattress on the bed. "Thanks. I'll take it from here."

Mia closed her door and leaned against it. This dig was full of surprises, and not all of them good. She toed off her shoes and dropped into the wing chair.

She connected with Mr. Gordon and quickly gave him a synopsis of the evening's events.

"I appreciate you calling and giving me your information. I'd heard from the security team, but didn't realize there'd been a break-in at the B&B. I still haven't had an opportunity to speak with DI Anderson about Dr. Carter's murder. I'll see if we can meet tomorrow."

"Are you coming to the dig?"

"I'd like to spend some time with the students and see how they're doing. I'll see when I can get there. What time are you at the dig?"

"We leave here at eight, and we don't usually return until four or five. It depends on how the day rolls out."

"Thanks, I'll plan on being at the dig. And if something comes up, I'll connect with you."

Chapter Seventeen

Mia sat at the breakfast table and watched as the students filled their plates. They didn't appear any worse for the break-in, and Mrs. MacDonald and her sister had put on a big spread of food. Mia wondered if they'd gotten any sleep the night before. Despite Mrs. MacDonald's reassurances that she was fine, Mia was sure the break-in had rattled her.

One of Mrs. MacDonald's many nephews had replaced the front door lock last night.

Luke set his plate across from Mia's seat. "Did you get any sleep?"

Mia put her coffee cup down. "I did. A solid six hours. How about you?"

"Yes, and I searched online for known artifact smugglers with that tattoo."

Mia raised an eyebrow. "And what did you find?"

"No one with an exact match. I sent messages to colleagues asking if they recognize it."

"Mr. Gordon's planning to meet with DI Anderson and then check on the dig later today. He said the security team had the attempted break-in at the dig on the video feed. I want to look at it this morning."

"Are you going to speak with the press?"

"Yes. I'm not waiting around for them to start asking questions again."

Luke nodded. "I think that's wise. It'll put you firmly in charge of the situation."

Mia snorted. "Yeah, right. You're dreaming if you believe that." Mia pushed her plate away. "Any news from Anderson about Ethan's murder?"

"No new leads that I'm aware of."

"It doesn't make sense. Why would someone kill him for the artifacts? There's no way Ethan would've put the artifacts over his life or the lives of the students. He had too much to live for."

"It's possible he didn't get the chance to tell them that. Knocking him on the head may have been accidental."

Mia frowned. "I don't think you accidentally knock someone on the head. And Ethan wouldn't have turned his back on a stranger. That's the other part that bothers me."

"Do you think Ethan could have been involved with smugglers? He did have significant expenses with Henry's illness."

Mia's eyes narrowed. "How dare you?" she hissed. "You knew Ethan. He'd never do that. And besides, he had money. His parents died a few years ago and left him everything. I remember what he told me. His parents had invested well, and their home sold for several million dollars. Money wasn't a concern for him."

Luke raised his hands. "Mia, I'm just putting it out there. Anderson's going to ask you the same question. And I hate to say it, but what we're seeing is that smugglers collaborate with individuals involved in digs."

"I'm aware of the rumors. But Ethan was above that." Mia stood. "If I can interrupt your breakfast?" she paused as the students stopped talking. "We'll be heading out in about fifteen minutes. Mrs. MacDonald informed me the box lunches would be on the counter when we leave. And she'll also be tidying up the bedrooms today. If there's anything you'd rather she didn't touch, please put it away before we head out. Also, Mr. Gordon, will be in sometime today to check in with you all."

"Is he going to participate in the dig?" Phil asked.

"Good question. I don't think he has any experience at a dig, but if he wants to try, we can teach him."

Arriving at the site, Mia noticed the parking lot was filled with several news vans. "Right, I'll be speaking to the news people and making it clear the artifacts are secure. Can you all please go directly to the tent?"

When the reporters caught sight of Mia exiting the van, they shouted her name. "Dr. Reid, a word!"

Mia ignored them and walked up to the head guard. "Good morning. There was a report of someone trying to break into the tent last night."

"They didn't make it in. But we couldn't catch them."

"Did they or anyone else come back?"

"No."

"I'd like to see the video from last night. But first, I'm going to address the reporters and assure them the artifacts are secure. Then we're going to get to work. Notify me if you encounter any trouble with them."

"Yes, Ma'am. Let me know when you want to view the video. It'll take a few minutes to queue up."

Mia approached the perimeter and set her daypack down. "I have a brief statement." She paused as the reporters gathered 'round. "Someone attempted to break into the site's tent last night. Security has a photo of the individuals and will share it with you. I'd like to note that there's a clear photo of a tattoo on the arm of one individual. If anyone has information that could lead to this person, we'd appreciate it if you would contact Police Scotland and speak with DI Anderson. As for the artifacts, I'm pleased to say they're in a secured location and are safe."

The reporters burst out with questions. Mia raised her hand. "That's all. I'm off to work."

Mia hurried to the tent and put her lunch in the cooler. "Okay everyone, game plan for today."

She waited as they stood around the table. "Rina, I'd like you to work in the closest square to the right in the broch. We're going to start sifting through the layers there. It'll be a bit more labor-intensive. Don't forget to take breaks. Phil and Diana, you're going to be in the square where we've found the coins."

"And where do you want me to work?" Luke asked.

"You and I will float between the two groups. We'll lend a hand where needed."

The team worked steadily for about an hour. Angus arrived, and Mia called a break.

"Good morning. Are you all well after last night's adventures?" Angus asked.

"Ah, you're aware of that," Mia said.

"Talk of the village. A break-in at Mrs. MacDonald's B&B has never happened. A break-in of any kind hasn't happened in the village for years." Angus sighed. "Not sure what the world's coming to."

"They attempted to get into the tent as well. At least we think it's the same people." Luke pulled his phone out of his pocket. "Do you recognize this tattoo?"

Angus checked the photo, "Is that one of the burglars?"

"Yes. And we think they might have something to do with Dr. Carter's death," Mia said.

"I've not seen one like this in a long time." Angus mused.

"Where did you see it?" Mia asked.

"Oh, it was twenty years ago. I was working in Edinburg, and there were several military officers at the uni. Including some Canadian officers. Several of the officers had this tattoo."

"Have you seen any of them lately?" Mia asked.

Angus leaned back on the table. "I saw one fellow about a week ago. He'd come in with his wife for a bit of a holiday. They were staying at the cabins outside of Portree, and he drove down to see the broch. He'd heard about the dig coming up. I ran into him and his wife at the pub."

"Do you remember what they looked like?" Luke asked.

"I've better. I've a photo of the three of us raising a glass." Angus pulled out his phone and found the photo. "This is them." He turned the screen toward Luke and Mia.

"Could you send me that photo?" Luke asked.

"Of course. Do you think they might've had something to do with Dr. Carter?"

Mia waited as the photo came across. "They look like a couple that was at the restaurant last night. There were two other men with them. They left shortly after we arrived. I remember the woman staring at me and then telling the men to hurry up. I'm wondering if they're the couple that showed up looking for artifacts."

Mia hurried to the students. "Can you look at this photo?"

"That's the couple that were here asking about artifacts. The woman spoke with Dr. Carter," Rina said.

"Yes. That's them for certain." Phil pointed to the man's arm. "That's the same tattoo I saw on his arm."

"Thanks. I'm going to touch base with Anderson." Mia sent Anderson a text with the photo and the information from the students. "Angus, do you know their names?"

"Aye. Malcolm Reeves and his wife's name was Freya."

Mia added that information and waited impatiently for a response.

Finally, the whoosh of Anderson's text came back: **"Great news. Will provide information to the team."**

Mia sighed. "Anderson will take care of this."

"Did he say what they were going to do?" Phil asked.

"He's going to tell the team. Whatever that means."

Luke interrupted, "It means the information will be distributed to Police Scotland. All officers will be made aware of this development. If these two people have anything to do with Ethan's death or antiquities smuggling, we'll find out."

Everyone left the tent and started working. The press was still outside the perimeter watching what they were doing, but appeared to be getting bored.

Mia called for a break shortly before noon. They stopped their work, picked up their tools, and headed to the tent.

Mia cleaned her hands with the hand wipes available and then opened the site laptop and began entering the information gathered from the morning.

Everyone chattered about their work and what they had found. Mia overheard Diana saying, "No gold this morning. I guess it's too much to expect to find some every day." And she laughed out loud.

Diana looked sheepish. "Oops, didn't mean for you to hear that, Mia."

"It's all right. Some levity is called for. I hope you don't think archaeology is all about finding treasure?"

"Dr. Carter emphasized that archaeology is the study of humans through their material remains. And we shouldn't expect to find a treasure like gold and jewels. Before we went on a dig, he always reminded us that our objective was history and not treasure," Rina said.

Mia's phone pinged with a text.

Gordon: Should be able to be at the site in an hour. Hope to chat with the students.

Mia: That's great.

Mia tucked her phone in her pocket and grabbed her lunch. As she ate her lunch, she listened to the banter between the students. Angus entertained them with some local legends.

Mia waited until everyone was ready to go back to work. "I've heard from Mr. Gordon. He plans to be here this afternoon, and he'd like to chat with you about your experience with the dig. He may even get his hands dirty and do some digging." She looked at the students, "Tell him about your finds and how excited you were. He'll like hearing about that."

Luke held her back a moment before going out. "Anderson will be here in an hour. He has some news about the two people the security cameras caught."

"Well, that's good, isn't it?"

"Maybe. He didn't tell me what the news was. He was driving here from Portree, and his phone reception was bad. I told him Gordon was coming in, and he wants to talk to him."

Mr. Gordon arrived shortly before two. Dr. Bateman was with him. The students and Angus stopped their work and spoke to both men briefly. Dr. Bateman had some questions about the finds of the day, and Diana and Phil took him through some of the artifacts they'd uncovered in their square. "We've found a few eating utensils that show the people here cooked their meals. And the vessels we've discovered show they stored their food." Diana pointed out some of the utensils and vessels.

Dr. Bateman nodded his head. "And how are you cataloguing the finds?"

Mia stepped up. "We have a laptop and a ledger in the tent for cataloguing the finds. The items are stored in bags that are labeled with the date, time, and finder's initials."

"Dr. Reid, is there somewhere we can speak?" Mr. Gordon asked.

"Follow me. Luke, could you come with us?"

Luke followed the three of them to the tent.

Once inside, Mr. Gordon turned to Luke and asked, "Is there a reason why you're here?"

"I'm with the AART branch of Interpol. I accompanied DI Anderson when he received the call about Dr. Carter. I specialize in the repatriation of stolen antiquities." Luke explained his connection to the dig. Mr. Gordon appeared to be satisfied with his answer.

"For the moment, I suggest we keep the artifacts secured. I'd like to have them all appraised so I can insure them properly. Dr. Forbes, do you have resources that could appraise them?" Mr. Gordon asked.

Luke took out his phone. "I'll make a note and connect with you soon."

"Excellent. Dr. Reid, can you provide me with the plan of action for the next few weeks?"

"Certainly. I've made some changes to the original plan Ethan and I put together." Mia pulled the site laptop to the center of the table and turned the screen toward Mr. Gordon and Dr. Bateman. She went through the plan, Mr. Gordon, asking a few questions along the way.

"That's well done, and it's clearly outlined. Now, do you have any idea what you might expect to find?"

"I would expect to continue to find the detritus of everyday life. I don't think we'll find more treasure, such as gold coins and gems. They were clustered in one area and were close to where the ring and the sgian-dubh were found."

"Do you think there's more to Bonnie Prince Charlie being here?" Dr. Bateman asked.

"History shows he was on the Isle of Skye. Different accounts of his travels exist. The ring and the sgian-dubh show that a person of wealth was here, as do the coins and gemstones. But it could have been payment to someone, or a thief could have taken them as well."

"Basically, you're saying it's difficult to prove the treasure belonged to him," Mr. Gordon said.

"Yes. We have a volunteer who is quite knowledgeable; he taught history at the University of Edinburgh."

"I'd like to speak with him if he's available," Mr. Gordon said.

"He's here today. Do you have time to talk this afternoon?" Mia asked.

"I don't. I have a conference call in about thirty minutes. Will he be here tomorrow afternoon?"

"It shouldn't be a problem. I'll check with him." Mia made a note in her phone to follow up with Angus.

DI Anderson walked into the tent. "Good afternoon. I'm DI Anderson in charge of the murder investigation of Dr. Carter. Mr. Gordon, I need to speak with you."

"I don't have a lot of time. As I mentioned to Dr. Reid, I have a conference call in thirty minutes."

"This won't take but five minutes. If you'd come with me?" DI Anderson led Mr. Gordon to the far end of the tent, where they sat down.

Dr. Bateman raised an eyebrow. "Mia, could you show me some of the other artifacts that have been found?"

Mia motioned for him to follow her and led him to their shelving units filled with the smaller, less valuable artifacts.

They spent a few minutes discussing the utensils, pots, and vessels they'd found. Mr. Gordon joined them when he was through speaking with DI Anderson. "I need to get back to the cottage. Dr. Reid, I'll return tomorrow."

Mia watched the two men leave.

"Who was the man with Mr. Gordon?" DI Anderson asked.

Mia explained. "He told me he was here on a vacation, and he plans on touring in Scotland. But I don't believe him. I'm not sure why he's here. Yesterday, he examined the valuable artifacts we've discovered."

"Is he really an expert on them?" Luke asked.

Mia shrugged. "I'm not sure. He appeared to know what he was talking about."

"Did you learn anything from Mr. Gordon?" Luke asked DI Anderson.

"Not really. He confirmed Dr. Carter was highly respected in the field and stated he would never work with antiquity smugglers. He didn't know why someone would kill him and wanted to know when we'd be able to determine who had murdered him."

"Well, that's the million-dollar question, isn't it?" Mia asked. "Come on, let's put the artifacts away. We won't figure this out now. We made it through this meeting with Mr. Gordon. Let's see what else he's going to do while he's here." Mia returned the artifacts she and Dr. Bateman had examined to their proper containers.

Mia looked around for Angus. Mr. Gordon wanted to touch base with him tomorrow.

"Angus, there you are. Mr. Gordon, the dig's sponsor, would like to speak with you tomorrow afternoon. He wants some background on the site and some more information on the history of the area."

Angus dropped into a chair and drank from his water bottle. "Yes, of course. I can speak with him. Is there anything specific he's looking for?"

"I think he's wondering if there might be more treasure to be found. And he means gold coins and gemstones."

Angus scoffed. "That's all they're interested in. Not about the people who lived here and worked the land." He sighed. "When and where does he want to talk?"

"I'll send him a message. Is it okay if I give him your phone number?"

Angus nodded. "Best to do it that way. Then you aren't running messages between us. You have enough to deal with here."

Mia sent a text to Mr. Gordon and then tucked her phone away. "Are you all right? You seem a bit out of sorts."

"It's the people gawking at the site. All they're talking about is the treasure. It would be grand if they could remember their history."

"I wonder..." Mia paused. "I'm doing a presentation on the dig early next week. Would you be willing to talk about some of the people who lived in the area? What they did and how they lived?"

Angus set his water bottle down. "I would love that. I can pull some information from the courses that I taught. There are a few key points I could make."

"Perfect. Let's plan some time tomorrow to talk about how we can work together. I think we can make an interesting and lively presentation which will help us keep people away from the dig and respecting the work we do here."

Luke stopped by. "Are you ready to head back to the B&B?"

"I am. Angus, we'll talk tomorrow unless you'd like to join us for dinner?"

"No, my wife has made plans for us tonight. I'll be here in the morning, and I'll let you know when your Mr. Gordon contacts me."

Mia and Luke hurried out to meet the others by the van.

Mia stopped by the office where Mrs. MacDonald was doing some paperwork. "Everything all right today?"

"It is, miss. The insurance agent came by and gave me a quote. The police assured me they'd keep monitoring things. And my sister is going to stay with me for a few more days. We're going to go through some of the storage areas and clean them up."

"Could I speak with you in private?"

Mrs. MacDonald stood and closed the office door. "What's wrong?"

"Nothing, but I'm worried that the items we uncovered at the dig connect to the break-in. People thought I'd stored them in the safe in your office. I feel terrible this happened." Mia winced.

"I understand you'd feel that way, but it's really part of doing business. Is the treasure safely stored?"

"It is. And if you'd rather, I can make sure it goes to a bank in Portree."

"That's not necessary, and I'd rather remain unaware of its location. How are things at the dig?"

"Our sponsor arrived yesterday; he's here for a few days. There's been a few more people watching us work."

"Does that create more work for you and your team?"

"Maybe a bit more, but nothing we can't handle. I'd better get cleaned up. We're going to the pub for dinner." Mia turned toward the door. "Thank you for your understanding."

Once in her room, Mia quickly sent a text to Gran and one to Alex, telling them all was well. A fast shower and then fresh clothes. It didn't take her long to do her hair and makeup.

She grabbed her phone and wallet, stuffing them in her jeans' pocket. And walked out the door.

Luke and Mrs. MacDonald were chatting by the office when Mia arrived downstairs.

"Ah, there you are. I told the students to go ahead to the pub, and I'd wait for you."

"Thanks. I'm famished. Are you ready to go?"

Luke turned to Mrs. MacDonald. "You have a good evening. And if you need anything, you have my contact information. Don't hesitate to use it."

Mrs. MacDonald blushed. "I'll be fine. Thank you."

Mia and Luke walked down the lane toward the pub.

"What was that all about?" Mia nudged Luke.

"Mrs. MacDonald was fussing about, and she reminded me of my mother. She does the same thing when she's upset or worried. I reminded her that I work for Interpol and if she has any concerns, to give me a call day or night."

"You're such a white knight." Mia grinned at him.

"Can't help it. It's ingrained in me to be there when people need help."

"You always were prepared for anything."

Luke grinned. "Well, that's a good thing. I recall it helped you out a few times." Luke slipped his arm through Mia's. "Come on, admit it. You've missed me."

Mia laughed. "I missed you, but, I was angry and upset when you didn't respond to my emails or phone calls."

Luke pulled her closer. "I certainly didn't win any awards for that behavior."

"My dad used a few choice words to describe you. I'm not sure he's forgiven you even if I have." Mia ducked her head to bite back a laugh.

"Ugh. I suppose I deserve that. I'm not sure when I'll cross paths with your father again, but before I do, I'd better apologize."

They arrived at the pub. "Are we good?" Luke asked.

"Yes. We're good. I've gotten past our relationship, and I'm fine working alongside you again. Has Anderson spoken about how long he's going to be here?"

"I think he's going to be here for at least another week unless they find Ethan's killer before then. My supervisor wants me to stay close. He's convinced there are smugglers operating in the area. So, you're stuck with me for a little longer."

Mia grinned. "I have no complaints. I can use your many years of experience on the dig."

"As if. My back is still sore." Luke opened the door to the pub, and they walked in.

Familiar with Phil's choice for a table, Mia strolled toward the back of the pub. The pub owner, Devon, raised his hand in their direction.

"Good evening, Dr. Reid. I wanted to tell you there's been some reporters hanging about asking questions about the dig you and your friends are working on."

Mia frowned. "Are they from around here?"

"No, they're from London and a couple from the United States. They showed up mid-afternoon and were comparing stories. They asked me about the treasure that had been found and who oversaw the dig."

"And what did you tell them?" Luke asked.

"I referred them to the site. And told them to speak with security."

"Anything else?" Mia asked.

"An older gent came in with two other men earlier this afternoon. He was Canadian and seemed knowledgeable about the dig. He spoke to the reporters."

Mia sighed and pulled out her phone. "Could it be this man?" She showed him a photo of Charles Gordon.

"No, wasn't him. This man had black glasses and a beard."

"How about this man?" Mia showed him a photo of Dr. Bateman.

"Yes, that's him."

"He's the dean of the school of archaeology at my university. Can you describe the two men with him?"

Devon described two men who sounded familiar.

"They sound like the two men who ran into me at the university. What are they doing here? And with Dr. Bateman." Mia tapped her hand on the bar. "Thanks for telling me. I don't suppose anyone overheard what they were talking about?"

Devon leaned forward. "They were talking about the dig and the treasures you found. The one with the glasses told the other two where they should search for the treasure."

Mia's eyebrows rose. "Search for the treasure? But that's in a secure location. I'll be talking to Dr. Bateman tomorrow morning."

"If I see him or the other two again, I'll let you know."

Mia reached in her pocket, "Here's my card with my number. I'd appreciate a call if any of them show up again."

Devon grabbed the card and stuck it by the phone mounted on the wall. "I'll let the staff know, in case they show up when I'm not here."

Mia and Luke settled at the table with the students.

"Everything all right?" Phil asked.

Mia told them what Devon had said. "I don't think there's anything we can do about it unless they show up with Dr. Bateman. We'll need to be careful about what we talk about."

The waitress arrived and took their orders.

Mia asked the students if they had plans for their afternoon off.

"I'm going to walk the trail to the ruins," Diana said. "I want to explore the area a bit more and take photos."

Phil nodded. "It's a nice area. I'm going into Portree to take in the sights. Rina, what are your plans?"

Rina swallowed her drink. "If Diana doesn't mind, I'd like to go with her. I haven't been to the ruins yet."

Diana nodded. "That'd be great. According to the information I've found, it isn't that long a walk."

Mia listened as they discussed their plans. She'd go to the site and do work and then relax.

Mia and Luke left the pub early, with Diana and Rina following along.

At the B&B, Luke suggested a nightcap. Mia agreed, the students went off to watch TV.

"I'll be right back. I want to put my coat away." Mia hurried upstairs.

Mia unlocked her door and checked that everything was in place. She hung up her coat and opened the backpack. Nothing had been touched. She sighed. "I'm getting paranoid. Enough already."

Luke had two glasses with generous servings of whiskey in them. Mrs. MacDonald had a fire lit, and the sitting room was warm and inviting.

"Everything all right?" Luke asked.

Mia took a sip of her drink. "Yes. Everything's secure. I'm doubting myself for having the stones and coins here. What do you think?"

"They're safe. Whoever broke in didn't find them, or they would've taken them. If you do take them elsewhere, someone could stop you along the way. Don't worry about it anymore."

Chapter Eighteen

The team had been working steadily for an hour before Mr. Gordon and Dr. Bateman showed up. Mr. Gordon headed straight for Mia when he arrived.

"Dr. Reid, anything new to report?"

Mia stood and stretched her back. "We've been busy cataloguing items we found yesterday. Most are pots and utensils." Mia walked toward the tent. "This morning, we're finding more of the same. If you'll come with me, I can show you what we've discovered."

Mr. Gordon and Dr. Bateman followed her to the tent. Mia took them to the table where Diana was cataloguing the information.

Mr. Gordon looked at the artifacts. "Good examples of everyday life. Did you discover anything else of monetary value?"

Mia shook her head. "Most of the discoveries are related to everyday life. We haven't found any more gems or coins."

Dr. Bateman picked up a pot. Celtic crosses decorated the outside of the pot and it had two handles on either side. "The workmanship is very good. And I'm surprised there are no breaks or cracks."

"It was buried amongst other pots and utensils. They were all in good condition." Mia picked up the camera. "Let me show you how we found it." She scrolled through the photos and found the one she was looking for. She handed the camera to Dr. Bateman.

"Great photo and a very good find."

"Thanks, I found it and took the photo," Diana said.

"There's been a change in my plans. Is the volunteer here this morning?"

Mr. Gordon asked.

"Yes, let me go get him." Mia strode out of the tent and found Angus.

A few minutes later, Angus was explaining the history of Bonnie Prince Charlie to Mr. Gordon.

Mia stood next to Dr. Bateman as she put the artifacts away. "I heard you were at the pub yesterday afternoon. It's good food, isn't it?" Mia wondered if he'd deny being there.

"I was. I ran into a couple of friends, and we went there for lunch. And yes, the food is excellent."

"That's fortunate, running into friends. Did you know they were nearby?"

Dr. Bateman shook his head. "They'd messaged me the day before asking if I was in the area. They suggested meeting at the pub."

"Are they locals?"

Dr. Bateman frowned. "No, they're from Lakeview City. They're working in Portree on an assignment from Mr. Gordon's company."

"I didn't realize he had someone working out here. Is it for a new project?"

"I'm not sure what exactly they're doing."

"Do they work at the university?"

"No. How are you coping with the loss of your colleague?" Dr. Bateman changed the subject abruptly.

"It's upsetting. He was a good friend. We're back to work, but we keep looking over our shoulders."

"Do the police have any leads?"

"Not at the moment." Mia glanced at Mr. Gordon and Angus. "Charles is taking this seriously."

"Interesting. He hadn't let me know you were coming. Are you staying with him?"

"Yes. He's rented a large cottage. There's plenty of room, and there's housekeeping staff." Dr. Bateman's phone buzzed with a text. "Excuse me, I need to respond to this."

Mia continued to put the artifacts away as she thought about their brief conversation. He hadn't given her the names of the two men. She wondered where exactly they were working. Mia wasn't aware that Mr. Gordon's company was interested in expanding their work in the area, and that was something she kept up with. Especially since she didn't know what was happening with her position at the university. Her phone buzzed with a text.

Luke: Anderson coming in to meet with your Mr. Gordon. Is he still here?

Mia: Yes. He's here for another hour.

Mr. Gordon walked back to Mia. "That man is an amazing source of local knowledge. How did you find him?"

"From what I understand, he volunteered when he learned about the dig. He spoke with Ethan, and they worked out what he would do. Since I arrived, he's been extremely helpful in dealing with the locals. He knows a lot of people here."

"He's well experienced."

Mia nodded. "Angus is a great help to us." Mia cleared her throat. "DI Anderson will be here shortly, and he'd like to touch base with you. I don't know the specifics, but he asked me to notify you."

"Not a problem. He's the officer in charge?"

"Yes. He's been working with Dr. Luke Forbes on the antiquities smuggling as well."

"Do they think this has anything to do with smuggling?"

Mia shrugged. "There's always a danger, especially with the valuable artifacts we've found. The Canadian smuggling ring might be connected to smuggling in Great Britain."

"I want to talk to the students. I enjoy learning about what they've discovered. It brings me back to the start of my adventures."

Mia watched as he approached the students. He spoke with each one, asking thoughtful questions that showed the students he was interested in what they were doing.

Luke showed up at her side. "Everything good?"

Mia glanced up at him, "Come with me." They walked away from the dig and students.

Mia told him what Dr. Bateman had said about the two men with him at the pub.

"And he didn't give you their names?"

"No, he received a text he had to deal with. I'm not even positive they're the same men who ran me down."

"Well, you know they're from Lakeview City."

"I can't do anything unless I see them. And questioning Dr. Bateman isn't going to help the situation. He might tell them I'm too curious about them, and they'd leave."

Mia heard the slam of two car doors and turned toward the parking lot. "There's Anderson. I should tell Mr. Gordon."

"Just wait. I'd like to speak with Anderson first." Luke raised his hand in greeting, and Anderson responded in kind.

"Do you have any news for us?" Mia asked.

"Nothing new, I'm afraid. I'm looking for information, and I'm hoping your Mr. Gordon can fill in some gaps."

"He's chatting with the students."

"I'll get to him shortly. Now, anything else happen at the B&B?"

"No. Mrs. MacDonald replaced her door. The artifacts are still in the same place. No one disturbed them. I don't think anyone has an idea where they are."

"Did you think about putting them in a bank?" Anderson asked.

"Getting them out in a timely manner would be an issue if I needed them. With Mr. Gordon and Dr. Bateman here, I want them close."

Anderson ran his hand through his short hair. "Fine. I just hope everything stays secure."

Mia watched his face. "You don't seem happy about something."

"It's taking longer to figure out what happened to Dr. Carter than I'd like." Anderson turned to look at the dig. "Who's the man with the dark glasses and beard?"

Mia explained who Dr. Bateman was.

"I'll need to speak with him as well. Can I use the tent?" Anderson asked.

"Sure. Diana is working in there. I'll ask her to come out while you speak with them."

"Perfect. Let's go."

Mia introduced Anderson to Dr. Bateman. Then went to the tent to get Diana to work out on the dig.

"Should I put everything away?" Diana asked.

"Let's just cover it all up. There's a security guard, and DI Anderson will be here. The artifacts should be fine."

Diana and Mia pulled a heavy fabric cover over the artifacts, and Mia took the site laptop with her to get some work done. They left the tent, and Mia noticed Anderson and Dr. Bateman accompanying Mr. Gordon toward the tent.

Anderson didn't keep them long, and he and Luke left for a video call about twenty minutes later. Before he left, Luke suggested to Mia they have dinner in Portree. Mia agreed.

Mr. Gordon and Dr. Bateman stayed until lunch time and then left to pursue other matters.

They spent the rest of the day getting ahead on the job. Mia closed the dig around three o'clock.

Mia hurried through her shower and getting her hair and makeup done. As she was applying her makeup, she stopped and gazed at her reflection in the mirror. *"Hmm, what am I doing? Do I think this relationship is going to start up again?"* She shrugged. "It's dinner. Don't overthink this," she said out loud to her reflection. Finishing up her makeup, she dried her hair and tamed the wavy curls.

Opening her armoire, she took stock of the clothes she had brought with her. Her black jeans, red long-sleeved shirt, and her black sweater would work well. She could dress things up with her necklace and earrings she'd worn at the Museum fundraiser before she'd boarded her flight.

Her choices made, she dressed and sent a quick text to Alex and Gran, letting them know about her day.

A: Have fun at dinner with Luke. I'm off to the lake this weekend. Keep in touch!

M: Enjoy the lake. Will chat later.

G: I'd like to talk to you about Mr. Gordon. Call me asap.

M: I can call now.

"Hi Gran. How are you?"

"Ah, Mia. I'm fine and glad the dig's going well. This will be quick. Fran Esly and I had coffee today and she had lots to say about Charles Gordon's company."

"What's happening?"

"Apparently, his company is in some financial difficulties. He's overextended in several departments, and his board of directors is calling a meeting next week."

"Really? He didn't mention that while he was at the dig today. Is Mrs. Esly certain of her information?"

"Her husband, Tom, is on the board of Charles's company. I don't know if they've contacted Charles about the meeting, but I can't imagine he doesn't know about the situation he's in."

"That might explain why he's so interested in the artifacts we've found at the dig. I wonder if he thinks he'll be able to sell them off?"

"Mia, I want you to be careful. I'm not hearing good things about Charles and some of his employees."

"Gran, you'd better elaborate. He's on the island and is spending time at the dig. And Dr. Bateman is here as well. I'm not clear what he's doing with Mr. Gordon."

"I've learned that Dr. Bateman is a member of the board as well. He's helped Charles get involved with digs around the world."

"Ugh. None of this sounds great, but there's nothing illegal about it. Maybe just bad business decisions." Mia pulled her sandals out of the armoire. "I'm going to do a bit of online digging tonight. Just to see what I can find on Mr. Gordon's business. When I originally checked it out, everything seemed legitimate. And I doubt Ethan would have signed on for something that wasn't legit."

"Well, let's hope everything is all right and Fran misunderstood. I know your parents had to deal with sponsors that went belly up, and it wasn't a pleasant experience."

"No, it wasn't, but that happened in Columbia. I'll be fine. I don't want you to worry. Luke and I can talk about this on our drive to Portree. He might know more."

Gran sighed. "Please be careful. And enjoy your evening out with Luke."

"Not a problem. I'll talk to you tomorrow, okay?"

Mia thought about what Gran had told her. There had been nothing in Mr. Gordon's company portfolio that indicated his company was on shaky ground. She hadn't done a deep dive in the company, but the Archaeological Society approved it. There shouldn't be any problems.

She grabbed her sweater, tucked her phone and wallet in her cross-body purse, and locked her door.

Luke met her on the landing going downstairs. "Perfect timing. And you look great."

Mia smiled. "Thanks. I'm looking forward to dinner."

Mia noticed Diana and Rina sitting in the breakfast room. "You guys okay?"

"We're just waiting for Phil. We're going to head to the pizza place for dinner." Diana said.

"Enjoy your dinner."

Mia and Luke stepped outside, and Luke unlocked his rental. He opened the door for Mia, and she slid into the sedan easily.

"I'm looking forward to some time away from the students."

Luke laughed. "Were we like that at their age?"

"I'd like to think we were. But we're not that old yet. We still have some good years ahead of us." Mia paused. "I learned something about Charles Gordon's company before I left." She told him what Gran had found out. "What do you think about this?"

"It might be good to do a closer check of his company. I can dig deeper than you can. And I'll tell Anderson about this."

"Do you think he might be responsible for the attempted thefts at the dig and the break-in at the B&B if he's struggling financially?"

"It's possible. He'd need a buyer for the artifacts." Luke shook his head. "That wouldn't be difficult. I'm sure he could line up a lot of buyers. Especially the gemstones and the gold coins."

"I don't enjoy thinking he's behind this. But I'm not sure what else to think. When Gran mentioned the antiquities smuggling in Canada, he admitted he'd heard about it, but that's all he said."

"It would be hard to believe that a person in his position didn't know anything about it."

"Can I sit in when you check your resources, or is that top secret?"

"Of course you can. You might see something I miss."

Mia snorted. "I doubt it. You've had a lot more experience than I have in this field. But thanks. I'd like to see what you can find online."

"Are you familiar with Portree?" Luke asked.

"Not really. This is my first time to this part of Scotland."

"It's a lovely community, and it certainly caters to tourists. The restaurant I've booked overlooks the water. I asked for a table with a view. Let's hope we can get one."

They arrived in Portree, and Luke drove around to find a parking space. "Are you okay with a short walk?"

"Sure, it's a nice evening."

A spot opened down the street from the restaurant, and Luke slid the car in it.

"That's not too far." He locked the car as they exited and started down the sidewalk.

Mia looked around the street. It was still light outside, with a few people strolling about. She overheard accents from around the world. "Lots of tourists." She pointed to three tour buses parked in a hotel parking lot. "I wonder where those groups are from?"

"Anderson mentioned the buses earlier today. Apparently, two of them met on a road, and one had to back up a fair distance so they could pass."

Luke pulled the door to the restaurant open. "After you."

Mia walked in and paused for a minute, her eyes adjusting to the change in light. The restaurant had wide plank wooden floors, a reception desk immediately at the front, and there was a short line up of people waiting to be seated.

Luke put his hand on her back and guided her to the hostess. "Reservation for Luke Forbes."

"Yes sir. Your table is ready." The receptionist handed two menus to a young woman with a long red braid. She wore black pants and a short-sleeved black shirt.

The woman smiled at the two of them and said, "This way, please." And led them to a table for two in front of a window overlooking the harbor. "Will this be satisfactory?"

Luke nodded. "Perfect."

They sat, and the waitstaff listed the specials for dinner. On the menu were several seafood dishes as well as beef and chicken.

"Would you like a drink before dinner?"

Luke looked at Mia. "Mia, would you care for some wine?"

"That would be nice. You go ahead and choose."

Luke glanced at the wine list and ordered a bottle of their finest white wine.

"I'll be back shortly." The waitstaff left them.

Mia sat back. "This is a nice place. How did you find out about it?"

"I asked Mrs. MacDonald. She recommended it, and I checked it out online. The menu has a range of options that would appeal to both of us."

Mia perused the menu. "There's a lot on offer. I'm tempted by the salmon."

"Looks like an excellent choice. I'll have the same."

The waitstaff returned with the wine and opened the bottle. She poured a sample for Luke and he tasted it, then nodded his approval.

After pouring their wine, the waitstaff took their orders.

Luke raised his glass. "To old friends."

Mia touched her glass to his. She wondered if he was talking about the two of them or Ethan. "Is that what we are? Old friends?"

"You tell me."

Mia sighed. "I don't know if I want to get into this now. There's a lot happening with the dig, Ethan's death, and now this antiquity smuggling ring." She took a drink of wine. "Honestly, I'd like to get to know you again before I decide if we're going to be more than friends."

"That's more than I could hope for. I can't apologize enough for the past."

"Apology accepted. We've both changed over the years." Mia put her glass down and leaned forward. "In a strange way, I'm kind of glad things worked out the way they did for us. I'm not sure I would have pushed myself so much in my career if we'd still been together."

Luke nodded. "Well, I know I wouldn't be working in the field I am now. Let's start fresh, shall we?"

Mia smiled. "I agree. And yes, old friends can be the best." She took a sip of wine. "How are your parents?"

Luke filled her in on his parents' activities. They had retired from teaching several years ago and spent half of their time in Spain and the other half with his brother's family in Wales. He had several funny stories about his nephews that had Mia laughing with him.

Dinner was served, and the food was excellent. They lingered over their decadent dessert and coffee.

Luke settled the bill, and they walked out. Luke offered Mia his arm, and they walked down the sidewalk, arm-in-arm. They fell into step with each other, and it reminded Mia of the long walks they took when they were dating. "Do you mind if we walk along the waterfront?" Luke asked.

"You read my mind."

Luke smiled, and they wandered down toward the waterfront. Shops were still open, and Mia could see a bookstore. "I need to check this out." She pointed at the bookshop.

Mia pushed the door open, and the bells on the door tinkled. The bookstore had a selection of contemporary books and there was a section of gently used books. Mia strolled toward the gently used books and found one on the history of the Isle of Skye. She picked it up and read through the table of contents.

"Found something?" Luke popped up next to her.

"Hmm, yes. I think I'll take this one and maybe a couple more as well. I didn't bring any reading material other than work."

Luke peered over her shoulder. "The history of Skye looks interesting. How far back does it go?"

"The early 1200s, I think. They have a section on the Jacobite Uprising. I'd like to learn a bit more about it." Mia glanced out the window and frowned. "That looks like Dr. Bateman." She leaned forward for a closer look.

Luke followed her to the window. "Did you see him clearly?"

"No, and now he's gone in the crowd."

Luke glanced at his watch. "We should think about heading back."

"Yes, of course. Let me go pay for this." Mia stopped by the display next to the cash register and picked out two novels she hadn't read. One was a police procedural, and the other a thriller.

She paid for her purchases, and then they walked back to the car. They started the drive back to the B&B.

"Has Anderson given you any more information about Ethan's murder?"

"The pathologists suggested that the drug was taken with either food or drink. He would feel tired shortly after taking it."

"Do they think someone accidentally administered the drug?"

"No. It was intentional. In fact, they believe he would have died from the overdose."

Mia's voice hardened. "They were going to kill him regardless. It didn't matter what he did. Then why hit him over the head?"

"To make it appear as an accident. That's what Anderson suspects."

"Would this be the work of a smuggling cartel or just regular treasure hunters?"

"That's the question, isn't it? I don't know of any treasure hunters who would drug someone, question them, and then kill them. They normally wait around and steal the items and then clear off."

"That's what I thought as well. And that leaves us with the smuggling cartel. And it sounds like it's big business."

"If it's a cartel, yes, it's big business. And they won't wait around. They'll be looking for the gemstones and the gold coins. Especially since the rumors about Bonnie Prince Charlie are everywhere." Luke cleared his throat. "Mia, is your seat belt buckled?"

"Yes, why?"

"There's a vehicle that's been following us since we left Portree, and they're moving closer to us. I want you to be prepared in case they try to overtake us."

"Should I call the police?"

"Call Anderson directly. And put him on speakerphone."

"Anderson here."

"It's Luke and Mia. We're on our way back from Portree, and we've picked up a vehicle that's following us aggressively." Luke's voice was loud.

The car that was following them pulled up next to them. Mia looked at the car and noticed that it was a dark-colored Range Rover. The car rammed into them, and Luke fought to control the car. Mia screamed.

"What's happening?" Anderson yelled.

"They just hit us with their car. It's a Range Rover. I can't see inside the car to see who's driving." Mia's voice cracked.

"Luke, are you okay to drive?" Anderson asked.

"I am. I've dropped back behind them. There's no one else on the road. We're about ten minutes from the B&B. I need to focus on my driving."

Mia watched as Luke dropped back and then he accelerated the car. "What are you doing?" she asked.

"I want to get close enough to see their license plate. Stay on the line with Anderson, but open your camera app. Get ready to snap a photo. The lights from this car should light it up enough to be clear."

Mia opened the camera app and increased the zoom. She waited as Luke sped up, trying to catch the car up ahead.

He pulled close enough that Mia snapped several photos.

Anderson called out, "Once you have the photos, pull back. Luke, do you hear me? Pull back. I don't want you getting into something you can't deal with. I'm on the road with one of the officers. We should be coming up to you soon."

The car stopped, and Luke slammed into them. The airbags in his car deployed and when they got free of the airbags, the Range Rover was gone.

Luke pounded his hand on the steering wheel.

"Are you all right? Luke, Mia, are you hurt?" Anderson yelled.

"I'm all right, a bit shaken up. Luke, are you hurt?" Mia asked.

Luke shook his head. "I'm fine. I'm just mad I fell for that. There's no way they were going to let us get that close."

"I took the photos, and I have the plate number." Mia checked her phone and then called out the plate number to Anderson.

"Please repeat it once more." The officer's voice came through. "I'll put it out immediately."

Mia repeated the number.

"Good work, Mia. Stay with your vehicle. We should be coming up to you shortly."

Luke turned on the hazard warning lights. "Are you sure you're not hurt?" he asked Mia.

"I'm fine. My shoulder's sore, but other than that, I'm good. How are you?"

Luke rolled his neck. "My neck feels tight. We should get out of the car and wait on the side of the road."

"Are there flares we can put out?" Mia asked.

"I'll check the boot." Luke pushed the car door open and stepped to the back of the car.

Mia climbed out of the car and stretched her back. This wasn't how she'd expected their evening to go.

Luke slammed the trunk closed, and he cracked a flare, then set it a few yards away from the car. He repeated the action toward the front of the car.

A few moments later, a police car and ambulance arrived on the scene.

The paramedics came out and ran Mia and Luke through a series of checks. After examining them for several minutes, they declared they were well enough to go back to the B&B. The police inspected the car and called for a tow truck.

One of the officers spoke with Mia. "I understand you have the license plate of the other vehicle?"

Mia pulled out her cell phone. "I took a photo." She showed her the photos of the Range Rover.

"Would you be able to identify the individuals in the vehicle?"

Mia shook her head. "It was two men. That's all I saw."

"Right. We're all looking for this Range Rover. DI Anderson has the license number out. We're to stay here with you until he arrives."

At that moment, a police car pulled over, and DI Anderson got out. He strode across the road. He stopped to speak to the paramedics and then hurried to Luke and Mia's side.

"We found the Range Rover discarded a couple of miles down the road. It was empty."

The officer who'd been nearby spoke up. "Sir, their car's going to be towed away. The front is destroyed too much to drive."

"Thank you, Officer. I'll see them back to their B&B. Luke, did you connect with the car rental agency?"

"I've left a message, and I've also contacted my insurer."

"Good. The paramedics say you're both cleared to go back to the B&B."

They arrived at the B&B just as the students were returning from their evening out.

As Mia and Luke stepped out of the car, the students hurried to them.

"What happened to your car?" "Are you all right?" Diana and Rina ran toward them, hurling questions.

Mia raised her hand. "We're fine. Had a run-in with an aggressive Range Rover."

DI Anderson interrupted. "I'm sorry, Dr. Reid. This was more than a run-in. They tried to force you off the road. The students need to be made aware of this new development."

Mia sighed. "You're right. Is Phil here?"

"He's coming up behind us," Diana said.

"I'm only going over this once. We'll wait until he gets here."

They didn't have long to wait, and when Phil arrived, Mia suggested they gather in the sitting room.

Mia and Luke recounted their eventful evening.

"The Rover was stolen. I believe this incident is connected to the death of Dr. Carter. It wasn't an accident. It was deliberate." DI Anderson looked at each of them as he spoke. "I want to urge you to use caution and be alert to your surroundings. If you feel as if anything is off, even just a bit, pay attention. Get somewhere where there are people."

"Do you think we could be in danger?" Rina asked.

"You should be fine at the dig."

"I'll talk to Mr. Gordon in the morning and let him know what happened. As for tomorrow, why don't you take the full day off? We've worked hard this week, and we've made up for the time we've lost. I just want you to remember to be careful when you're out. Stay safe."

"Luke, I'll touch base with you as soon as we obtain more information on the driver of the Range Rover. The local officers are on it. I'm off and will see you tomorrow." DI Anderson left, followed by the officer who was helping him.

Luke walked to the bar and helped himself to a whiskey. "Anyone else?" he asked as he lifted the bottle.

"I'm up for one," Mia said.

The students nodded in agreement and Luke did the honors.

They sat in the sitting room. Mia listened as the rest of the group chattered about the evening. Luke fielded the questions from the students with relative ease. Mia frowned and rubbed her forehead.

"Headache?" Rina asked.

"Yes. This wasn't what I expected this evening." She sighed. "I don't understand where they came from. I didn't notice anyone following us."

"If they were following you, they'd be careful not to be seen," Rina said.

Mia finished her drink. "That's true. I'm heading to bed. I still plan on going to the dig in the morning. Are you firm with your plans?"

"Rina and I are going to the ruins for a hike and then maybe to the beach, depending on the weather," Diana said.

"I'm going to Portree. There's a bus that goes from the village. I'll be gone until after dinner." Phil added.

* * *

"Good; I want you all to be vigilant, but have a good time as well."

The following morning, Mia was in the breakfast room enjoying a hearty meal. She'd had a decent sleep last night despite the accident. Her upper back was a bit sore, but she hoped that moving around would help. She finished her breakfast and received a text from Mr. Gordon.

Mr. Gordon: Need to speak with you regarding last night's accident.

M: of course. When?

Mr. Gordon: Will be at dig at 10 am.

M: Will see you then.

Mia sighed. She'd sent him a text earlier this morning letting him know about the accident. Anderson may have talked to him as well. She wasn't sure. She got up and poured herself another cup of coffee and sat at her table. Taking her time, she went through her notes. She'd printed out Ethan's as well. There wasn't anything odd in his scribblings. He'd mentioned the interest from the historical society and the help Angus had been giving him. Angus had provided him with information the society had gathered over the years.

There was correspondence from Mr. Gordon outlining the work he expected from Ethan and the students. Mia wasn't surprised by Mr. Gordon's decision to extend the timeline to next year. The plan was for Ethan, herself, and the students to carry out the dig for six weeks this summer, and then resume next year. She hoped to come back, but there was a lot of uncertainty about her future. Her stomach contracted at that thought. Mia shook her head. Nothing to be done about that now. She knew she wouldn't go back to the university. The politics of academia were difficult to maneuver. She preferred the field. Opportunities would come up, and if she had to leave the Lakeview area for work, she would.

Luke arrived in the breakfast room as she was looking over Mr. Gordon's correspondence. "Good morning. How's your neck?" he asked.

"Morning. I'm sore and stiff. How are you?"

"My back is sore, and my head aches. But that could be from the whiskey. I owe Mrs. MacDonald a bottle. I'll need to make good on that today."

Mia raised an eyebrow. "That's not like you."

"Phil joined me, and he had a lot of questions about my work with Interpol."

"Ah, so he plied you with whiskey to hear about your adventures. How late were you up?"

Luke took a deep drink of coffee. "It was well past midnight when I turned in."

"Are you sure you're up to coming to the dig?"

"I will be after breakfast. I've taken something for the aches and pains. Coffee instead of tea will help clear my head. And some fresh air and activity will help me get back on my feet." Luke drank more coffee. "What time do you want to leave?"

Mia glanced at her watch. "Mr. Gordon is coming in at ten this morning. He wants to discuss yesterday's accident. Will you be ready in thirty minutes?"

"Yes. Are we going to be there all day?"

"Probably until one or so. It depends on how many people are queueing up for information." Mia picked up her coffee cup. "I've asked Mrs. MacDonald for a couple of thermoses of coffee and some muffins to take with us."

Chapter Nineteen

Mia informed security that she and Luke would be working in the tent. "Please let me know if there are questions from anyone who stops by."

"Will do, ma'am."

She set up the laptop and started looking through notes from the previous week. Luke busied himself, cataloguing the artifacts the group had found. They worked steadily and quietly for the next hour and a half.

Mia reached for the thermos and poured herself a coffee. "Do you want some?" she asked Luke.

"That'd be great."

Grabbing their cups, they walked outside to the dig to see if there were any passersby. The parking lot was empty except for their van and the security vehicles.

Luke glanced away from his phone. "I've received a message from Anderson. They caught a break on the driver of the Range Rover. The traffic camera captured his image." Luke handed Mia his phone. "Take a look."

Mia enlarged the photo and gasped. "He looks like one of the guys who cut me off when I was biking to work."

"Are you certain?"

"Yes. I'm positive. And he followed me when I took my bike to the shop and then to lunch." Mia frowned. "He also looks like the man I saw at Glasgow airport. I thought he seemed familiar at the time but couldn't place him."

"Did the police do anything about your accident?"

"I didn't report it. They gave me more than enough money to repair my bike, and then they left quickly."

"That's unfortunate. I'll let Anderson know, and he can consult with the police in Canada to see if they have any information on them."

Mia handed Luke his phone back, and he called Anderson.

Mia's phone pinged with a text from Mr. Gordon.

Mr. Gordon: "Will be at the dig shortly."

M: "I'm here with Luke."

"Mr. Gordon will be here soon. I wonder if he'll recognize the man in the photo."

"I'll make sure to show it to him." They returned to the tent and worked steadily until Mr. Gordon arrived. Dr. Bateman was with him as well.

"Mia, I'm glad you weren't injured in last night's events," Mr. Gordon said.

"We're a bit sore, and Luke's rental suffered quite a bit of damage."

"Do the police have any information on who tried to run you off the road?" Dr. Bateman asked.

"They caught a photo of the driver." Luke pulled out his phone. "Here it is." He showed it to Dr. Bateman and Mr. Gordon.

"Not a great picture." Dr. Bateman peered the phone. "May I take a closer look?" he asked.

Luke handed him the phone, and Dr. Bateman enlarged the photo. "He certainly seems intent on what he's doing. Where was this taken?"

"Just outside of Portree. I'm certain they followed us from there."

Dr. Bateman handed the phone to Mr. Gordon, "Charles, do you recognize this man?"

Mr. Gordon glanced at the phone. "I'm afraid I don't. I don't know many people in Scotland except the ones I've worked with on this dig."

Luke took the phone from Dr. Bateman. "If you spot this man, please contact the police. DI Anderson is anxious to speak with him."

"I have the detective's contact information. Now, have any other problems cropped up?" Mr. Gordon asked.

"The crowds have been picking up around the dig, but security is keeping them under control. Was Angus able to fill you in on the history of the area?" Mia asked.

"He was. I'm looking at how we can use the history to call attention to the finds. It's adding interest with potential investors."

"Mia, I'd like to look at the ring, and the sgian-dubh today. Is that possible?" Dr. Bateman asked.

Mia shifted her feet. "I could have them here around two this afternoon."

"And could you bring the gemstones and gold coins? As you're aware, I'm somewhat of an expert in gemstones."

"Of course. How long will you need to look at them?"

Dr. Bateman pursed his lips. "An hour should be sufficient."

"Luke, will you join us this afternoon?" Mia asked.

"I'd welcome the opportunity."

"I'll be here as well. I'm curious to learn about Dr. Bateman's opinion. Well, I must run. I have a conference call about another project shortly. Dr. Bateman, are you returning with me?" Mr. Gordon asked.

"Yes. Mia, I'll meet up with you later this afternoon. At two, correct?"

"That's correct."

The two men left the tent. Mia growled. "I didn't want to do that. I'm not comfortable parading those artifacts around."

"He seemed anxious to see them. I wasn't aware he was an expert in gems."

"He's written several articles on gems found at different digs." Mia shrugged. "It isn't like I could say no, especially with Mr. Gordon here. Let's wrap things up and get a bite to eat."

They left for the pub a short time later. A hearty lunch put Mia in a better mood, and Luke's headache disappeared.

"What have you learned from the car rental company?"

"They'll be providing me with a new vehicle and dropping it off at the B&B around four o'clock. They were concerned about my safety. My insurance covered the damages."

"Nice that they're delivering it to the B&B. We should get back there."

Mia stopped at the B&B and hurried upstairs to her room. Luke followed her. She pulled out the bags of artifacts from the compartment in the backpack. She placed them on top of the desk. Luke examined them thoroughly. "They're in good condition. And Angus and Rina did excellent work in cleaning them up."

Mia grinned. "They did. Now, let's figure out what Dr. Bateman wants with them. I'll be watching him carefully while he has them."

They drove to the dig, and Mia parked as close as she could to the tent. Mia spoke with the head security guard.

"Could you send a guard to the tent?"

"Not a problem, ma'am. I'll send Tim."

Mia and Luke headed for the tent. Mia put the artifacts on the table. A few minutes later, Mr. Gordon and Dr. Bateman walked in, accompanied by the security guard.

"Mia, do you have the artifacts?" Mr. Gordon asked.

"Yes, come take a look."

Bateman and Gordon walked to the table and started examining the artifacts. Bateman pulled out a jeweler's loupe. "May I take them out of their bags?" he asked.

"Of course," Mia watched as Bateman opened the bag, and the gemstones tumbled out on the cloth.

He began examining them one at a time. Halfway through, he stopped. "These are amazing. Your team did excellent work in cleaning them." His eyes gleamed as he looked at Mr. Gordon. "And they're quite valuable."

Mr. Gordon smiled. "Great to know that. It's good to have more information to share with the public and with my investors."

Mia cleared her throat. "I hope the information on the value of the artifacts doesn't get out. It's difficult enough to keep the public out of the dig."

Mr. Gordon clicked his tongue. "You're right. But I will make my investors aware of the finds."

Bateman continued examining the artifacts and moved on to the ring. "This ring was made by an excellent craftsman. The large stone is a ruby. I had thought it might be a garnet, but it's not. And the smaller stones are emeralds and diamonds. A very valuable piece."

He picked up the sgian-dubh. "A nobleman used this piece. The

165

craftsmanship shows that this piece was made for someone of wealth."

Bateman spent the next thirty minutes examining all the pieces. Mia watched him carefully, making sure that each artifact was returned to the correct bag.

"Great finds, Mia. Charles, this will certainly go a long way with increasing your reputation and securing additional investors. You should be happy."

Mr. Gordon nodded. "I've received messages from collectors around the globe requesting to view the items. I've confirmed I'll be taking the gemstones, gold coins, ring, and the sgian-dubh on a tour."

Mia was taken aback by the news. "I thought you were still waiting for permission."

"My contacts with the Scottish government are working to make sure I can take them. Of course, I'll make the appropriate payments in order to accomplish that." Mr. Gordon clapped his hands together. "Well, we'll leave you to it. I'm returning to Canada this evening. It's been a productive trip."

The two men left. Mia watched as they walked to their car. Dr. Bateman answered a call on his phone, and Mr. Gordon hurried to the car.

Tim, the security guard, asked, "Do you need me here any longer, ma'am?"

Mia shook her head. "Thank you for being here. I'm going to call it a day."

As they were walking up to the van, Mia's phone pinged with a text.

Diana: We're going to have dinner at the Castle restaurant. Did you want to join us?

"The girls are having dinner at the Castle. Did you want to join them?" Mia asked Luke.

"I'm still tired from yesterday's events. I was hoping for a quiet dinner with you here in the village."

"That sounds like a plan. I'll let Diana know."

M: Thanks, but we're going to eat in the village. Chat later.

D: later.

"That was kind of them to invite us," Luke said as they climbed into the van.

"Yes. Overall, the students are a good bunch. Diana's fitting in nicely with them."

Mia parked the van at the B&B. "What time did you want to go for dinner?"

"Mmm, does six o'clock work? That way, if the rental agency is late, it isn't an issue."

"That sounds good. I want to call Gran and Alex before we go out. I'll meet you in the sitting room."

They parted at Mia's door, and she dropped her daypack on the floor. She opened the armoire, took out her backpack, and hid the artifacts. Tucking her backpack away, she glanced at herself in the mirror. Her hair had come out of her braid, and she had dirt on her shirt. Hazard of the job, but it was time to do laundry. She opened the desk drawer and found an information sheet with the facilities at the B&B for guests. A glance at her watch showed she had enough time to wash her clothes before dinner with Luke.

She changed into her cleanest shirt and shorts and hurried downstairs with her dirty laundry.

Back in her room, she called Gran to see how she was doing.

Gran was happy to hear from her and wasted no time on pleasantries. "I have more information on that cartel I spoke to you about."

"Gran! Who are you talking to? I don't think it's a good idea for you to be asking questions."

"I didn't ask any questions. I was at the last board meeting for the Arts Council two nights ago and after they gave me my award, one of the new members cornered me and gave me the latest gossip on a couple of antique dealers I've worked with." Gran paused for a moment.

"Are you still there?" Mia asked.

"Yes, dear. I was just having some water. Now, the two dealers have been under investigation by the police. One is Tim Fraser, of Timeless Treasures, and the other is Martha Jones of Jones Antiquities. Tim and Martha are newcomers on the antique market, and people don't know a lot about them."

"I remember seeing Timeless Treasures on Queen Street. The shop's been there a couple of years. It looks like it has a lot of floor space."

"It does. A lot of *empty* floor space."

"Well, maybe he has trouble keeping up with inventory. It happens."

"Please. It's rumored he has soirees at his store twice a month. And he has one happening this week. I'm going."

"Gran! Don't do that. Especially if you think he's into smuggling items."

"I'll be perfectly safe. Tom and Fran Esly are going and have offered to bring me with them. No one pays attention to little old ladies, but I might be able to learn something. "

"Not a good idea. Would you object if I ask Alex to join you?"

"No, Alex is welcome to join us. I was told I could bring a guest." Gran cleared her throat. "Now, about Martha's shop. As far as I can tell, it's a legitimate business. She and her husband lived in Washington, D.C., for fifteen years. She moved back to Canada after they divorced. And apparently, she had enough from the divorce settlement to start this antique shop. The items in the shop are of good quality, but they're overpriced. There's been talk around the antique circles that she's moving items privately between collectors."

Mia frowned, "But Gran, isn't that what antique dealers do?"

Gran coughed. "Well, in some cases, yes. But it appears she does more business with the private collectors than with people coming into her shop."

"Do you think the shop is a front?"

"No. I'm simply telling you what the word on the street is." Gran sighed. "It was so much easier to do business when I ran my little shop. There wasn't talk of cartels. If someone wanted to purchase from a collector, well, it was a simple thing to organize. There wasn't this fear of doing something wrong."

"Tell me you aren't going to go to her shop?"

"Well, not this week. I won't have time. Enough about me, what's been happening at the dig."

Mia updated Gran on her work, and about Mr. Gordon being in Scotland. She didn't tell her about her and Luke's mishap the previous evening. Mia didn't want to worry her. They hung up and Mia went downstairs to switch her clothes to the dryer.

Then she called Alex. Alex put her on speakerphone as she was driving to the lake.

The difference between the call with Gran and the call with Alex is that Mia told Alex everything. Including how she was starting to feel about Luke.

Alex reassured her she would go to Timeless Treasures with Gran and would keep an eye on her activities.

"So, are you thinking you and Luke might get together again?"

"I'm not sure. It's not something I had thought about, and I'm wondering if it's just circumstances and being thrown together that's making me think like this." Mia pursed her lips. "We haven't talked about a future together. And he lives in Great Britain, and I'm in Canada. I'm not looking for a long-distance relationship. But it has been nice to see him again. We've talked about being friends again."

"And how did you feel when you were in the accident? Were you worried about him? Scared?"

Mia groaned. "Come on. Of course, I was worried and scared. It wasn't fun getting pushed off the road. And he had blood running down the side of his head."

Alex chuckled. "Right. Mia, you're a sensible person. What's the harm with a fling? If you both know it isn't going to go anywhere, there's no harm."

Mia sighed. "I think I still have feelings for Luke, and I don't want to get hurt again. The last thing I need right now is this kind of complication in my life." Mia blew out a breath.

"Okay. You don't have to do anything you don't want to. Just relax and see what happens next. You're in charge of you and your feelings." Alex paused for a moment. "Maybe this is a good thing. You can take some time to explore the relationship. From what I remember, the two of you were good together."

"We were. Until he went back to England. I think I'll take your advice and see where this goes. I don't have to make any long-term promises to anyone."

They chatted for a few more minutes and then disconnected the call. Mia leaned against the headboard of the bed. Alex knew her well, and Mia wasn't about to discount her advice. This week felt like it had been a month long but had sped by like a race car. It had been awful to learn about Ethan's death, and then when last night's accident happened, Mia was afraid Luke had been gravely injured, or worse. Her timer went off on her watch, and she hurried downstairs to get her laundry out.

Chapter Twenty

Back in her room, she spent a few minutes putting everything away and considered her options for dinner. She hadn't planned on a dinner companion other than Ethan and the students, and she hadn't packed much in the way of dressier clothes. Mia sighed. Alex was right yet again. It was past time she updated her wardrobe.

Mia took a long, hot shower and groaned when she noticed the bruises along her shoulder from the seat belt. No wonder her upper back and shoulder were sore. She grabbed an analgesic cream and liberally applied it to her shoulder and upper back.

She did her hair and makeup and then got dressed. Her jeans were clean and presentable. They fit her well. She added a black tank top and a long-sleeved plaid shirt. More than suitable for dinner at the pub. She tied the shirt at the waist and made certain none of the bruises on her shoulder were visible.

Mia grabbed her cross-body bag and tucked her wallet and phone in it. She pocketed her key in her jeans and hurried downstairs.

Luke waited for her by the door.

"Did you get the new rental?" Mia asked.

"I did. They were prompt. Want to walk or drive to the pub?"

"Let's walk."

She caught him up on Gran's news.

"I don't blame you for being concerned about her going to this auction. Although I suppose if she's with her friends, she'll be fine."

They had a pleasant dinner at the pub and Phil showed up just as they were finishing their meal.

"Any word from Rina and Diana?" Phil asked.

"They're having supper at the restaurant in the Castle."

The waitress brought the pitcher of beer they had ordered and included a couple of bowls of nuts.

They spent a pleasant evening talking about archaeology and some digs they had worked on.

"We're going to head back. Are you staying out longer?" Luke asked.

Phil glanced at his watch. "It's after ten. I guess Diana and Rina aren't coming here tonight. I'll walk back with you."

Arriving at the B&B, Phil asked Mrs. MacDonald if she'd seen the girls come in.

"I haven't been out front all evening. I was visiting with my cousin who dropped by."

Mia's phone buzzed with a text.

"It's from Diana." She opened the message.

Diana: We have the women. Get the treasure from the dig and bring it to the ruins tomorrow at noon.

"Oh no! What is this?"

Luke hurried to her side. "What's wrong?"

Mia turned her phone to him. "Read this message. It doesn't make sense."

Luke frowned. "Is this a joke?"

"I don't think so. Diana wouldn't joke about this." Mia's fingers flew over her phone.

Who is this? Diana, are you all right?

Mia watched as three little dots flickered, showing someone was answering.

No joke.

Followed by a photo of Diana and Rina bound to chairs in what appeared to be a cave.

What do you want?

The treasure. Ring, sgian-dubh, gemstones, gold coins. Noon tomorrow. The ruins. Come alone, and no one gets hurt. Dr. Reid

must make the exchange. No one else.

"Mia, what is it?" Luke asked.

Mia drew a deep breath. "Someone has Diana and Rina and they're holding them prisoner. They want the treasure we found at the dig in exchange for their release." She handed her phone to Luke. "Look at the photo."

"No way! This can't be happening." Phil cried out.

Luke looked at Mia. "I'm calling Anderson."

Mia nodded. "I'll contact Mr. Gordon and advise him about this. Then, I'll get the artifacts ready. I hope they don't get hurt before we can make the exchange."

Phil brushed his hands through his hair. "How did they get them?"

Mia shook her head. "Mrs. MacDonald, how far are the ruins they went to?"

"It's not far. Maybe three miles. It's an easy walk there and back. And if they wanted to use an Uber, there are plenty around." Mrs. MacDonald's face was pale.

"Are you all right?" Mia asked Mrs. MacDonald.

"I'm scared for the girls. This hasn't happened before."

"We'll get them back. Could you look at the photo to check if you know where they might be?"

"Of course. Hand me your phone." Mrs. MacDonald put on her cheaters and peered at the photo. "Hmm, this could be a cave on the far side of the island. There are a few scattered everywhere."

Luke disconnected his call. "Anderson will be here shortly."

Mrs. MacDonald handed Mia her phone back. "Let me get a map of the island. There are caves, and there are tunnels too."

Mia sent Mr. Gordon a brief message.

Two of the students are being held in exchange for the ring, sgian-dubh, gems, and coins. We have to make the exchange at noon tomorrow.

Mia waited a few minutes, but Mr. Gordon didn't reply immediately. "Ugh, I forgot he's flying back to Canada tonight. I'm not sure when he left."

"But he'll let us make the exchange for them, won't he?" Phil asked.

"He should. Let's just calm down. We can't do anything right now. Let's try to figure out where they might hold them." Mia turned to Mrs. MacDonald. "Did you find the map?"

"Yes. Let's go into the breakfast room." Mrs. MacDonald led the way and quickly lay down a map of the island.

"This one shows the caves that are open for people to visit." Mrs. MacDonald pointed to the legend on the map.

"I don't think they'd keep the girls in a tourist spot," Mia said.

"Aye, but some of these are closed because of the danger of falling rocks or animals that have made them their homes."

Phil groaned. "Not good! They could be in a dangerous place."

Luke bent over the map. "What's this area?" he asked, pointing to a section close to the water.

"It's private property. Owned by a foreigner. I'm not sure who it is, but there are signs all over saying no trespassing." Mrs. MacDonald sniffed. "As if anyone would harm a pasture."

"Are there buildings on the land?" Mia asked.

"Of a sort. There are ruins of an old farmhouse and some outbuildings."

"Is there any way we can find out who owns the property?" Mia asked.

"Anderson should be able to find out. Why are you asking?" Luke asked.

"I'm just wondering if they're in a tunnel and not a cave. It could be that this farmhouse has an underground tunnel, and that's where they are."

Luke shook his head. "That's a reach. We can ask Anderson if he can gather information, but I wouldn't put too many resources at looking into it."

Luke made a call to Anderson. "He'll be here shortly," Luke reported to the group.

They waited for Anderson impatiently. Mia walked back and forth in the breakfast room, worst-case scenarios going through her head.

"Right then. Mia, what exactly is happening." Anderson's voice was calm and reassuring.

Mia informed him about what had happened and when they'd been contacted. She forwarded the text message string to him.

"I'm going to ask our tech department if they can triangulate the message's origin. It's possible we can pinpoint the location. We're going to start a search in the area where the girls were today."

Phil spoke up. "They planned to visit the ruins and go to the beach. They texted me photos from both places. The last message was that they were going to a nearby restaurant for dinner."

Anderson nodded. "Those would be helpful. Phil, can you show us the photos they sent you?"

Phil showed him the photos he'd received earlier that day.

"Please send them to this officer. I'll have him go through them as well. I'd like you all to examine the photos and if you can identify anyone or anything in them." Anderson handed out a business card to Phil.

"Do you think someone followed them?" Luke asked.

"It's a possibility. My officer will go through the photos. If there's anyone who appears in the background in more than one, we'll check them out." Anderson eyed Mia. "We're going to do everything we can to find them. But they could be anywhere."

Mia nodded. "I understand. We've been looking at a map of Skye. The photo the kidnappers sent shows them in a tunnel or a cave. Mrs. MacDonald has a map showing different caves on Skye."

"Tourists enjoy exploring the local caves. I always warn them to be careful close to the water. The tide comes up very fast." Mrs. MacDonald folded her arms across her chest. "Some of them come back wet."

Anderson smiled. "I doubt they have them in a cave close to the water. That leaves tunnels."

One of the officers came in. "We have the flyers with the girls' photos. We're going to send them to the other stations on Skye."

"Send them across Great Britain. There isn't a guarantee they're on Skye. Have the rest of the officers come in?" Anderson asked.

"They're waiting outside."

"I'll go speak with them and get them started." Anderson walked toward the door.

Mia and Luke followed him out. "I have a vested interest in what you're going to say next. Can we help with the search?" Mia asked.

Anderson shook his head. "I want you to stay here and wait for them to provide you with instructions. Have you heard back from Mr. Gordon about the exchange?"

"Not yet. He's flying back to Canada tonight."

Anderson stopped in front of the officers. There were fifteen of them from the surrounding area.

"Right, you're all aware of why you're here. The information's on your phones, and we'll distribute the flyers. Time is important. You should also have a photo of where we believe the women are being held. If any of you have an idea where that is, tell us. Any questions?" Hearing none, Anderson continued. "You'll work in teams of two. It's late, but a sweep of the beach area by the ruins is necessary. I'll contact the Castle, it's near the ruins, and advise them about what's happening. They should have security cameras, and we'll get access to the feed. We may find something on the cameras that will help. Any questions?"

The officers shook their heads.

"Right then, Officer Murphy will send you on your way. Keep in touch, and if you find anything, contact me immediately."

Mia watched as they left the grounds of the B&B. She put her hand on her stomach and felt it flip. If anything happened to Diana or Rina, she'd never forgive herself. Mia hoped they'd find them soon and that they'd be unharmed. She hurried back to the B&B.

"Phil, can I see the photos they sent you?"

"Sure." Phil opened his phone for Mia.

Mia scrutinized the pictures.

"What are you looking for?" Phil asked.

"I'm checking the background in case there's someone who's trying to stay out of the picture." Mia pinched her fingers and enlarged a photo. "Like this one." She showed Phil the photo. "The man in the background turns his head away. He's wearing a black T-shirt and blue jeans."

"I see him. Is he in any other photos?" Phil asked.

Mia scrolled through the photos. "Here he is. You can make out some of his features." Mia gasped. "He looks like the man who tried to run us off the road."

"Anderson needs to be told about this." Luke strode out to the parking lot to speak to Anderson.

Anderson returned with Luke.

"Good catch. With this photo and the one from the highway camera, we might get lucky." Anderson made a call.

"That's good that you found that," Phil said.

Mia smiled. "It's a start."

Mrs. MacDonald came in. "I've put coffee on in the breakfast room, and I'll bring out some muffins shortly."

"Thank you. I doubt any of us will be sleeping tonight," Mia said.

Chapter Twenty-One

Mia's phone rang, startling everyone in the room. She grabbed it, wondering if it was the kidnappers.

"Mia Reid."

"Mia, it's Charles Gordon. I'm calling from my plane. I just read your text. What happened?"

Mia filled him in.

"Are the police involved?"

"Yes. I contacted DI Anderson, and officers are out looking for them."

"Have they discovered anything?"

"Not yet." Mia bit her lip. "I need your approval to exchange the artifacts for the girls."

"It breaks my heart that we're going to lose the artifacts, but yes, go ahead. Their safety is more important."

"Thanks."

"Who's making the exchange?"

"I am."

"I'm not comfortable with that. Isn't there an officer who can go in your place?"

"No, I'll be fine. I can take care of myself, and I have a responsibility to my team. Diana and Rina need me there. I'll make sure they're released."

"My pilot's telling me we'll be arriving shortly. Keep me informed."

"Ah, Mr. Gordon, we cannot allow the press to realize what's happening."

"Of course." Mr. Gordon hung up.

Mia rubbed her face and rolled her shoulders.

CHAPTER TWENTY-ONE

"What did he say?" Phil asked.

"He gave the go-ahead with the exchange. And he wants me to keep him informed."

"And is he going to keep this quiet?" Luke asked.

"I hope so. I didn't feel comfortable telling him that, but he's the one who talked about our finds."

"Can you get the artifacts in time to make the exchange?" Phil asked.

Mia explained the hidden compartment in her backpack.

"Wow, have you used it before?"

"Yes, quite a bit. Ethan and I were in a remote location in Central America last year. The artifacts were small and valuable. They fit easily in the compartment. Ethan had one as well."

They moved to the sitting room, where the chairs were more comfortable. They talked quietly between themselves until about three in the morning, when Phil fell asleep in his chair. Mia worried about Diana and Rina's fate.

Anderson came in around five o'clock. "I thought you'd still be up. Is there coffee?"

Mia pointed to the sideboard. "Mrs. MacDonald has kept us supplied all night. Help yourself."

Anderson poured himself a cup and added cream and sugar. "Nothing on the beach. We spoke with the waitress who served them at the restaurant. She said they'd had supper around six-thirty, and it was just the two of them. We're still going through the security footage at the Castle." He pulled out a chair and sat. "They've been very cooperative. The photo Phil sent with the man in the background is being circulated as well. We've used facial recognition, and he shows up at Glasgow airport on the same day you and Diana arrived."

Mia gasped. "I thought I'd seen someone who looked familiar, but I couldn't place him."

"He and another man were on the same flight as you and Diana were. His name is Brent Marshall. From Canada, and he has a record for theft and assault. Not a nice person."

"So, was he following us?" Mia asked.

179

"Possibly. But why would he follow you? Who was aware of the artifacts Dr. Carter had discovered?"

"Well, I knew, and Shelly did too. Ethan told Mr. Gordon."

Phil sighed. "It wasn't a secret. We talked about it at the pub. People were at the dig when we found them. Lots of people could have known."

"True. But this sounds like it's organized. Someone sending them here to get the artifacts. I wonder if they're the ones who broke into the B&B?" Mia asked.

"It's possible. We'll be showing his photo to the local businesses when they open this morning. I'm hopeful someone will remember him." Anderson took a long drink of coffee. "Did you report your accident to the police?"

Mia shook her head. "It didn't warrant a report. No one got seriously injured. Their car wasn't damaged, and they gave me money to repair my bike."

"Why did they run you down? What happened when they came to help you?" Luke asked.

Mia told them what had happened.

"And one of them had your daypack?" Luke asked.

"Yes. I remember looking up, and he was holding it by the zipper. And he nodded at the guy giving me money. The guy giving me money is the one in the photo Rina sent to Phil."

"Where's your daypack?" Luke asked.

"In my room. Why?"

"I'm curious. Do you mind getting it?"

Mia made her way to her room. None of this made sense. How was her accident related to the dig? She pulled out her daypack and brought it down to Luke.

"Do you mind if I search it?" Luke asked.

"No, what are you looking for?"

Luke checked the pack carefully. "I'm wondering if they put a tracker in your bag. You say someone broke into your office that morning?"

"Yes. Do you think they used it to follow me?"

"It's possible. Is your office number listed in a directory anywhere?"

"No. You go through the department's switchboard."

"It could have helped them find your office. Found it." He tugged at the inside pocket of the daypack and then showed them a small electronic tracking device that was blinking.

"What's that?" Phil asked.

"That's a tracking device. We've discovered these in several shipments of stolen artifacts. The thieves use them to track the artifacts when they leave the museum or the homes of the artifact's owners. It's small, quiet, and effective."

Anderson looked at it. "Once it's installed on the item, it begins tracking. For at least thirty days."

Mia shook her head. "I can't believe it. That's been in my bag all this time?"

"Yes. And I suggest we leave it there. You'll be using this daypack to make the exchange, and we'll be able to follow you when you go."

"How are you going to do that?" Mia asked.

"I go to the manufacturer's website, add the number, and click on it. I'll be able to track it from my phone. Keep your daypack with you." Luke grabbed a loupe on the table and located the serial number. Then, using his phone, he scanned the number and waited a few moments. A beep, and then he smiled.

"Gotcha. The tracker's added to my phone, and we'll be able to follow you."

"And I think the kidnappers will keep your daypack. That way, if they make their escape before we can reach them, we'll be able to follow them," Anderson said.

Mia rubbed her eyes. "This all sounds unbelievable. I never thought they'd be tracking me."

Luke's eyes narrowed. "But why would you have thought that?"

"Ethan told me to be careful. He thought he was being followed."

Anderson grimaced. "I'm not sure why you would have thought you'd be followed. You didn't have any information or artifacts."

"He was concerned. And he was right to be. I'm going to lie down for a bit. I'm not sure I'll sleep, but my brain is whirring too fast. What should I do with the artifacts?"

"Leave them here with us. We aren't going anywhere." Luke said.

Mia went up to her room and peeled off her clothes. She climbed into bed, set an alarm on her phone, and pulled the blankets over her head.

An hour and a half later, she woke up feeling rested. Time to get moving. A hot shower and breakfast would clear the cobwebs.

In the breakfast room, Mia saw that Mrs. MacDonald had replenished the breakfast items. Phil was nowhere to be seen. Luke and Anderson had remnants of breakfast on their plates.

"Did you get some rest?" Luke asked.

Mia walked to the sideboard. "I did. But I'll feel much better when the girls are back." She heaped breakfast on her plate and filled her coffee cup.

"Any updates?" Mia asked Anderson.

"No one's seen them, and we haven't found anything that belongs to them. The waitress who saw them at the restaurant said the men in the photos spoke with them as they left. She didn't hear what they said, but it didn't appear to be threatening."

Mia ate her breakfast, Luke headed upstairs to shower and change, Anderson worked the phone talking to the officers who'd been out in the field.

Phil came downstairs an hour later for breakfast.

"What are your plans?" Mia asked.

"I'd like to go down to the beach and walk around. Who knows, I might see something that was missed," Phil said.

"That's fine; the police still have a presence there. I expect you to be back here by eleven. I want to know you're safe when I'm delivering the artifacts."

"Agreed. I'll grab some breakfast. Is it okay if I use the van to get to the beach?" Phil asked.

"Of course."

Phil ate breakfast and then left for the beach. Mia watched him leave. "I hope he stays safe."

Anderson overheard her. "He'll be fine. There's still a police presence there. I've sent them a message to keep an eye on him."

"Thanks. I can't afford to lose anyone else."

"You haven't lost Rina and Diana. You're going to get them back," Luke said.

Mia's phone buzzed with a text.

Ruins parking lot at noon. Bring the artifacts, or you won't see the girls again.

Got it.

Mia swallowed hard. It was really going to happen. She rubbed her face and showed Anderson her phone. "From the kidnappers."

"Right. We'll set up our people at the ruins. Some will be maintenance workers, others will be tourists."

Mia glanced at her watch. "I'd better get ready. I'm going to change into warmer clothes and hiking boots. I'll be down shortly."

Upstairs, Mia tied her hair back in a braid. She dressed in her jeans, a T-shirt, a plaid shirt, and her hiking boots. She tucked her driver's license and a credit card in her jeans. Mia paused before leaving her room. She noticed her reflection in the mirror and nodded. "You can do this. The girls need you."

With a deep breath, she hurried downstairs.

Chapter Twenty-Two

"I'm ready to go." Mia strode into the breakfast room. Luke and Anderson were examining the map.

Mia stopped at the table and placed the artifacts in the large pocket of her daypack. Checking the smaller pocket for the tracker, she zipped everything up.

"Officers are at the ruins. They're dressed as groundskeepers and are working in the gardens. We have two couples posing as tourists. Don't search for them. They know what you, Diana, and Rina look like. And they have the photos of the two men we think took them," Anderson said. "Are you certain you want to do this? We have an officer who can take your place."

"The kidnappers were clear. I need to make the exchange."

"I don't doubt your abilities, but I'm concerned for your safety as well. We'll be tracking the daypack." Anderson rubbed his face.

"I'll be fine. I'll be back soon."

Phil stood by the door. "Good luck, Mia."

Luke walked behind Mia. "I'll escort you to your car."

They left the B&B, and Luke opened Mia's door. "Please be careful." Luke paused. "Mia, I've missed you, and I want to get to know you again. So, don't take any chances. Give them the artifacts, get the girls out, and come back safely." He pulled Mia into a hug; then he gently kissed her.

Mia sighed. "I care about you, too. We'll figure this out, I promise. Now I've got to leave. I can't be late." Mia dropped the daypack in the car, turned, and wrapped her arms around Luke. "I'll be back, don't worry."

Mia hopped in the car and waved at the group assembled outside, then headed toward the ruins.

The drive didn't take long. She pulled into a vacant spot in the parking lot and pulled out her phone, checking her messages. Nothing from the kidnappers. She'd have to wait until they contacted her.

A few moments later, her phone pinged with a text.

Get out of your car. Follow the path on the left. Keep walking. We'll contact you when we're sure no one is following you.

"Well, here we go," Mia muttered to herself.

She grabbed the daypack, slung it over her shoulder, locked the car, and found the path.

She followed the path through the woods and was mindful of the surrounding noises. Or rather the lack of noise. No birds singing, no squirrels chattering. Just the wind blowing through the trees. She could smell the sea air in the wind. The path meandered toward the sea. She stopped when the path forked in two directions. Which way was she supposed to go? She stood waiting and searched for a sign.

A branch cracked behind her. Whirling around, Mia faced one of the men who'd run into her in Lakeview. She adjusted her stance with one foot slightly in front of the other and slipped her phone in her jeans pocket.

"Dr. Reid. Nice to see you're prompt. Turn around and arms out to the side."

Mia complied, and the man patted her down thoroughly. "What are you doing?" she asked.

"Making sure you aren't wearing a wire." The man pulled out her cell phone and checked it. "Turn this off." He turned her to face him.

Mia took her phone and turned it off. The man grabbed it and shoved it in his pocket. He pulled out a black pillowcase. "To make certain you can't lead anyone to our hiding place." He put the pillowcase over Mia's head. "Not a sound out of you." He grabbed Mia by the arm, and they started walking.

They'd walked for what seemed like five minutes when they started going downhill. Mia could feel the pull on her body as they walked on rocky terrain. The wind whipped the pillowcase against her face, and she heard waves crashing close by. Suddenly, everything became muffled. The man pulled the pillowcase off her head and pushed her forward. "You'll need to duck down."

Mia swiftly scanned her surroundings. They appeared to be in a cave by the water. It was low tide, but Mia's eyes noticed pools of water along the edges of the cave.

"Come on, get moving. I don't have all day." The man planted his hand in the middle of her back and pushed.

"All right. I'm just getting my bearings." Mia spat out as she started walking forward.

They walked for, what Mia thought was about nine hundred feet, and then he called out. "Stop. See the wall in front of you?"

Mia nodded. There were signs of water reaching the top of the wall at high tide.

"Move to the right and stay put." He waited until Mia complied, and then he walked to the far-left wall and twisted a large ring. The rock wall in front of Mia opened. Behind the wall, another man stood armed with a gun.

The man with the gun motioned Mia toward a bench. "Move over there and hand me the daypack."

She walked to the bench.

"Drop it on the ground and kick it to me."

Mia did as he asked, surveying the room carefully. It appeared to be a large cell with two doors leading down two separate paths.

He handed his gun to the first man. He opened the daypack and pulled out the artifacts. "Sweet. We've got them. Well done, Dr. Reid."

"What happens now? You have the artifacts. Let the students go."

"That depends on our boss. But hey, you can see the students. You can join them. Get up." He motioned towards one of the doors.

Mia stood and walked to the door he'd pointed to.

"Open it."

Mia opened the door and discovered a dungeon-like room. It had stone walls, a barred door, a small window several yards above the floor, and Diana and Rina sitting on the floor.

The second man followed Mia in and shoved her toward the barred door. "Here they are. They've been waiting for you." He pulled out a key and, unlocked the door, and pushed Mia inside with them. She fell to the ground.

"Hey. You said you'd let them go. That was the deal." Mia struggled to get up.

The man with the gun stood in front of the door. "No, it wasn't. I said if you wanted to see them again, you'd have to give us the artifacts. And you did, and now you're seeing them." He laughed. "A professor should be able to read information accurately, shouldn't she?"

Mia glared at him. "What are you going to do with us?"

"Nothing. The sea will deal with you. The tide's rising, and in a few hours, none of you will be a problem anymore."

Diana gasped, and Rina sobbed. "No, don't do this. We won't say anything to the police."

"Right. And the Easter Bunny and Santa are friends with the Tooth Fairy." The man with the gun sneered. "Enjoy your time together." Turning away, he left the heavy door open. "It won't take long."

"Stop! We can make it worth your while. We have money." Mia called out.

The man with the gun turned around. "Money isn't the issue. I don't want to cross our boss." And walked away.

Rina moaned. "Oh my God. We're going to die here."

Diana walked to the barred door and shook it. "I don't want to die. I'm not done living yet."

Mia looked around the cell. Searching for a break somewhere. "Are you okay?"

"My head hurts. I think they drugged us last night. But I'm not sure what they used," Diana said.

Rina nodded. "And my ankle is swollen. I think I twisted it last night."

Mia checked Rina's ankle. Pressing along the sides, she watched Rina's face. Rina inhaled a breath. "That hurt."

"Can you keep it elevated for a bit?"

"Yes. You sound like you have a plan."

"I do. There's a tracker in my daypack. Anderson and Luke can track me.

I don't know if they could follow me in the cave. But, they should be able to follow the trail to the mouth of the cave."

"Do you think they'll come looking for you?" Diana asked.

"When I don't check in with them, they will. There were officers at the ruins as well. They'll be watching for me. My car's still in the parking lot." Mia walked along the wall with the door. "Have you tried to get out?"

Diana shook her head. "We didn't have a chance to. When we got here, they tied us up and took photos. Then they drugged us. The last I remember, we were sitting on the chairs. They must have untied us last night."

"Do you think the tide is going to reach this room?" Rina asked.

"Oh yeah, it will. There are high tide water marks in the outside room, and they've left the heavy door open. The water will come in." Mia pointed at the wall behind them. "See those water marks? High tide will cover up to that point."

Rina's eyes widened. "No! We can't drown. We've got to get out of here!" She scrambled to her feet and hopped to the door, pulling on it and trying to open it.

Mia hurried to her. "Rina, calm down. Panicking won't get us anywhere. Let's search for something that could help us get out of here." Mia walked to the door and examined it closely. She noticed the door's hinges were rusted. If they applied enough force, they might pull the door off. Mia grabbed the door and yanked on it. Nothing.

Diana was watching. "Let me help. You want to loosen the hinges, right?"

"Yes. Maybe if we all pull at the same time."

Together, the three of them pulled hard.

Mia felt the door shift. "It's moving. Again."

They heaved hard and then twice more. One hinge gave way.

"It's working!" Rina yelled.

"One more time ought to do it." Mia wiped her hands on her jeans.

They pulled again, and the hinges gave way with a screech. The door collapsed toward them.

They pushed the door into the cell and gave a whoop of joy. "That was amazing!" Rina said.

"Make sure there's nothing left behind, and let's go. Rina, do you need help walking?"

"I think so. My ankle feels like it's on fire."

"I'll help you out." Mia grabbed Rina by the waist and supported her.

"They took our bags and sweaters from us. I don't know where they are." Diana looked around the cell.

"They might have kept them in their car. I didn't notice them when we were coming here through the cave." Mia led them out of the dungeon. She glanced to the right and noticed a closed door. "What's in here, do you know?"

Diana shook her head.

"Rina, lean against the wall. I want to check and make sure no one else is in here." Mia tugged on the door, and it opened. Mia gasped. "Wow. Check this out."

Inside the room were shelves filled with artifacts. Mia walked in and examined a shelf. "These are artifacts that were reported stolen over the last year. I remember reading a report sent to the university."

"Why are they here?" Diana asked.

"I wonder if there's a smuggling operation here on Skye. Although that doesn't make a lot of sense. Whoever's running this would have to get it to a major airport."

"Not if they used ships to transport them." Rina was holding herself against the wall.

"That's true. They could get them on board and smuggle them in through customs in various countries." Mia mused.

"What are we going to do about them? Aren't they in danger of getting damaged by the water?" Diana asked.

Mia glanced at the walls and the floor. "There aren't any water marks in this room. I think it's safe from water damage. Do either of you have your phones?"

"No. They took them from us," Diana said.

"They took mine too. Okay, let's get out of here. I have my car keys and license. If we can make it to the parking lot, we'll be fine."

Mia helped Rina hobble to the main cave. Diana followed behind them. Mia spotted the bench and her daypack was thrown on the floor next to it. "Why did they leave this here? Rina, sit on the bench for a minute." Mia picked up the daypack and shook it. It was empty, and they'd removed the tracker. Mia looked around the bench and spotted her phone. "Why would they leave this behind?"

"Maybe because we're supposed to die here. It would have gone out with the tide. Could they have left our phones, too?" Diana asked.

"They might have. Look around for them. I'm going to take a couple of photos of the room with the antiquities. I'll be right back. Rina, don't move." Mia scooted back to the room.

"Please hurry," Rina called after her.

Mia snapped the photos and then shut the door securely. She hurried back to the girls. Diana had found their phones by the entrance of the cave. "I'm going to check on the tide. I'll be quick." Mia hurried to the mouth of the cave.

At the mouth of the cave, the water had started to come in. Mia searched for the trail. There was a path, but part of it was under water. The rocks would be treacherous, and it didn't look promising. Raising her phone in the air, she realized there were no bars. She wouldn't be able to get in touch with Luke or Anderson. They'd have to get out on their own.

"All right, we're going to get wet. Rina, how's the ankle?"

Rina had her foot on the bench, and her face was pale. "It hurts, but I'm not staying here. Let's go." Rina stood and leaned on the wall.

"We'll help you. Diana, the path is to the left. The first few feet are under water. The rocks will be slick, go slow and be careful. You'll go first. Rina, you're next. I'll help you manage the path. You may need to crawl up part of it. We can't wait much longer, the tide's coming in. If you run into trouble, let me know. I don't want either of you falling into the water."

Diana and Rina nodded. "Do you have any bars on your phone?" Diana asked.

"None. I take it neither of you do either?"

"We tried. Nothing."

"We'll check again when we reach the top of the path. It's time to move."

Mia held her breath as Diana sloshed her way forward. The undertow was strong, and Mia could see Diana wobble. She reached the start of the path and turned to wave at Rina and Mia. "Made it. Rina come on. Be careful; the water really pulls at you."

Mia grabbed Rina by the waist. "I've got you."

Mia calculated it took them twice as long as it took Diana. When they reached the edge where the path started, Diana pulled Rina toward her. Mia felt the cold water on her legs. She glanced down and saw the water was well above her knees. She scrambled up next to Rina.

Rina was breathing hard and had her eyes closed. Her face was white, and the sides of her mouth pinched.

"How's the pain?" Mia asked.

"Not good. But I'm not staying here."

"Give me your phone. It might save it from getting wet. Diana, put your phone in your pocket."

Rina handed Mia her phone, and Mia buttoned it securely in her shirt pocket. Her own phone was safely tucked away.

Diana complied and started up the path. Mia watched her carefully before giving Rina the go-ahead.

Rina dropped to her knees and started to crawl up the path. Mia kept her hand on Rina's back to support her, and Diana turned around a few times to pull Rina up. It took them fifteen minutes to get up to the lookoff point on the path. They dropped to the ground and looked back where they climbed. Rina was gasping for breath and tears were running down her cheeks. "I couldn't have made it without your help. Thank you both."

"No worries. We weren't going to leave you behind," Diana said.

Mia pulled out her phone. There was one bar. She tried calling Luke, but the call dropped. She sent a quick text.

Need help. Have the girls but Rina is hurt. Meet at parking lot.

She held her phone up in the air and hit send.

"Did it go through?" Rina asked.

"Still waiting. I'll try again when we get on the path." Mia watched Rina carefully. Her face was pasty. "We can rest for a few minutes, then we'll need to keep moving."

Mia waited until Rina's breathing was steady. "All right. Let's keep going. The path should be easier now."

She was right. The path rose, but it wasn't steep, and although the ground was gravel, they could manage. Mia and Diana supported Rina. Mia didn't want her to put any weight on her bad ankle. They'd eventually get to a forested path that would be easier on Rina and she encouraged them on.

Mia's phone pinged. The sound reverberated, and all of them stopped in their tracks.

Luke: At parking lot. Where are you?

Mia tried calling him again, and this time, it went through.

"Where are you? Are you hurt?"

"Rina has a badly sprained ankle. Diana is fine except for a headache. I'm okay. We're on a path heading toward the parking lot. It's along the edge of the sea."

"Are you safe?"

"I think so. The two men left a while ago. They took the artifacts and left us to drown in one of the caves."

Luke swore. "Stay where you are. One of the officers knows exactly how to get to you. We're on our way, and we'll have equipment for Rina."

"Thanks. We're in the middle of the path, and we aren't moving."

"What did he say?" Diana asked.

"They'll be here soon. They know where we are. Rina, sit down and rest your ankle. They're bringing equipment to help you out."

Rina dropped to the ground with a sigh. "Thank you. My ankle is killing me."

Diana raised Rina's jean leg and exclaimed, "Rina, it looks like a grapefruit!"

Mia glanced at Rina's ankle. "That's going to take time to heal. It might be broken."

Diana sat next to Rina and propped Rina's ankle on her legs. "This might help a bit."

"You don't have to do that," Rina said.

"It's a good idea," Mia said. "Now, the police will want to talk to you both and get as much information as they can get about the two men. And Luke will want to know about the artifacts we found in the cave."

"Do you think they'll be safe from the water?" Diana asked.

"They should be. I closed the door securely." Mia walked a bit, stretching her legs.

Mia turned her head to the right. "Someone's coming." Mia stood in front of Diana and Rina. If it was the kidnappers, she'd do her best to fight them off. To her relief, it was Luke, Anderson, and a team of emergency response people.

"Mia!" Luke called out and then ran toward her. He grabbed her in a hug. "Are you all right?"

"Wet, but otherwise fine. Diana and Rina need some attention, though."

The emergency response officers were already dealing with the girls. Blood pressure cuffs were on their arms; two of them were examining Rina's ankle, and a third was checking Diana's pupils.

Anderson came up to Mia. "Good work getting them out. Do you know where the kidnappers went?"

"No, they talked about meeting with their boss. But they didn't give a name." Mia glanced at Luke. "We found some artifacts in the cave. I'm sure they're the ones I saw in a report on missing artifacts a few weeks ago."

"Where did you find them?"

"They were in a different room from where we were held. There was a heavy door that kept everything waterproof. There weren't any signs of water damage in the room. I took photos and closed the door tightly. We can go back when it's low tide." Mia opened the photo app on her phone and showed the photos to Luke.

"Thanks, Mia. We'll go down later. Can you send me the photos? And Anderson, will you come with us?" Luke asked.

"That I will. I'll bring some officers with me." Anderson pulled out a notepad. "Mia, I'd like to ask you some questions about what happened."

Mia answered Anderson's questions as best she could. He was surprised she had been abducted so close to the parking lot.

"Did you see any of our officers?" he asked.

"I did, but the kidnappers had me go off to the path by the parking lot. The officers weren't anywhere near that path. It's almost as if the kidnappers knew what you were going to do."

Anderson nodded. "That shows they're organized. It wouldn't surprise me that they've done this before. Did you recognize them?"

"Yes. It was the two men who ran me down in Lakeview."

"Well, that's helpful. Now let's check to see if they're still in the area."

"Do you think they're part of this cartel Gran heard about?"

"They could be. I'm also thinking someone from Charles Gordon's company could be involved with this," Luke said.

"Sir, we're ready to move the young lady," an officer said.

"Excellent. Let's get them to the hospital."

The emergency officers carried Rina on a stretcher to the parking lot. Diana followed behind her with Mia by her side.

They put Rina in an ambulance and told Diana to get in as well because she would need to be checked by a doctor.

"I'll be following the ambulance to the hospital, and I'll meet you both there. You can come back to the B&B with me when we're done," Mia said.

Luke held out his hand for her keys. "I'll drive. Anderson's following in his car."

Mia handed over the keys and slid into the front seat. She was shaking. Luke hurried to get a blanket from the emergency crew.

He came back and wrapped her in the blanket and then turned on the heat. "Are you sure you're okay?"

Mia nodded. "I'm just cold."

"The hospital isn't far, and we'll get some hot tea in you." He pulled out behind the ambulance.

Mia saw Anderson follow behind them.

They arrived at the hospital in twenty minutes. Mia and Luke didn't talk much on the drive.

At the hospital, Mia watched the medical team take Rina into X-ray, and then Diana went into a cubicle to be examined.

"I'd like you to get checked out." Luke led Mia to the waiting area.

"I'm not injured or hurt. And I'm much warmer. I've stopped shaking." Mia smiled. "Honestly, I'm fine. If I wasn't, I'd get checked out."

They sat down to wait, and Luke put his arm around her.

"I want to be there when Anderson talks to Rina and Diana. I know he's not going to browbeat them, but I want to be there to support them," Mia said.

"I'm sure he won't have any objections. He was quite upset when we couldn't find you. The tracker worked well until it didn't. I assume it stopped working when you went underground?"

"I think so. They took out the tracker and left my daypack on a bench. I don't understand why they left our phones behind. That wasn't bright."

"Well, thank goodness for stupid criminals." Luke grinned.

Anderson stopped in front of them. "I'm going to chat with Diana. Mia, did you want to be there?"

Mia stood. "Yes."

Luke followed them as they headed to the cubicle where Diana was.

There was a doctor with her, and she had just finished examining her. "Not too bad for the ordeal she's been through. Unless something shows up in the blood work, we won't be keeping her. A good meal, some rest, and she'll be right as rain. I'll be back shortly."

Mia smiled. "That's good news."

Diana grinned. "I'll be very glad to return to the B&B."

Anderson cleared his throat, "I have a few questions to ask. Are you up to it?"

Diana nodded.

"Did you overhear any calls they made?" Anderson asked.

"We could hear them talking in the cave. They seemed to be arguing about something, but I couldn't make out what it was. It was just before they gave us food this morning."

"Anything else?"

"Can't think of anything." Diana leaned back on the pillow.

The doctor returned. "Good news, you can leave the hospital. All bloodwork came back clear, telling us that whatever was in your system is gone. I'd suggest you take it easy for the next couple of days. How long are you on Skye?"

"I leave in another week. I'm working at the dig just outside of Dunvegan."

"If you experience any ill effects, come back."

"What's happening with Rina?" Diana asked.

"We think her ankle is broken. We've called our orthopedic surgeon in. She'll determine if surgery is required."

Diana's face fell. "She must have been in a lot of pain."

"And she climbed with that ankle. Can I see her?" Mia asked.

"Of course. Follow me."

"I'll be right back." Mia hurried after the doctor.

Rina was in a room down the hall. Mia poked her head in. "Can I come in?"

"Mia, yeah, come in." Rina tried to scoot up in her bed and winced.

"Don't move. The doctor told us your ankle may be broken. I'm sorry to hear that."

Rina shrugged. "I can't do much about it now. They're bringing me some pain medication. I spoke with the surgeon a few minutes ago. She's going to operate tonight. She says it's not a bad break, and I should be fine."

"Do you want me to stay with you?"

"No, the doctor said I'd be asleep until tomorrow morning. I'd appreciate it if you came by later tomorrow. I just spoke with my mom and dad. They'll be here as soon as they can, but it probably won't be until late tomorrow afternoon."

"I'll be here by noon. Get some rest." Mia held Rina's hand for a minute. "You sure you're okay?"

"I will be." Rina's eyes were almost closing. "I'm just really tired."

Mia left the room. She noticed a police officer sitting next to Rina's door. Good, Anderson was taking steps to make sure she'd be safe. She stopped in Diana's room, and they made their way to the entrance.

Luke was waiting for them by the door. "Anderson's going to want to debrief both of you. He's on his way to the police station in the village. He told me to bring you both there."

Mia nodded. "I expected as much. Let's get going."

They hurried to the car. Once they got on the road, Mia turned in her seat to ask Diana a question and realized she was asleep.

Mia leaned back in her seat and sighed. "What a mess this is. Nothing about this dig has gone well."

"You found treasure. And we've reconnected. I'd like to think that's good."

"You know what I mean. And yes, it's been nice to be with you." Mia took a sip of water. "I'm going to have to let Mr. Gordon know what's been happening. I'm surprised he hasn't been calling me."

"Ah, about that. Anderson got in touch with him when we lost you. Mr. Gordon told him to get you and the students out, no matter what. I know Anderson's let him know you're out and safe."

"Good. I'll send him a text and set up a time for a call. I don't really want to deal with this now." Mia sent a text and was surprised to get a return message immediately.

Please call asap.

"Ugh. Do I call now or not?" she mused.

"We'll be at the police station in fifteen minutes. You'll only have to speak with him for a brief time."

Mia placed the call.

"Mia, are you and the students okay?" Mr. Gordon barked.

Mia grimaced. "Rina's in the hospital with a broken ankle. Diana's unhurt and she's resting now. I'm not injured. And I'm sorry this happened."

"Not your fault. Your responsibility was to get the students back, and you did. We'll find the artifacts. No doubt they'll be up on the dark web soon. I have some of my people watching for them."

"Thanks for that. I don't have long to talk. We're on our way to the police station to speak with DI Anderson. Is there anything else you need?"

"I'm afraid so." Mr. Gordon paused a moment. "I need you to close the dig. Unfortunately, there have been too many challenges with this project, and my board of directors isn't happy. My office will be in touch with the local government to advise them of our plans. Your job will be to make certain the dig is closed properly."

Mia drew a breath. "I'm sorry to hear that."

Mr. Gordon continued, "The notoriety associated with the dig and Dr. Carter's murder is having an adverse impact on my company."

Mia was stunned. He was concerned about how Ethan's murder was impacting his finances.

"I expect you to close the dig by the end of the week. Please ensure an arrangement to store the artifacts. Do you need help with this?"

"No. I've done this before and can get it finished." Mia bit out the words. Ending the dig like this was disappointing.

"I'll speak with you again tomorrow." Mr. Gordon disconnected the call.

Mia put her phone down. "That didn't go well."

"He wants to shut it down?" Luke asked.

"Yes. And I can't blame him. Ethan killed; Rina and Diana kidnapped; antiquities stolen. It's not good. We were lucky Rina and Diana got out alive."

"And that's to your credit. Your quick thinking got them out. What are you going to do?"

"I have no choice. He's the dig sponsor and has all the money. I'll wrap things up and work with Angus to display the artifacts in the local museum."

Luke pulled out in front of another car. "The first thing to do is speak with Anderson. After that, you can talk to the students and let them know what's happening. This isn't your fault, you know that, right?"

Mia took a long drink of water. "I do. But it doesn't help the situation."

Diana stirred in the back seat. Mia turned to check on her. "Hey, we're almost there. Do you want some water?"

"That'd be great."

Mia grabbed another water bottle and handed it to Diana. "Did you get some rest?"

"I did. How long will we be with the police?"

"It shouldn't take too long. Anderson and his team will want as much information as you can provide. He knows you're anxious to get back to the B&B." Luke pulled into the parking lot at the police station. They entered the station and Anderson noticed them arrive.

"Mia, Diana, if you'll come with me?"

They followed him to the back of the police station. Luke stayed behind in the entrance. Mia noticed there were small offices along the hall and two conference rooms on either side of the hall.

Anderson stopped in front of the one on the right side. "Diana, if you'll have a seat in here, Officer Murphy will take your statement. Mia, you'll be in here with me."

"Diana, if you're done before I am, just wait for me. We'll go back to the B&B together."

Diana nodded her head and took a seat at the table. After closing the door, Anderson led Mia to a different room.

Anderson asked Mia to tell him everything that had happened since she left the B&B that morning. Mia gave him a thorough reporting and clear descriptions of the two men. She also mentioned the second room with additional artifacts that were left behind. She showed him the photos of the room she'd taken before leaving the cave.

"I have a team waiting for the tide to go out, and then we'll go check on the cave. Luke will come with me to verify the antiquities."

"What happens now?" Mia asked.

"We'll send a description of the two men to Police Scotland. Luke will take care of working with AART, and he'll send the description of the men to Interpol. We'll do our best to capture the two men and to locate the missing artifacts."

"I spoke with Mr. Gordon, and he mentioned members of his team are searching the dark web for the stolen artifacts."

"Luke's reaching out to his contacts to find out what they know."

"Mr. Gordon also informed me that he's closing the dig. And he wants us to leave by the end of the week."

Anderson nodded. "I'm aware of that. The local government isn't happy with him."

Mia sat back. "Unfortunately, he controls the funds." Mia was quiet for a minute. "What's happening with Ethan's death?"

"There are no new leads, and the woman who wanted to purchase the antiquities seems to have disappeared." Anderson stood. "We're not giving up. I contacted Mrs. Carter. Dr. Carter's body is being returned to her today. Mr. Gordon has taken care of the arrangements."

As Mia left the conference room, she saw Diana and Luke talking at the entrance.

"Ready to head back?" Luke asked.

"Yes. A hot shower will be nice."

Anderson walked them out. "I'll be in touch. Luke, we'll need to leave at around nine this evening."

Chapter Twenty-Three

Phil came running out of the B&B, followed closely by Mrs. MacDonald and her sister.

Mia and Diana got out of the car.

"Are you guys all right?" "Where's Rina?" "What happened?" The questions flew at them.

Mia raised her hand. "Let's grab a seat, and I promise we'll answer all your questions."

Mrs. MacDonald led them to the breakfast room. "Let me get you some food and drink. Please don't start until I get back."

"Oh, food would be lovely. Thank you," Diana said.

Mrs. MacDonald and her sister brought out trays laden with tea, coffee, and pastries. They poured two cups of tea for Mia and Diana. "First, drink this, then you can have whiskey."

Mia smiled. "Thanks."

"What happened?" Phil asked.

Between Mia and Diana, they told them. When they stopped for a moment, Phil whistled. "Wow, you guys are lucky to be alive. Will Rina be okay?"

Mia nodded. "There's a police officer on her door, and the surgery's being done tonight. I'll be in touch with the hospital later this evening, and I'll see her around noon tomorrow. A broken ankle means she'll be laid up for some time."

Diana swallowed her tea. "Tell them about Mr. Gordon."

Mia sighed. "I have some bad news."

When she was done, Phil's eyes narrowed. "I guess I'm not surprised he's shutting it down. When do we have to leave?"

"He wants everything shut down by the end of the week."

"That's not a lot of time." Phil pushed back his chair. "What are we supposed to do with the artifacts we have here?"

"We'll work with Angus and donate them to the local historical society. Which is what was going to happen at the end of the summer." Mia looked at the students. "I know this isn't what you wanted, but it's out of my hands. Mr. Gordon's pulling back the funding, and since this is a privately sponsored dig, there's nothing we can do."

"It's not your fault. I understand." Phil walked to the window. "What's happening about Dr. Carter's death? Are the police still looking into it?"

"They are." Mia gave them the information she'd learned from Anderson.

Mia's phone rang. She glanced at it and saw Dr. Bateman's number. "I need to take this call. Excuse me." She walked to the lobby.

"Mia, I heard from Charles. Are you going to close the dig on your own?"

"Yes, I've closed digs before. I just wasn't planning on doing it quite so early."

"If you need help, let me know. I'm here for the next two days."

"Sure. I'll know more after tomorrow morning. I'll let you know if I need help."

When she walked in Phil and Diana were looking at her expectantly. "That was Dr. Bateman, advising me he's available to help if we need him. I told him I'd let him know."

"Are you going to have him help?" Phil asked.

Mia shook her head. "We can do what needs to be done ourselves. I'm counting on Angus to help us."

"Is anyone else hungry for a meal?" Luke asked.

A resounding chorus of "Yes" provided an answer.

"I need to shower and change clothes. Can we meet in about thirty minutes?" Mia asked.

"I need to clean up too. I'll feel better after that and clean clothes," Diana said.

"Sounds good. Is going to the pub all right with you?" Phil asked.

They all agreed, and Mia hurried upstairs. When she reached her room, she was surprised to find Luke at her heels.

"I'd like a minute before you have your shower."

"Come in then." Mia unlocked her door and stepped into her room.

Luke closed the door behind him. "Mia, I just want to say how glad I am you're safe. And to explain what I meant before you left for the exchange."

Mia sat in the chair, and Luke leaned against her desk.

"I'm not very good at this. Seeing you again has brought a lot of feelings that I thought I'd left behind. You were the best part of my grad school years. When we were together, I felt alive. When I had to make the choice to be with Jacklyn, I tried contacting you. But I couldn't get through or find you."

Mia frowned. "When was this?"

"Late 2013. Your email accounts didn't work, your phone number had been disconnected. And I'm ashamed to say, I didn't reach out to your Gran or your parents."

"We'd talked about spending the rest of our lives together. When I found out you and Jacklyn were married, it felt like someone had pulled my heart out of my chest."

Luke hung his head. "How did you know Jacklyn and I were married?"

"She sent me an email after I left the university. There was an attachment, and it was the engagement announcement. The email came from your personal email. And when I saw it, I thought you sent it. Alex is the one who read it through and realized it was from Jacklyn. I didn't want to hear from you or her again. I blocked you on my email accounts and I wasn't in Canada in late 2013. I was working in remote South America for over six months. Even my parents had difficulty reaching me."

"Now that I've connected with you, I'm determined to get to know you again. When you left this morning, I was afraid I wouldn't see you again. And I didn't like it."

Mia rubbed her forehead. "I don't know what to say. I'm not sure how we'd make a relationship work. You're based here in Great Britain and I'm in Canada. And I don't have any idea what I'm going to be doing in the next six months."

"I understand. But I'd like us to figure out if we can make it work again."

"I haven't been in a relationship for a while. I'll need some time to think this through." Mia glanced at her watch. "I'm tired and I need to clean up before we eat. I don't want to keep Phil and Diana waiting. Can we talk about this later?"

"Right. I'll wait for you downstairs. I wanted to make sure I let you know how I felt before anything else happened."

"Well, you've given me a lot to think about." Mia smiled. "I'll see you shortly."

Luke left, and Mia blew out a deep breath. "So, not what I was expecting today." It was too early to talk to Alex or Gran. She hurried through her shower and dressed carefully.

Luke and the students were waiting for her. Phil had the keys to the van, "I'll drive. I don't think you and Diana should walk anymore today."

"Thanks, Phil."

At the pub, cheers greeted Diana and Mia. Devon MacLeod, the pub's owner, came to their table and plopped a pitcher of beer in front of them. "On the house. And so's your dinner. We're so glad you're safe."

"Thank you, much appreciated," Mia said.

"How is Miss Rina?" he asked.

"A broken ankle, but she'll be out of the hospital soon," Diana said.

The waitress arrived and took their orders. The talk around the table centered on what was going to happen next.

"There's a position with a CRM in my home state. It starts next month. Nothing as exciting as what we had here, but it's experience in an area I haven't much time in." Phil put down his beer.

"I have a job in Sault Ste. Marie with the city. My grandparents live there. I'll be helping them organize artifacts for their museum," Diana said.

"What are you doing, Mia?" Phil asked.

Mia shook her head. "I haven't decided yet. I'll be spending time with Shelly and Henry, then returning home to Lakeview. My position with the school isn't firm yet, so I'll probably look for work somewhere else."

"Would you work for our school?" Phil asked.

"Maybe. I enjoy spending time with students, but I'm not comfortable working with departments and politics." Mia glanced at Luke. "Or I might take some time off and travel a while."

Their meals came, and everyone focused on their food. As soon as their meal was done, Phil said, "Why don't we head back to the B&B? You guys must be tired."

At the B&B, Mia waited to speak with Luke. "I want you to know I'm going to think about what we discussed. But I need some rest. I'm going to see Rina at the hospital tomorrow. Could we meet for dinner after?"

"Yes, I'd like that."

"Are you still going with Anderson to the cave tonight?"

"I am."

"Will you let me know what you find? I'm almost positive I saw those artifacts reported as stolen in one of the bulletins I read a few months ago."

"Of course."

"Please be careful. We know those two men weren't working alone."

"We will."

"All right then, will I see you in the morning?"

"Of course."

Mia went up to her room. She was exhausted, both physically and mentally. She took off her shoes and sweater and leaned back on the bed. "I'll close my eyes for a minute."

* * *

Mia woke up the next morning sprawled across her bed, fully dressed. She smiled, "Wow. I must have been tired." She looked out the window and saw the sunshine. As she reached for her phone, she realized it was past six. She called the hospital in Portree, asking for an update on Rina. The nurse told her she'd had surgery, and the surgeon was happy with the outcome. Rina was still in the recovery room and would be moved to her room later in the morning. Mia hung up, relieved at the good news.

After a hot shower, she ran through her day while she dressed. Artifacts would need to be transferred to the historical society. Angus could help with that. And she needed to see Rina at the hospital. At the end of her day, dinner with Luke. She still didn't know what she was going to tell him. Mia shrugged. "I don't have to decide right now."

She packed her daypack with the items she'd need for the day and headed downstairs.

Phil was finishing up breakfast.

"Good morning. Is Diana up yet?"

Phil pushed his plate away. "She's outside talking with Rina. Rina called to let us know the surgery went well."

"Good. I spoke with the nurse and plan on going to see her around noon."

Mia put together her breakfast from the options on the sideboard and poured herself a large cup of coffee.

Diana returned to the table. "How's Rina?" Mia asked.

"She's dopey from the pain medication. But glad the surgery happened. Her parents are on their way."

"Did she say when she'd be able to leave the hospital?" Phil asked.

"Maybe tomorrow." Diana took a drink of juice. "Isn't that awfully soon after surgery?"

Mia raised an eyebrow. "It depends on a few factors. Hospitals don't keep patients in too long anymore. I'm glad her parents are coming. We'll need to pack her things for them. I'm sure they're going to want to get back home as soon as possible."

They finished their meal quickly.

"Phil, can you take the van to the dig? I'm going to take my car and then leave before noon to see Rina."

Phil nodded. "Do you want us to stay at the site and keep working?"

"Yes, please. I'd like to get as much done as we can. Have you been able to change your flights out?"

"I got a flight out of Inverness on Saturday. I'll need to leave no later than Friday evening."

"Diana, what about you?"

"I've got a flight out from Inverness, but not until Sunday. I'll go up with

Phil. Have you heard if DI Anderson found the artifacts in the cave?"

Mia shook her head. "Not yet. I'll send Luke a message to see if there's anything to report."

They put their dishes away and left for the dig.

Before leaving, Mia sent Luke a message.

M: Did you find the artifacts?

L: Yes. And you were right. They were from the reports you read. Did you sleep well?

M: I did. Where are you?

L: Debriefing w Anderson at the police station. Will talk to you soon.

"Well, that's good news to let the students know." She thought to herself.

Mia walked to the head security guard. "Good morning. Have you heard from Mr. Gordon?"

"Aye, ma'am. He's let us know you'll be closing the dig. Do you know exactly when you'll be done?"

"Mr. Gordon told me he wanted everything done by the end of the week. The students are leaving on Friday, so it will be done before then."

"Will that be enough time?"

"Yes. I'll be working with the historical society, and covering up the grid won't take us too long."

Mia walked into the tent and told the students about the artifacts Anderson and Luke had found.

"That's one good thing about these last few days!" Diana smiled.

"Do you think we'll be able to see the artifacts?" Phil asked.

"I don't see why not. I'll send a message to Luke asking about us seeing the artifacts."

M: Students would like to see artifacts. Can they?

L: Yes. Was going to suggest tomorrow afternoon?

M: Perfect.

"Tomorrow afternoon to see the artifacts. Luke will let us know where."

"Awesome." Phil grinned.

"Right, let's get to work." Mia delegated the chores. Angus arrived at the site, and Mia filled him in on the changes. Angus worked closely with her to make the transition of artifacts from dig to museum as smooth as possible. The morning passed quickly.

Mia called for a stop just around eleven. "I'm going to head to the hospital to check in on Rina. I don't know how long I'll be gone for. Thanks for the hard work this morning. If you can do another couple of hours this afternoon, we'll be ahead of schedule, and our side trip tomorrow afternoon won't put us behind."

Phil nodded. "Sounds like a plan. Please say hi to Rina."

"I will. I'll talk to you later today."

Mia called Rina from the parking lot. Rina sounded alert and was looking forward to Mia's visit.

She stopped for a bite to eat at a cafe just outside the hospital. She was getting ready to leave her table when she overheard a voice that sounded vaguely familiar. Mia slowly glanced around. Sitting at a table along the side of the cafe was the man who had grabbed her at the parking lot. Mia drew a deep breath. She had to get a hold of Anderson and let him know where they were.

Mia casually took her phone and snapped a photo of the two men. Then she sent it to Anderson with the message,

M: These are the two men who took me and the students. At the Three Cups Cafe in Portree, just outside the hospital.

A minute later, Anderson replied.

Alerted police in Portree. Have they seen you?

M: No.

A: Get out now.

Mia didn't like the thought of leaving the cafe without knowing what they were planning. But she also didn't want to get caught. There was a menu on the table next to her, and she grabbed it and held it in front of her face. They wouldn't notice her if she stayed hidden.

Mia watched them for a few minutes worrying the police wouldn't show up in time.

One of them got a call on his cell, and Mia watched as he looked around the cafe. She ducked her head behind the menu and held her breath.

The two men got up and left the cafe quickly. Police arrived a few minutes later. Mia was upset they hadn't been faster, and she sent a message to Anderson.

M: They left before the police got here. One of them got a phone call.

A: The police have their photo. They'll find them.

Mia hurried to the hospital and made her way to Rina's room. She was finishing lunch, and her ankle was in a cast.

Mia and Rina chatted about what was happening with the dig. The surgeon came in to talk to them just as an older couple arrived.

Rina introduced her parents, and the surgeon gave them an update on Rina's condition. The surgeon indicated she'd provide all the records to Rina's physician and would give them copies to take with them when they left the hospital.

Mia told Rina everyone was leaving on Friday, and they would come by to see her before they left.

Rina's parents were happy to meet Mia, and she was able to provide some information to them on what had happened.

"What about the treasure we saw in the other cave?" Rina asked.

"DI Anderson, Luke, and a team of officers went in last night at low tide to recover the artifacts. I'm going to check them out tomorrow afternoon. I'm not sure if they got all of them or not." Mia noticed Rina's eyes closing.

"I'm going to head back to the site. I'm relieved the surgery went well. I'll come back and check on you before you leave." Mia stood.

Rina's mom reached out to Mia. "Thank you for being here with Rina. Is there anything we can do to help?"

"We have it all in hand. The site's being closed. And I'm uncertain what's going to happen with it next year. I'm available to discuss any questions or concerns Rina has about the dig any time in the future. And I'll provide her with references as well. I'm glad you were both able to come here."

"No problem. We'll see that she gets home as soon as we can move her."

Mia dug in her pocket and pulled out a business card. "Here's my contact information. Please let me know if you need anything. Diana and I will pack Rina's things, and we'll have them ready for you."

Mia left the hospital and drove back to the dig. She arrived just as Angus and the students were getting ready to leave.

She provided them with an update on Rina's surgery and that her parents had arrived.

"Rina must be glad to see them?" Phil asked.

"Yes, she was. I told them we'd pack her things and have them ready for them to pick up. Diana, would you mind helping me with that?"

"Not a problem. I'll throw her clothes in the wash tonight, and then we can pack them."

"I'm going to look at the dig before joining you back at the B&B."

"We've got the artifacts organized. They're all logged in the site laptop," Phil said.

"You did a lot of work. I'll check the ledger against the laptop. I'll bring both back with me tonight."

They left, and Mia strolled to the tent. She found boxes that needed to be put together off the right-hand side of the tent. They'd deal with that tomorrow morning. The boxes looked sturdy enough to carry the artifacts. They'd still need packing material to protect the artifacts when they were being transported. Angus might know where to get the material. The ledger was sitting on the table next to the laptop.

She quickly flipped the pages, checking them and noted they had followed procedure. All artifacts had numbers, descriptions, and the initials of the person who discovered them and the person who logged them in the ledger. There was a column to indicate which box the artifact had been placed in for transportation or storage. That column would be completed in the next few days.

"Mia. There you are. I wasn't sure anyone was still here."

Mia turned around and saw Dr. Bateman standing in the tent entrance. A man and a woman were with him.

"Dr. Bateman. What can I do for you? Were we supposed to meet?"

He walked toward the table where the laptop and ledger were. "I wanted to stop by and see if you needed any help. But it appears you have it all in hand."

The couple stopped a few feet behind Dr. Bateman.

"Everything's under control. I was in Portree earlier checking on a student." Mia nodded at the couple. "I'm Dr. Mia Reid. And you are?"

"Malcolm Reeves and my wife Freya."

"Malcolm is a friend of mine from Lakeview City. We ran into each other at the pub the other day. It's a small world. I didn't realize they were in Scotland."

"Are you archaeologists?"

"No, I'm in the security business. And Freya is my right-hand person in my business."

"Do you work for Mr. Gordon?" Mia closed the ledger and tucked it in her daypack.

"We've done some work for him in the past. I was curious what the set up was here. I've mostly worked on jobs in the city for him."

Mia noticed Freya was looking at the artifacts that were in boxes.

"We'll be taking those to the historical society tomorrow. Mr. Gordon is shutting down the dig early. Are you interested in artifacts?"

Freya's eyes met Mia's. Mia felt a shiver go down her spine and wished Luke was close. Freya didn't give off warm, friendly vibes.

"I've a passing interest in antiquities. I always think they're so overvalued. I mean really, a lot of this is just rubble. Broken pots and weapons. I can't believe people spend as much money as they do on them."

"Well, those bits of rubble show how people lived in history. And it has merit. As for how much people spend on them, most people who purchase artifacts do so to own a piece of history. And to them, it can be priceless."

"Mia, have you heard about the find the police made?" Dr. Bateman asked.

Mia raised an eyebrow. "You mean the discovery in one of the nearby caves? It's all over the village. I managed to rescue two students who had been kidnapped from the cave. Before we left, I discovered a chamber filled with stolen artifacts. I reported it to the police, and they recovered them. The students and I are going to the police station tomorrow to view them.

According to Luke Forbes, the artifacts were stolen from different museums and collections in Europe."

Dr. Bateman glanced around the tent. "None of them are here, are they?"

"No. They're at the police station."

"Are the ring and the sgian-dubh part of that find? Or the gemstones and gold coins?"

"Not to my knowledge. The kidnappers have those, but I've been told the police are looking for them, and they hope to apprehend them soon. How did you hear about that?"

"It's all over the news. And Charles contacted me about it. He wanted me to verify with the police if his artifacts were part of the collection."

"Have you seen them?"

"Despite my credentials, the police won't allow me to look at them. I've heard a cartel is involved with it."

Mia frowned. How did Dr. Bateman know about a cartel? She was sure DI Anderson hadn't said anything about it.

"Where did you hear about a cartel?"

Dr. Bateman glanced at Malcolm and Freya. He shrugged. "I assume a cartel is involved. There's been rumblings in Lakeview City about underground auctions involving antiquities." He paused and then looked directly at Mia. "I'm sure you've heard about them. There's even a rumor someone at the university has been involved."

"With the auctions? How?"

Freya moved closer to the table.

Mia's feet shifted. Her stomach tightened, and the hair on the back of her neck prickled.

MacAllister pushed through the tent opening. "Ah, Dr. Reid. I wanted to let you know we'll be here for the next two days. Will that be sufficient time for you to close up?"

Mia drew a breath. "Yes, that works well. I need to head out. Dr. Bateman and his companions were just leaving." She looked at Dr. Bateman. "Unless there's something else?"

"No, that's fine. We'll be heading out. Thank you for your time."

Mia watched as they left. She rubbed her forehead. It felt sticky with sweat.

"Dr. Reid, are you all right?" MacAllister asked.

"Yes, thank you for coming in. I was ready to leave when they arrived, and I'm quite tired. Please make certain no one enters the tent until we return tomorrow."

"Will do."

Mia checked the filing cabinets, locked them, then picked up the laptop and left the tent. She stopped by the squares. They still needed to be cleaned up and closed off. There wasn't anything she could do to prevent other people from coming in and digging around. And she was certain someone would. The talk of the treasure was enough to guarantee that.

Looking at the squares, she felt her shoulders slump. Her eyes dampened. So much had happened here. Not just in the past, but right now. Ethan had lost his life. Someone had threatened them. And Diana and Rina had been kidnapped. Was digging up the past that important? Was it worth Ethan's life? Mia shook her head and felt tears prick in her eyes. She still didn't know who had killed Ethan, and she didn't want to leave without knowing who had done it and why.

The why she could figure out. Artifacts. She knew the killer couldn't have been the two men who kidnapped Diana and Rina. They weren't in the country when Ethan died. But could the killer have been working for the same people they'd been working for? Was it a smuggling cartel? Or was it a greedy collector?

She brushed at her eyes and straightened up. This wasn't solving anything. Time to go back and review what she knew. Mia sighed and turned away from the squares.

She drove to the B&B and hurried upstairs. She and Luke were supposed to meet for dinner, but she hadn't heard from him since earlier this morning. As if he'd read her mind, her phone pinged with a text.

L: Dinner at six-thirty?

M: Sounds good.

L: I'll pick you up at the B&B.

M: great.

She put the laptop and ledger on her desk, and grabbed a quick shower, and changed into clean clothes. She pulled her hair out of her braid and applied some light makeup.

That done, she called Gran to tell her in on what had happened in the last thirty-six hours.

As expected, Gran was upset by the recent events. Mia reassured her she was fine and would be back in Canada soon.

"Gran, have you heard anything more about the cartel that's rumored to be working out of Canada?"

"I met some friends from the Arts Council for lunch, and it came up."

"What did they say?"

"Margaret Appleby mentioned she had received an invitation to a special auction happening in three weeks. She mentioned that there would be artifacts never seen before, some of which date back to Bonnie Prince Charlie."

Mia gasped. "That could be the artifacts we had!"

"That's what I thought. I asked Margaret if she was going, and she said no, the entry fee was much too high. To secure a seat, anyone attending must pay ten thousand dollars, non-refundable. Margaret wasn't comfortable with those terms and turned it down."

"Did she give you a contact person?"

"No, and I couldn't figure out how to ask for one without raising suspicion. They're aware of my opinion on special auctions."

"I'm going to pass this information on to Luke. He may have contacts that he can work with."

They chatted for a few more minutes and then hung up. Mia was eager to talk to Luke about this latest news. Gran had provided Mia with Margaret's contact information.

Mia sent a text to Alex.

M: Can we talk later?

A: Yes. Heading for a meeting. How about six my time?

M: That works. Talk then.

Mia had another hour before she and Luke were to meet. Pulling out a notebook, she began listing the people involved with the dig and those who might be connected to Ethan's death. She didn't think she'd figure out who did it, but listing the people showed her who might have had an opportunity. She included the two men who'd been involved in the kidnapping and then scratched them out. If they were the same men who had run into her in Lakeview, they would have been in Canada when Ethan was killed. The obvious ones to Mia's mind were the man and woman who wanted to buy the artifacts. Could they be the couple with Dr. Bateman? She'd have to ask the students. Mia sighed and glanced at her watch.

She checked her appearance in the mirror and grabbed a sweater from the armoire.

Luke was waiting for her in the lobby.

"Hi. I hope I didn't keep you waiting."

"Not at all. I just got here. Are you ready to go?" Luke asked as he opened the door.

"Yes. How was your day?"

Luke chuckled. "Busy, and I know yours was too."

They settled in his car. "I've made reservations at the restaurant at the Castle. I hope that's okay with you?"

"Sure. Is that the restaurant Diana and Rina went to?"

"It is. I don't think we'll wind up like they did." Luke drove out towards the highway. "Anderson told me you'd seen the two men who kidnapped you and the students."

"I was having lunch in a cafe near the hospital, and they were sitting at a table. I don't think they noticed me. And they left before the police arrived. Someone might've tipped them off because they received a call a few minutes before the police showed up."

"Did you follow them?"

"No. Anderson told me the police would go after them. They had their description. Do you know if they were found?"

Luke pulled into the parking lot of the restaurant. He parked the car. "No. So, we need to be careful."

"What about the students?" Mia asked.

"The police are keeping them under observation, and Rina's police guard is still at her door. I assured Anderson I could take care of us and wouldn't need a police escort tonight." Luke smiled.

"Do you really think they're still around? If I were them, I'd get out of the country."

Luke got out of the car and walked around to Mia's door. Opening the door, he said, "Anderson has their description and names out everywhere, including train stations and airports. Through Interpol, we discovered their names and nationalities. They've been working in smuggling for some time now and are well known. We'll catch them this time."

They walked to the restaurant and were seated immediately.

When the waiter arrived with their wine and appetizers, he took their orders.

Luke raised his glass. "A toast, to us. Wherever this takes us, I'm very glad we reconnected."

Mia smiled. "I can drink to that."

The wine was excellent, and Mia told herself to relax. "I must admit, I was surprised you were here when I arrived. This entire week hasn't been what I expected." Mia took a drink of wine. "I told you I'd let you know where I stood about us tonight. But I don't have an answer except that I know I want you to be a part of my life."

Luke put his glass down and leaned across the table. "I don't know where I fit in with your life or where you fit in mine. But I'd like the opportunity to explore the possibilities."

"There are a lot of things happening right now that I don't have answers to. I'm not sure where I'm going to be working this fall. And while I have the financial means to take care of myself, I need to work; that's part of who I am."

"I understand that. When I left the museum for Interpol, I wasn't sure how it was going to work out. But it's been the best decision I made."

"And that's part of the problem. You're based here. I'm in North America. When would we see each other?" Mia frowned. She needed Luke to understand how she felt. "I'm interested in learning where the relationship can go, but not at the expense of my career."

The waiter arrived with their entrees. Mia sat back and waited until he'd left.

"Any suggestions? Because honestly, I'm not sure I can see a way forward that works for both of us." Mia placed her napkin on her lap and hid her shaking hands.

"Do you need to leave for Canada at the end of this assignment? Could you take some time off and spend it with me?"

"I could, although I want to spend time with Shelly and Henry. Can you get time away from work?"

"Yes. What if we went to Chicago to see Shelly and Henry together? I'd like to pay my respects to Ethan's family."

"I want to spend time with you, and that might be the perfect solution."

They chatted about what had been happening in their lives and their mutual friends in the archaeology world. Mia enjoyed the evening.

They indulged in dessert and coffee and then called it a night.

Luke drove them back to the B&B, and they went to the sitting room for a nightcap. Phil, and Diana were there.

"Hi. How was dinner?" Diana asked.

"Excellent. What are you guys up to?" Mia sat in one of the chairs.

Luke walked to the bar. "Mia, did you want a whiskey?"

"No, I'm good, thanks."

"We're just finalizing our plans for the rest of the summer. The CRM that I applied to responded that they have a position for me." Phil grinned.

"Oh, that's great. Good experience, for sure." Mia smiled. "Diana, when do you start?"

"I start in a couple of weeks. I'm going to drive up to Sault Ste. Marie earlier and spend some time with my grandparents." Diana looked up from her notebook. "I've been making notes of things I'd like to do in the Soo."

They sat chatting quietly for a while, and then Mia got up to leave. "I'm off to call a friend at home. We'll leave around eight tomorrow morning. We'll get most of the work finished up and then check out the treasure the police recovered."

"I'm going to start packing Rina's things. Laundry's all done," Diana said.

"Did you want some help?" Mia asked.

Diana shook her head. "There isn't too much to pack. Rina's a lot neater than I am."

Mia toed off her shoes when she got in her room and made herself comfortable. She had a lot to talk to Alex about tonight.

Mia spoke to Alex for almost twenty minutes, filling her in on what had happened.

"So, what's happening with the kidnappers?"

"The police are still looking for them, and they've set up watches at the airports, and train stations. I doubt they'll get away. There are too many people looking for them." Mia took a sip of the tea she'd made earlier. Her throat was dry.

"And you're okay? You weren't hurt?"

"Rattled, but I'm all right." Mia filled Alex in on what she'd decided as far as the relationship with Luke.

"That sounds like a good plan. There's an opportunity for the two of you to reconnect without the stress of the dig. What do you hope to get out of this?" Alex asked.

"Just to get to know each other again. There's still a lot to work out if we decide to go ahead with a relationship. We're still going to be on two continents."

Chapter Twenty-Four

Mia pulled into the parking lot at the dig. "I'm going to check with security, just to make sure everything's all right. Angus is bringing the historical society's van, and we can use that and ours to transport the artifacts later this morning. I'd like us to pack up as much as we can before we transport them. I don't want to lose any of the artifacts."

"I'll make up the boxes," Diana said.

"I'll ensure that the artifacts are organized chronologically by the date they were found and then packed," Phil assured.

"Excellent. I'll give Diana a hand putting boxes together, and if you need help, let me know."

They hustled out of the van and made their way to the tent. Mia peeled off to speak with the security guard. "Any issues last night?"

"A few people stopped by to look at the dig after hearing about the antiquities found in the cave, curious if any artifacts from this dig were included.

"It's probably a good thing we're wrapping up early. We'd have to spend too much time talking to people. We'll be here most of the morning and then back tomorrow to close things up."

Mia dropped her daypack on the table and marched over to help Diana put the boxes together. They had a good system going and soon had a stack of thirty boxes ready for packing.

Angus arrived whistling as he came in. "Morning, how are you all today?"

Diana grinned. "Great! We're going to see the antiquities Dr. Reid found this afternoon."

"Angus, you're welcome to join us. You've been part of this dig since the start," Mia said.

"I'd enjoy that. Are they at the police station?"

"Yes. Anderson will let us know when we can go."

"Well then, let's get these artifacts packed up, and we'll take them to the museum. I have the museum keys."

The four of them worked quickly and effectively and were at the museum before noon. They unloaded the boxes of artifacts and brought them into the museum's storeroom.

"Dr. Reid, would you have time to lend me a hand in setting these up sometime this week?" Angus asked.

"Yes. I'd enjoy the opportunity to help you set them up."

Mia received a text.

A: You and the students can come to the station at 2 to see the artifacts.

M: Excellent.

"Okay, we're set for two this afternoon at the police station to see the artifacts they found in the cave."

They drove to the station, and someone directed them to the larger conference room. Luke met them at the door. "Come in and see what we recovered. We haven't been able to identify them all, but we've made some headway. Most of the artifacts are from Great Britain and France."

The artifacts were spread across four long and narrow tables. Each table was covered with specific artifacts. One table had weapons such as knives, swords, shields, bows, and arrows. The second had gold artifacts, including jewelry, goblets, bowls, and crosses. The third table held coins and jewelry with stones in them. And the last table held tablets with Celtic markings and language on them, and books.

Mia was happy with the recovery they'd made. She recognized some of the artifacts from the shelves in the cave. The artifacts were priceless and there was no doubt in Mia's mind that they'd made a significant recovery.

The students and Angus closely examined the artifacts and peppered Luke with questions that he was pleased to answer.

As they were leaving, Luke pulled Mia aside. "I'm going to be here into the evening. I'm waiting for a colleague to come in and help me with the artifacts. We'll be transporting them back to London and determining their origins. I won't be able to meet you for dinner."

"Don't worry. You have a lot of work to get done here. I'll have dinner with the students and make an early night of it. Will I see you in the morning?"

"Yes, I'm not driving to London. My colleague will return tomorrow. Breakfast at seven?"

"Sounds good. We'll talk then."

"Did you want to meet for dinner at the pub?" Mia asked Diana and Phil.

"Sure. I need to finish up some laundry before I go. Phil, can you wait for us?"

"Not a problem. Does six-thirty work for you both?"

"I should be done my calls by then. Let's meet in the sitting room."

Phil and Diana agreed, and everyone dispersed.

Mia checked her messages and noticed a text from Lottie Myers, Dr. Bateman's administrative assistant.

L: Could you call me please?

Mia frowned. Why did Lottie want to talk to her? The text had come through while they were at the police station. Glancing at her watch, Mia figured out the time difference and called Lottie.

"Dr. Bateman's office. Lottie Myers here."

"Lottie, it's Mia Reid. I just received your message. What can I do for you?"

"Dr. Reid, thanks for calling me. I'm trying to reach Dr. Bateman, but he seems to have his phone off. Have you seen him today?"

"No, I haven't. But that's not unusual. He hasn't been at the dig every day. Is there a problem?"

Lottie sighed. "I don't know. The police have been here asking questions."

"About Dr. Bateman?"

"Yes, and how often he's been away and where he's been. I don't like this. There's been some discrepancy in his expenses with the university, and now the police are here."

Mia sat in the wing chair. "Why are they asking about his travel?"

"There's an investigation with the university on mismanagement of travel expenses. Dr. Bateman has been away frequently this year, and he's traveled to Europe, Asia, and Central America at least once or twice a month. Some of the travel was approved by the university, but not all of it. And the travel that wasn't approved is what's in question."

"Do you know when and where he was on his travel?"

"Yes. I booked it all. Why are you asking?"

"It might help me here. We've just discovered a rather large cache of stolen antiquities. I'm wondering if Dr. Bateman knew anything about them."

"I know he's flown to London several times, and he was in France a few months ago. I can send you the dates he's traveled in the last year. Wait, do you think he had something to do with stolen antiquities?" Lottie's voice rose.

"No, of course not. I'm just wondering if he might have heard about any thefts when he was in the region. Was he traveling for university business while he was here?"

"That's the problem. No one at the university approved those trips, but he charged them to his travel budget."

"Do you know who he met while on his trips?"

"I might be able to find information in his calendar. Is that important?"

"It could be. Do you mind looking and sending me any information you find?" Mia knew this was a big ask. Lottie was loyal to Dr. Bateman, to a fault. "I might be able to shed light on his travels and that could help with the explanations to the university and police."

"In that case, yes. I have it ready. I'll send it to you straight away." Lottie hung up a few minutes later having confirmed Mia's email address.

Mia hurried through her shower and got dressed quickly. She opened her email program and there was the email from Lottie with Dr. Bateman's travel.

While quickly reviewing the information, she discovered that Dr. Bateman had been present at several locations where thefts of valuable historical items had been reported. Did that mean he was involved with the thefts? Or was it simply a coincidence? Diving into a more careful examination, she discovered that thefts had occurred at every location he had visited. Checking the dates confirmed that information. Mia sat back, chewing on her bottom lip. She had to be careful. His behavior while he'd been in Scotland had made her suspicious. He hadn't shown up at the site when he'd said he would. And his claim of jet lag didn't sit well with her. So where did he go? And then finding the stolen artifacts in the cave where Diana and Rina had been held. Mia tapped her chin. Had anyone else traveled with him? How could she find that out?

Maybe Luke could help with that. He had access to databases she didn't. She knew he was tied up for the evening, but she could always send him a message.

M: Could you check if Dr. Bateman traveled with anyone on the following dates from last year? 08/15 09/25 10/14 11/20 12/05 01/28 02/15 03/12 04/28

L: Why?

M: He's traveled to locations where antiquities have disappeared. Wondering if he has anything to do with it. Plus he was here when we discovered the cache.

L: Will check but might not get an answer tonight.

M: He told me he's leaving tomorrow.

L: Right, will do my best.

M: Tks

At dinner, Mia and the students chatted about the artifacts they'd seen and how large a cache it had been.

"I wonder where they all came from?" Diana asked.

Mia shook her head. "I don't know. Luke mentioned that he and his colleague will examine the artifacts and compare them to reports of stolen artifacts. But there's a possibility that not all of them were reported missing."

Mia noticed Dr. Bateman walk into the pub with Freya Reeves. They sat at a table across the room. "There's Dr. Bateman. He told me he's leaving tomorrow morning. I suppose I should speak to him before he leaves."

Phil shifted his attention to Dr. Bateman and did a double take. "Whoa. That looks like the woman who was talking to Dr. Carter about buying artifacts."

"Are you sure?" Mia asked.

"Yes. The hair's different, but that's her for sure."

Mia sent a text to Anderson.

M: Woman who wanted to buy artifacts from Ethan at the pub with Bateman.

A: Will send two officers to pick her up.

M: Thanks.

"Is DI Anderson coming?" Diana asked.

"He's sending two officers. I want to keep an eye on her. Are you guys all right if we wait here?"

"Sure. We're not in a rush to get to the B&B," Phil said. Diana nodded in agreement.

The waitress arrived to take their plates away.

"May I have a cappuccino, please?" Mia asked

"Anyone else?" the waitress asked.

Diana and Phil requested cappuccinos as well.

Phil glanced at Dr. Bateman's table. "It looks like they're going to have a meal. Is it going to be obvious we're just hanging around?"

Mia shook her head. "We've ordered a coffee, so it's not a big deal. I'd prefer that we didn't make it obvious we're watching their table."

They enjoyed their cappuccinos and chatted quietly among themselves. Mia monitored the door and checked her watch.

Freya got up from their table and walked toward the back of the pub.

"I'm going to go talk to Dr. Bateman. I want to make sure he stays here and isn't going to leave while she's in the ladies' room." Mia pushed her chair away and strode to Dr. Bateman's table.

"I didn't think I'd have an opportunity to speak with you before you left." Mia pulled a chair out and sat next to Dr. Bateman.

"Mia, this is a surprise. How are things wrapping up?" Dr. Bateman glanced around the pub.

"We're almost done. Artifacts are packed, and we've taken some to the museum. The remainder will go tomorrow. Did you have an opportunity to see the recovered cache of antiquities?"

Dr. Bateman shook his head. "I'm afraid not. I've been extremely busy with a project, and unfortunately, it looks like I'll have to return to Canada tomorrow. So, I won't be able to see them. From what I've heard on the news, it's quite a recovery."

"The students and I were able to see them. It was an amazing find. Interpol is actively working to return the stolen items to their rightful owners." Mia wondered how far she could push things with him. "Do you know anything about them?"

Dr. Bateman's eyebrows rose, and he stroked his beard. "What do you mean?"

"I was speaking with Lottie Myers this afternoon. It appears the university and the police are investigating some of your travel in the last year. I've checked on the dates in question and where you were. Artifacts were stolen from museums and archaeological digs in every location you went to."

"I told you she was going to be a problem." Freya's voice came from behind Mia.

Mia felt something poke her in the side. She glanced down. Freya had a gun stuck in her side.

"Time for us to leave. Mia, you'll be coming with us. Don't make a sound or Freya will shoot you. And those two students you've been working with? Well, there are two men here watching them as well. And they won't hesitate to get rid of them. Now, quietly, get up and come with us." Dr. Bateman threw some bills on the table to cover their meal. Freya grabbed Mia by the arm, and they left the pub.

Mia glanced back and saw Phil and Diana looking at her in puzzlement. She shook her head and hoped they understood not to follow her.

Chapter Twenty-Five

Outside, Dr. Bateman unlocked a car, and Freya pushed her in the back seat and sat next to her. Dr. Bateman started the car and drove slowly out of the village.

"Where are you taking me?"

Dr. Bateman looked at her through the rear-view mirror. "We're going to the cottage, and we'll chat about what you know and what we're going to do with you."

Freya had the gun trained on Mia. "I won't hesitate to use this. So don't try anything."

The cottage was close by, and Mia barely had time to think through her options before they pulled into the driveway.

Dr. Bateman stopped the car. "Let's get her inside with minimal fuss. Mia, you'd do well to remember Freya has a gun."

As they got out of the car, Mia had her phone in her hand. She stumbled and managed to press Luke's phone number. She hoped he'd hear the call and find her in time. She tucked the phone in her pocket.

Freya grabbed Mia by the arm. "Come on, move it." And pushed Mia toward the door of the cottage.

Inside, Mia's eyes adjusted to the lights. The cottage had a foyer and then opened to a living area and kitchen. On the kitchen island were three large duffel bags.

Dr. Bateman dragged a chair from the kitchen and pointed Mia to it. "Sit, now."

He took a tea towel from the kitchen and tied her hands behind her back.

"Now, Mia, you're going to tell us everything you know about the recovered artifacts. Including when they're being transported back to London and who's transporting them."

"I don't know. Honestly, I don't."

"Don't lie. I know you and that Interpol agent have gotten chummy. I'm sure he's told you everything about it. Maybe you need some convincing?" Dr. Bateman reached across the island and Mia saw he had a syringe in his hands.

Her eyes widened. "What are you doing?"

"A little help with your memory, perhaps? I don't want to resort to drugs, but we will if we must."

Mia bit her lip. "What did you do to Ethan?"

Freya laughed. "He wouldn't work with us. We offered him money for the sgian-dubh and the ring. He kept saying they weren't for sale. Malcolm drugged a glass of whiskey and gave it to him when everyone was celebrating at the pub. Then, we followed him to the dig. We'd already tossed the tent. When he saw that, he went out to the squares to see what else had been damaged. Malcolm went up to him and asked some questions. He would only say Professor Jones had them. He pushed against Malcolm, and I hit him with my walking stick. He dropped to the ground." Freya shrugged. "He wasn't any use to us anymore."

Mia's eyes filled with tears. Ethan hadn't deserved that. And she wasn't going to let them do anything to her. She glanced at Dr. Bateman.

"All right. What do you want to know?"

"Who knows that we're involved with the antiquities?" Bateman put the syringe down.

Mia shrugged. "I'm not sure. I can tell you the university and the police are looking into your travel. That wasn't such a smart thing to do. Traveling without it being authorized. You had to realize that would catch up to you."

"Water under the bridge. Who else knows? Did you talk to Dr. Forbes or the police about me?"

"The police don't know anything about you unless they've been contacted by the police in Canada. And I don't know why they would."

"What about the students?" Freya asked.

Mia shook her head. "They don't know anything about who's involved with the smuggling. And Luke doesn't know, either. I haven't talked to him about it."

"I don't believe you." Dr. Bateman glanced at his watch. "I need to get things ready. The other two will be here soon to get to the boat."

Mia heard a car pull in the driveway.

"That should be them now," Dr. Bateman said.

He hurried to the front door and let two men in. Freya followed him. Mia wasn't surprised to see the two men who'd run into her at the university walk into the cottage. Could this get any worse?

Dr. Bateman led the men toward the kitchen. One of the men was speaking with Dr. Bateman. "Yeah. I rented a small motorboat. We'll meet the ship at midnight. But we need to leave in a few minutes."

"The artifacts are packed in the bags. They're ready to go." Dr. Bateman pointed to the duffel bags.

"Too bad we can't take the ones the police confiscated, but these will make people take notice." The man speaking stretched his back.

"What do you want me to do with this one and the students?" Freya asked.

Dr. Bateman sighed. "Dr. Reid will meet up with an accident while she was out walking. I'll need you to arrange that. I don't need the particulars. With the students, we'll stick with the original plan. You'll need to wire the dig with enough explosives to take down the rest of the broch once the students show up for work tomorrow."

Freya nodded. "Shouldn't be difficult. I have access to dynamite, and I can set it up later tonight after I take care of this one. The security at the dig isn't the greatest. I'll set up the charges in the tent and where they're digging. They'll explode thirty seconds after someone walks into the area."

Mia's body shook. They were talking about killing her and the students as if they were nothing. She looked around carefully. Dr. Bateman and Freya accompanied the two men to their car. Freya carrying one of the duffel bags. Mia pulled her arms and twisted. The tea towel loosened. Keeping her eyes on the front door, Mia pulled again and felt the tea towel drop. Her arms freed, she stood up quietly and headed toward the back of the cottage. There had to be another way out.

She pulled her phone out of her pocket and saw that her call had gone through. So where was Luke and the police? Mia saw French doors off the dining area and hurried toward them. She opened them and hurried around the side of the cottage.

She heard the slam of the trunk of a car and then two car doors closing. Peering around the corner of the cottage, Mia saw the two kidnappers get in their car, and she snapped a photo of the license plate. She forwarded the photo to Luke and Anderson with an explanation of who was driving and where they were. Then she took a photo of the second vehicle and its license plate and sent that as well, telling them that Bateman or the woman would be driving this one soon. That done, she gazed around her. The cottage wasn't too far away from the village, and she should be able to get back to the pub quickly.

A twig cracked, and Mia jumped at the sound.

Freya was holding a gun on her and called out. "Found her. I'll bring her in." She waved the gun at Mia. "Hands up and walk to the front door. We're going to have a chat."

Mia raised her hands and walked to the front door. She had to believe she was going to get away.

Dr. Bateman was waiting for them. "Ah, Mia. There you are."

Freya pushed Mia ahead, and Mia stumbled into the living room. "Right here's good." Freya pointed to a kitchen chair with her gun. "Sit down."

Dr. Bateman followed them in and picked up the syringe. "Freya, can you handle things here?"

"With pleasure. I'll take care of her and set things up at the site. I'll meet you in Lakeview."

"Excellent. Mia, I'd like to say it's been a pleasure, but, unfortunately, it hasn't been."

Mia felt a prick in her neck. "Ow! What was that?"

Dr. Bateman tossed the needle on the kitchen counter and grabbed his bags. "Just a little cooperating juice. Freya can get overzealous. Have a good chat, ladies."

"I'll be in Lakeview tomorrow evening," Freya called out to Dr. Bateman.

Mia waited until Freya turned to face her again. She wasn't going down without a fight. Freya leaned over Mia and grabbed her by the chin. "You and I are going to have a talk."

Raising her arms, Mia broke free from Freya's hold on her chin and stood up. She head- butted Freya in the stomach, and Freya fell backwards. Freya stood up quickly and went on the attack. Mia took a step back and felt woozy. Whatever Bateman had stuck her with was starting to have an effect. She needed to get away.

Freya tried to grab Mia. Mia bent forward and down, grabbing Freya behind the knees, and lifted. She flipped Freya backwards. Freya's head hit the edge of the coffee table; she groaned and lay still.

Mia leaned on the couch and drew a deep breath. She noticed Freya was still breathing but not moving.

The crunch of gravel in the driveway told her someone had arrived. She stumbled to the door. Opening the door, she fell into Luke as he and Anderson pushed in.

"Mia, are you all right?" Luke caught her as she fell.

Anderson ran ahead and called out, "Police. Don't move."

"Did you get Bateman? He was on his way out." Mia's voice was slurred.

"We did. What's wrong with you?" Luke leaned Mia against the wall and checked her pulse.

Mia's eyes struggled to focus. "Bateman injected me with something." Mia drew a breath. "It's on the kitchen counter."

Luke called for the paramedics. "I'll be right back."

Mia's head rolled to the side as she watched him hurry to the kitchen. He picked up the ampule and spoke to the paramedics. Mia glanced toward the living room and realized Anderson had handcuffed Freya. She sighed and closed her eyes.

Chapter Twenty- Six

Mia felt a sharp pain in her left hand. She woke up and noticed an IV line in her hand and a paramedic sitting next to her.

"How's your head?" the paramedic asked.

"Hurts. But not as bad as my hand." Mia squinted at the paramedic's name tag. "Smith, where am I?"

"In the back of our ambulance. We've been checking your vitals and everything seems to be fine. You were injected with benzodiazepine. That caused you to get sleepy and dizzy. We're going to monitor you to ensure there aren't any adverse effects."

Luke popped his head in the ambulance. "How's she doing?"

"She's awake. Her vitals are good. We'll keep her on the IV for a little longer and check in with the hospital about follow-up."

"Mia, are you up to talking to Anderson?"

"Yes." Mia moved up the stretcher.

"Just stay there. I'll go get him." Luke hurried off.

Anderson climbed into the back of the ambulance. "Just a couple of questions. Do you know where they got the artifacts from?"

Mia shook her head. "No. They talked about getting them on a boat. Did you find the two men?"

"Thanks to your quick thinking, we tracked them down using the license plate. We caught them before they reached the water. Now, can you tell us what else you learned?"

Mia recounted what Bateman, and the woman, Freya, had talked about and how Ethan had died. And what the two men were going to do with the

231

artifacts. "It sounds as if this is part of a bigger organization. Could they be part of the cartel operating out of Canada?"

Anderson rubbed his face. "They might be. We'll see if Freya will give us some information."

"She admitted she hit Ethan with her walking stick. And she was planning to load the site with dynamite to get rid of the students. Maybe leverage that."

"Not to worry. She won't get away with what she's done. It's been my experience that in a group, one person always turns on the others. She might be the weak link." Anderson turned to go back to his car.

"How much longer do I have to stay here?" Mia asked the paramedic.

"We'll give it another fifteen minutes and then speak with the doctor. If she says you're good to go, then you can leave with assistance."

The medical staff discharged Mia twenty minutes later and advised her not to drive until the next day.

Luke was waiting to take her back to the B&B.

"I'd like to go to the police station," Mia said.

"I thought you'd want to. You know they won't allow you to sit in on the interview."

"I know. But I want to listen in. Surely there's a way to do that?"

"There's a room where you can watch and listen to the interviews taking place. I doubt you'll be able to listen in on all of them. Just let me touch base with my colleague."

Mia watched as he hurried back into the cottage, and then he returned shortly.

"Right, he's going to lead a thorough search of the cottage and the grounds. We're hoping we'll find something that will give us more insight into this group. I'll stay with you at the police station, and I may be called in to question Dr. Bateman or the others."

They pulled into the police station parking lot. Luke accompanied Mia inside. They stopped at the front desk, and Luke showed his credentials. "I believe DI Anderson has made arrangements for us to listen in on the interviews."

The desk sergeant stood. "Follow me."

He led Luke and Mia to a small room between two other rooms. He opened the door. "If you turn up the control, you'll be able to hear what's being said in either room. You won't be able to speak, and you must be quiet while you're in here."

"Got it. Thank you." Luke pulled a chair for Mia, and they sat.

The window in front of them showed Anderson and Dr. Bateman. There was a man sitting next to Dr. Bateman, and Mia assumed he was his lawyer.

"Ready?" Luke asked.

Mia nodded, and Luke flipped the control.

Anderson's voice came across. "Dr. Bateman, what were you doing with three duffel bags of antiquities?"

Dr. Bateman crossed his arms and didn't say a word.

"We're not talking until we have a guarantee of Dr. Bateman's freedom, and all charges dropped against him." his lawyer announced.

Anderson shook his head. "Not going to happen. We have enough information from the other three to keep you tied up for quite a while. I just thought you might want to make life easier for yourself. After all, if you provide us with details, we may be able to help you out. If you don't, well, I'm afraid you'll be going to prison for a long time."

Dr. Bateman glared at him and didn't say anything.

"Fine. I'll be back." Anderson closed his file and walked out of the room.

Luke opened the door as Anderson walked by.

"Ah, there you are. Dr. Reid, how are you?"

"I'm okay. But why isn't Dr. Bateman talking? Is he going to get out of all this?"

"Don't worry. We'll be able to send him away to prison. Freya's ready to talk, and so are the other two men that we captured. We've been letting them sit and think about what's going to happen. You'll be able to listen in on my interview with Freya. She's in the next room."

Anderson left, and Luke crossed the room and set them up to listen to Freya's interview.

"Freya Reeves. What can you tell me about why you're here?" Anderson sat across from Freya.

Freya shrugged. "I'm not sure what you mean."

Anderson opened a file and looked at it for a few moments. "It says here you arrived in Glasgow ten days ago with your husband, Malcolm. Why are you here? And please don't insult me by saying you're tourists. We have you on kidnapping Dr. Reid and assault. Likely a lot more."

Freya took a moment before answering. "We work for Dr. Bateman. Have for a few years. Malcolm met him through friends, and he had some work for us. We were supposed to pick up some artifacts and bring them to Canada."

"What about Dr. Carter?"

"What about him?"

"How did he die?"

Mia held her breath. Was Freya going to tell Anderson the same thing she'd told Mia?

Freya shifted in her seat. "That was an accident. He wasn't meant to die. Malcolm gave him too much of the drug in his whiskey. He was stumbling around the dig and then he pushed Malcolm hard enough that Malcolm fell. I hit him over the head with my walking stick. I didn't think I'd hit him that hard."

Mia let her breath out. There it was. She felt tears fall on her cheeks. At least now they knew who was responsible for Ethan's death.

Freya kept talking. "He wouldn't tell us where the treasure was. It wasn't in the tent. That's why we stayed around this area. We knew it was still here. As for kidnapping the students, that's on Bateman. I didn't want to have anything to do with it. He had those two guys from Lakeview snatch the students. And it worked. He got the treasure. I didn't know he was going to take Dr. Reid tonight. That wasn't planned."

Luke put his arm around Mia. "Are you all right?"

Mia nodded and leaned into him for a minute. "I'm good. We know who killed Ethan and who took the artifacts. What happens next?"

"We'll keep building the case. As far as Interpol is concerned, we'll make sure they're prosecuted and serve time for the thefts. My colleague from London will deal with that. I think it's pretty much a done deal."

"What about Dr. Bateman's role?"

"With statements from Freya and the other two, he'll be arrested and charged as well. It will be up to his lawyer where he goes to trial and serves his time."

Mia nodded. "I want to speak to him."

Luke raised his eyebrows. "I'll see what I can do."

Thirty minutes later, Luke escorted Mia to a holding cell. He looked at her. "You have five minutes to talk to him. You cannot touch him. Make sure of that. I don't need you up on assault charges. Do you understand?"

"Thanks. I won't need much time."

Mia stepped closer to the cell. "Dr. Bateman, I have something to say to you. I will make sure, if it's the last thing I do, that you're held accountable for your actions and the actions of the people you hired."

Dr. Bateman sneered at her. "Really? And how are you going to do that?"

"I have all the information I need. I'll be sharing it with the police here and in Canada. And there's the matter of Freya telling the police everything you did and wanted her to do. You'll rot in jail. You won't last long." Mia took a long look at him. "I don't know why you did this. Maybe greed. But you'll pay."

"Ha. I have powerful friends. They'll make sure I'm well taken care of."

Mia shook her head. "I'm done with you."

Mia walked out of the holding cell area and found Luke. "I'm ready to go back to the B&B."

"I'll take you there. And I want you to get some rest." Luke took her hand, and they left the police station.

Mia and Luke walked into the B&B. Mia was surprised to see Phil, Diana, and Mrs. MacDonald and her sister, in the sitting room.

"Where did you go?" Diana demanded. "We've been worried sick!"

Mia raised her hands. "Okay. Why don't we sit down, and I'll tell you what happened."

Luke pulled a chair out for her.

An hour later, Mia had answered all their questions.

"I think Dr. Carter would be proud of how you figured this all out," Phil said.

Mia smiled. "Thanks." She glanced at her watch; it was past midnight. "I need to get some sleep. Why don't we plan on a later start tomorrow morning? Say around nine-thirty?"

"Works for me," Diana said.

"I'll put the breakfast items out at eight instead of seven." Mrs. MacDonald rose from her chair. "Thank you for including us in your conversation. It's a relief this has been resolved."

Luke helped Mia out of her chair. "I'll escort you upstairs. After that, I have to go to the police station."

Mia opened the door to her room, and Luke followed her in. "Are you sure you're feeling well?"

"I am. I want to talk to Gran before I go to sleep."

Luke leaned forward and pulled Mia in a hug. "I want your word you'll get some rest."

"I will as soon as I talk to Gran. I'm exhausted."

Luke bent down and kissed her. "Take care, and I'll see you in the morning."

Mia toed off her shoes and dropped in the chair. Luke was certainly letting her know he cared about her. She had to figure out how she felt about him. A chat with Gran might help.

Mia hit Gran's number and waited until she answered.

"Mia, is everything all right?"

"It is now. I need to talk to you about what's happened."

"Let me get my wine. And we'll have a long chat."

Gran didn't interrupt while Mia told her of her latest adventures, and Mia appreciated that.

When Mia had finished, Gran sighed. "Mia, this dig has been a bit more than you expected, isn't it?"

"I'd say that's an understatement."

Gran cleared her throat. "I have news about Charles Gordon. It appears he's closed his business and left the country."

"What? That's not possible. I just spoke with him. He's the one who told me to shut down the dig."

"Mia, I'm telling you what I've heard. I had coffee with Fran and Tom Easly this afternoon. They're the ones who told me he'd closed everything down and that he isn't to be found. Tom said the board of directors of his company is furious. All of them made investments in his company, and apparently, he's taken the money and fled."

"Wow, Gran, that's hard to believe."

"Unfortunately, Tom knows a few people on the board, and they've been cheated out of a significant amount of money. They've contacted the police, and the RCMP's fraud department is investigating."

Mia was checking her news feed on her laptop. "Gran, I can't find anything online about this."

"The police haven't released any information, and the board isn't talking to the media. The only reason Tom told me is he knew you were working for Charles."

"This isn't good at all. Luke and Anderson need to know about this."

"And what are you going to do about Luke, dear?"

"I'm still not sure. I'd like to spend some time with him, but that may change because of these latest developments. And there's Ethan's memorial to consider as well. Once I know, I'll tell you what my plans are."

"Taking some time with Luke sounds like a good idea. I always liked him."

Mia chuckled. "Just put it out there, Gran. Don't hold back."

"He was good for you. You haven't been the same since the two of you broke up. Sometimes, revisiting an old flame is a good thing. Let your guard down again, Mia. It's time."

Mia sighed. "I'll let you know. I'd better go. It's late here. I'll talk to you soon, Gran."

Looking at the time, Mia realized she was supposed to call Alex. She sent her a text letting her know she was fine and would talk to her the next day. Alex responded with a smiley face. Mia chuckled, Alex wouldn't be happy with her when they did connect.

She still had to call Anderson and give him the latest information from Gran. But before doing that, Mia called Charles Gordon's office line and his personal cell. Both calls went unanswered, and no message option was available. *"Well, that isn't good,"* Mia mumbled to herself. She called Anderson and left a message about the latest information on Charles Gordon. Then, she slid into her pajamas, and into bed.

The next morning, Mia tried contacting Gordon's office one more time. This time, she received a notification that the number had been disconnected. She grabbed her laptop and looked for the company website. Another red flag. She couldn't find it. Gran's information appeared to be accurate.

She hurried downstairs and saw that Luke and Anderson were finishing breakfast.

"Did you get my message?" Mia asked Anderson.

"I did. I've contacted the RCMP to see what they can share with us. Someone's supposed to get in touch with me today." Anderson put his coffee cup down. "I'm going to use this when I talk to Dr. Bateman. He may decide to talk if he thinks he's going to be left holding the bag."

Mia opened her laptop and hit the bookmark with the company address. "The company's website's gone."

Luke leaned forward. "May I?" He typed a few keystrokes and then frowned. "Someone disabled the website late last night. It appears Mr. Gordon has closed shop."

"How can he do that? It's a big company."

Luke clicked his tongue. "I've seen it happen overnight. Especially with smugglers. We may have found the head of the cartel. Mr. Charles Gordon."

"Was Dr. Bateman working for him?"

Anderson shook his head. "Bateman hasn't spoken one word except to ask for a barrister. He's been in his holding cell. I'll try to get him to talk this morning."

"We'll get to the bottom of this." Luke returned the laptop to Mia. "How are you feeling this morning? Any ill effects?"

"No. I'm fine." Mia frowned. "I can't believe I was working for a smuggler. How didn't I know?"

"He worked hard to hide what he was. As for Dr. Bateman, I think his problem's greed. He saw a way to make money and jumped at it. Both Mr. Gordon and Dr. Bateman's credentials were excellent."

Mia narrowed her eyes. "I hope you can catch him."

"We'll do our best." Luke put his napkin on the table. "You'll be at the dig today?"

"Yes, we need to wrap everything up. I'll ask Angus to bring in some additional volunteers."

"Right then. I'll keep you informed about what's happening." Luke leaned over and gave her a kiss. "Hang in there. We're going to figure this out."

Chapter Twenty-Seven

As soon as the students were done with breakfast, they left for the dig. When they arrived, Mia noticed there wasn't any security left. "Ugh. Why am I not surprised? Everything will need to be moved today. Hopefully, Angus can get some additional volunteers this afternoon."

They hurried to the tent, where Mia gave them their assignments. Then Mia called Angus and explained the situation. He assured her he'd be at the dig within the hour with additional volunteers.

By two o'clock that afternoon, every item had been delivered to the historical society.

"Thanks everyone for your help. We're going to wrap things up tonight with dinner at the pub." Mia looked at all the volunteers. "You're welcome to join us."

Angus nodded, "I may do that. When do you all leave for home?"

"I fly back to the States on Saturday. I'm going to do some sight-seeing before I leave." Phil said.

Diana pipped up. "I'm heading back on Sunday."

"When are you leaving, Mia?" Angus asked.

"In a few days. Luke and I will be driving to London."

Before leaving the dig, Mia sent Shelly a text asking to speak with her.

"Hi Shelly, how are you doing?"

"Okay. I just got word that Ethan's remains have arrived. I spoke with the funeral director, and they'll be taking care of everything."

"Do you know when the memorial will take place?" Mia hated to press for an answer, but she needed to know.

"Not until a week from now." Shelly sighed. "There's still a lot to do. Thank goodness for mom and dad. Will you be able to make it?"

"I'll be there. Luke mentioned he'd like to attend. Are you all right with that?"

"Of course. I'd like to see him again."

Mia ended the call a few minutes later. With this information, she'd be able to decide on her next step.

She called Alex and updated her on what had happened in the past twenty-four hours.

"Mia! I can't believe this. Are you certain you're all right?"

"I'm fine, really I am. I got some work done today at the dig, and tomorrow, I'm going to work with the historical society to help set up the exhibit."

"And what's happening with Luke?"

"I've decided to spend some time with him here and then in London later this week and next. He's coming to Ethan's memorial service in Chicago. We'll see what happens after that. I'm not making any promises to anyone. We both want to get to know each other again. It's been a long time since we've seen each other, and we've both changed."

"That sounds like a wise decision."

They chatted a few minutes longer, and then Mia hung up to get ready for dinner with the students at the pub.

That evening at dinner, Luke and Anderson joined Mia and the students.

"I have some news for you." Anderson had the table's attention. "We've charged Freya Reeves with Dr. Carter's death. We have an alert out for her husband, Malcolm. She and the two men we captured are talking about the smuggling ring. The two men admitted to putting a tracker in your daypack in Lakeview. They were acting on Dr. Bateman's orders. And apparently, Bateman had someone working with the local police providing them with information. That's how they knew about the police coming to the cafe in Portree. The noose around Bateman's neck is tightening."

"Has he talked about anything?" Diana asked.

"Not a word. His barrister is with him and working hard to make a deal. All the information Dr. Bateman has on the smuggling ring for a lighter sentence and that he serves his time in Canada."

At the end of the evening, Luke and Mia walked back to the B&B. "Have you decided about coming to London?" Luke asked as he reached for her hand.

"I have. I'd like a couple of days to finish up here. Angus has asked if I could help with the display at the historical society museum, and then I can leave. Shelly told me Ethan's service is in a week, and I want to be there."

Luke nodded. "Did you ask if I could attend?"

"Shelly said she'd be glad to see you."

"I'll make the arrangements. We can fly from London."

"I'm looking forward to our time together in London."

"Have you decided what you're doing this fall?" Luke asked Mia as they arrived at the B&B.

Mia led the way to the sitting room. "Not yet. I know I don't want to go back to academia. I'll take some time and look at options."

Luke poured them a drink of whiskey. "Who knows what will turn up, so long as you keep an open mind." Luke touched his glass to Mia's and smiled. "Here's to the future."

The next morning, Mia drove to the hospital in Portree accompanied by Phil and Diana. Diana had packed all of Rina's belongings, and they were looking forward to chatting with her.

The doctor was just leaving Rina's room when they arrived.

"We brought your stuff." Diana put the suitcase next to the window and then hurried to Rina's bedside.

Phil stood by the door until Rina noticed him and waved him in. "Come on in, Phil. Mom, Dad, you met Dr. Reid earlier. These two are the other students that worked with me on the dig. Diana Scott and Phil Brown."

"Nice to meet you." Rina's mother smiled at them.

Phil walked over and shook their hands. "I'm sorry to meet under these circumstances."

"Rina, how are you doing?" Mia asked.

Rina grinned. "Great, I'm leaving the hospital tomorrow. Thanks for bringing my stuff. Now tell me what's been happening. The nurses have been chattering about treasure, but they don't have details."

Diana laughed. "It's been quite the ride. Mia can tell you all about it."

With some prompting, Mia explained what had happened in the last twenty-four hours.

"So, the sponsor is the head of a smuggling cartel? And Dr. Bateman was working with him? That's awful!" Rina shook her head. "But wait, what does that mean with the artifacts we found?"

"Luke has told me they've recovered the artifacts. The ring, the sgian-dubh, the gold coins, and the gemstones were found in one of the duffel bags that Dr. Bateman was going to smuggle out. Luke spoke to his supervisor at Interpol, and it was decided the historical society can display them. If they're needed as evidence, the police will collect them." Luke had given Mia the news at breakfast that morning. She hadn't told anyone else and was happy to be able to tell the three students together.

Phil grinned. "I'm so glad. Dr. Carter would be pleased."

"Yes, he would."

Rina's parents filled them in on their travel plans and offered to help Phil and Diana get to the airport. Plans were made, and shortly after that, Mia and the students left the hospital.

The drive back to the B&B was lively, with discussion on when they'd all be leaving Skye.

"Are you going to be able to change your flights again?" Mia asked.

Phil shook his head. "I can't afford to do that, but I can stay at a hostel for an extra day. I'll do some touring around. Diana, what are you doing?"

"I'm doing the same. I've checked with the hostel online, and there's room. There are a few places I want to check out. I've got to pack my things tonight."

"Yeah, same here. It'll be a quick supper at the pub. The bus to Portree leaves early in the morning."

"What are you doing, Mia?" Diana asked.

"Angus asked if I'd help with the exhibit, and tomorrow works for both of us. Later this week, I'm going to London with Luke, and then we'll be flying to Chicago for Ethan's memorial."

They pulled into the parking lot of the B&B. "The pub for dinner tonight?" Mia asked.

Phil nodded. "Let's meet at six-thirty. I need to get laundry done."

"That works for me. I want to pack my stuff and make sure I don't forget anything." Diana closed the car door.

Mia followed them in. Her phone buzzed with a text. She was expecting Luke to connect with her and was surprised to see it was a Lakeview number.

She closed her bedroom door and checked the message. It was from one of her friends who worked at the Lakeview Museum.

Jill: Hi, do you have a minute to chat?

M: Sure, what about?

Mia's phone rang immediately after she sent the text. "Mia Reid here."

"Mia, Jill Addington. How are you?"

"I'm well. What's happening with you?"

"I'm calling in my capacity as HR manager at the museum. We have a special project coming up, and I'd like to know if you'd be interested in working on it."

Mia grinned. Jill was always direct and to the point when she was talking about work.

"What's the project?"

"We have several exhibits that are coming in this fall, and we're going to need someone to manage them. We don't have enough experienced staff to lead this project."

"What kind of exhibits?"

"We have one coming in from Central America, one from Great Britain, and one from Asia. We'd need you to oversee the current staff that we have and work with our marketing team to promote the exhibits."

"I have experience in all three areas that you've mentioned. What's happened to your staff?"

"Unfortunately, we just learned two of our senior staff will be out with a long-term illness. They'll both be gone for a minimum of eight months. We're scrambling and I heard from a reliable source that Lakeview University is implementing changes to the archaeology department. I don't know whether you're interested in moving from the university, but I thought I'd reach out to you."

"I'm interested in going in a new direction. Can you provide me with more information on what exactly the position will entail and when the expected start date would be?

"I can send you the position description and all pertinent information, including the benefits and compensation package. As for a start date, we'd need you to be ready for work the first week of August. The contract will run for eight months with a possible extension."

"All right. Send me the information. When do you need an answer?"

"As soon as you can. If you can't do this, we're going to have to look at hiring a recruiting firm, and I'd rather not go that route."

"I'm in Scotland and then heading to London in a couple of days. I'll look over the information. If I have any questions, I'll contact you."

"Great. Can you provide me with your email address? I look forward to hearing from you."

"I'll text you my email. And I'll talk to you soon. Jill, thanks for thinking of me."

"Mia, you were at the top of my list. I really hope you can work with us."

They disconnected the call, and Mia sent Jill her email address. This was an unexpected turn of events and would give her something to consider. She opened her email program on her laptop and saw Jill's email.

The attachments included a position description and a complete package with salary, benefits, work schedule, and expectations from the museum.

Mia read through the documents carefully and felt her excitement grow. This was a project she could get behind. The position was a mix of curator, conservator, and educator. All work she was comfortable with. There would be some evening and weekend hours expected, but overall, she thought it would be an excellent opportunity. The salary and benefit package were both generous. She composed an email to Jill with several questions she had and then closed her laptop.

Mia went downstairs to wait for Phil and Diana. Luke sent a text.

L: dinner at the pub?

M: Yes, heading out soon with Phil and Diana.

L: see you there.

Phil and Diana clattered down the stairs.

"We're ready. All packed and good to head out in the morning," Diana said.

"I can take you to the bus stop in the morning. Just give me a time, and we'll leave from here."

"Thanks, Mia. That would be great." Phil opened the door as they headed out.

They let Mia know what they were planning for their tour in Inverness. Phil showed her a couple of sights they had marked. "Rina and her parents aren't flying out for a couple of days. They weren't able to get a flight to accommodate her that fast." Phil put his phone away.

"Are they staying in Inverness?" Mia asked.

Diana nodded. "Yes, I'll spend a bit of time with Rina. I enjoyed getting to work with her."

They found a table, and the waitress promptly brought them a pitcher of beer. Luke joined them a short time later. Dinner was lively with talk about the next few days. Phil planned to attend Ethan's memorial service before working with the CRM he'd signed on with. Diana would be off to Northern Ontario for a summer job. Mia told them about the offer from the museum. They all agreed it was a good opportunity. When they were ready to leave, Phil and Diana searched out Devon, the pub's owner, and said their goodbyes.

Mia and Luke followed them back to the B&B, walking hand in hand.

"The offer from the museum sounds like an excellent opportunity."

"It is. I'm not sure how it would impact us seeing each other, though."

"I'm capable of traveling to see you. I don't want to stand in the way of your career."

"I'd like to think we can have both a career and a relationship."

"I think spending time together is going to be exactly what we need. Mia, I'm not worried. I believe we crossed paths for a reason. Let's enjoy our time together."

They joined Phil and Diana in the sitting room.

"When do you meet Angus?" Diana asked.

"He told me to be at the museum after nine tomorrow morning. I have the address for the historical society museum, and I'll meet him there. I'm looking forward to setting up the artifacts."

They chatted a while longer and then dispersed to their rooms. Luke made plans for the two of them for dinner the next evening. "I should be done by four tomorrow. We can have dinner and plan our trip to London."

"That's good. Can you leave the next day?"

"Should be able to. I'm planning a two-day road trip. Does that work for you?"

"Perfect."

After breakfast, Mia drove Phil and Diana to the bus stop. They were looking forward to the quick trip to Portree and then going on with Rina and her parents to Inverness. Both students promised to keep in touch with Mia.

Mia arrived at the historical society's museum shortly after nine. Angus was waiting for her in the parking lot.

"Good morning, lass. How are you doing?"

"I'm well. Looking forward to setting up the displays. Do we have to build any of the cabinets?"

"No, we have plenty of cabinets and glassed-in shelves to store the items. We've been fortunate to rotate our exhibits with other museums in Scotland. We've had a lot of interest in what was found at the dig. I think we'll have a tremendous amount of people coming through our doors."

"Oh, I'm glad to hear that." Mia grinned. "Are you going to include the information on Bonnie Prince Charlie?"

"Yes. I know we can't prove the artifacts were his, but it seems logical that they were." Angus unlocked the door and turned on lights as he walked through the entrance. "Here we are."

Mia glanced around. They were in a large room with windows overlooking the road. The walls had several large glass-fronted cabinets. There were six columns of different heights with museum display cubes on top. And there were tables with display cases on top of them. The wall closest to the door had boxes stacked up. Mia recognized them from their dig. "Is this where the artifacts are going to be displayed?"

"Aye. We've been working on the signage for the displays as well." Angus crossed the room to a desk. "I'd like you to look at the signage before we set it all up." He opened the middle drawer and pulled out a manila envelope. Mia reached for the envelope and saw that it contained labels with information on the various artifacts. She tipped the envelope, and the labels fell on the desk.

"These look great. I'll check them for accuracy as we install the exhibits." Mia examined a few of the labels and noted they conformed to museum quality labels. Information on the item, where it was found, and the approximate date of the object. She tucked them back in the envelope and left it on the desk.

"Should we get started?"

"Let's start with these boxes. They have the artifacts we believe are Bonnie Prince Charlie's." Angus opened one of the boxes, and Mia saw the artifacts.

"I didn't realize the police had already handed them over to you."

"That was Dr. Forbes's doing. He spoke up for our museum yesterday, and everyone agreed. We may have to return them to the police later, but for now, we can display them."

"Where are we going to put them? On the columns or in the cabinets?"

"We'll use the cabinets. That way, everyone can see them."

Mia walked to the cabinets. They were lined with a dark cloth and had forms that would hold the artifacts to display them well. The glass fronted doors were heavy to open and when she opened one, the lights went on in the cabinet. "Do the lights in the cabinet only come on when the door's opened?" she asked.

"No, they're on a timer and will be on the entire time the museum's opened. Once we finish setting up the display, the cabinet alarm system will be armed. It goes directly to the local police station and our insurance company."

"Is it armed manually?"

"It can be. Let me show you." Angus walked to the back of the room, where there was a concealed panel. He unlocked it with a passcode and then the panel opened, revealing the alarm system. "I just need to key in the passcode a second time, and the system is armed."

"That's a good system. Who has the passcode?"

"Myself and two other people with the society. And we change it frequently."

Mia and Angus worked together to set up the artifacts in the cabinets. The sgian-dubh and the ring held a place of honor in the middle cabinet. Lights gleamed on the metal and the gemstones in the handle of the sgian-dubh shone brightly. The ruby in the ring sparkled.

Mia found the labels with the information on the artifacts and placed them carefully where people could read them and learn about them. Mia was touched to see Ethan's name on the label, giving him credit for the find.

They showcased the gemstones and gold coins in a different cabinet. Angus turned on the lights in the cabinet, and the gemstones sparkled. The gold coins seemed dull in comparison, but up close, they were impressive. Mia made sure both sides of the coins could be seen clearly.

They worked steadily through the morning. Angus had brought lunch, and they stopped to eat the meal.

"When are you going back?" Angus asked.

"Tomorrow." Mia told him of her plans and the new position that had been offered.

"The new position sounds like it would be a good match for you."

"I could make it work. It's an eight-month contract, and it might be extended."

They spent the rest of the afternoon setting up the exhibit. By the end of the day, most of the artifacts were displayed.

"Well, thank you for your help, Dr. Reid. It's been a pleasure working with you." Angus shook Mia's hand as they wrapped up their day.

"I've enjoyed myself today. Thanks for giving me this opportunity. I hope the display has many visitors come through." Mia was pleased with the day's work. Installing the exhibits had been fun and bittersweet. She couldn't help but think of Ethan when the ring and the sgian-dubh took their place in the center of the display.

Mia arrived at the B&B shortly before four. Luke wasn't back yet, and that gave her time to think about the job offer at the museum. Jill had responded to her email and clarified the points Mia had questions about. She read through the documents once more. Everything appeared to be in order. The position was something that would stretch her a bit and would give her experience in areas that she didn't have. There was flexibility in the daily tasks, and that appealed to her. And she wouldn't have to start work until the beginning of August.

After reviewing the contract once again, she electronically signed off on it. Her work life was in control.

She closed her laptop and freshened her hair and makeup to get ready for dinner with Luke.

The drive to Portree was quick. At the restaurant, Luke asked for their finest bottle of red wine.

"A toast to your new future," Luke said as he raised his glass to Mia.

"Thank you. I hope to have you in my future as well."

"We'll make it work. We'll start tomorrow with our drive to London."

Mia smiled. She was looking forward to a future with a new job and Luke a part of it.

A Note from the Author

I'm not an archaeologist, but I've had a keen interest in archaeology ever since reading Agatha Christie's *Murder in Mesopotamia.*

As a believer in lifelong learning, I've taken several archaeology and antiquity smuggling/trafficking courses throughout the years.

There are countless resources online that provide reputable information on archaeology and archaeological digs.

Some resources I've used include:

- Ontario Archaeology Society
- The Archaeology Channel, YouTube
- Archaeology at George Washington's Farm, YouTube
- AIA Archaeology Hour
- Future Learn
- Open Learning

This is a work of fiction, and I have changed some location names in the manuscript.

Any errors or omissions are mine.

—Rose Kerr

Acknowledgements

There are several people I'd like to thank for their help.

My beta readers, Patricia Middleton and Diane Shore, provided me with invaluable feedback. Their keen eyes helped clean up the manuscript.

Olivia Foran answered my many questions about what life at an archaeology dig is like.

Kaitlin McCaw's photos and coffee chats about her visits to Scotland provided inspiration for the location.

Rachel Epstein's photos helped me see a different side of the Isle of Skye. Breathtaking.

My late agent, Dawn Dowdle. She was so excited about this book. Every one of us who worked with you misses you and your positive outlook.

To the team at Level Best Books: Shawn Reilly Simmons, Verena Rose, and Deb Well, thank you for all you do for us as authors. It's a pleasure working with you!

To my family, who've supported me throughout this journey, thanks doesn't seem quite enough! I appreciate you so much!

About the Author

Rose Kerr grew up reading Trixie Belden, Nancy Drew, Hardy Boys, and Agatha Christie. These books sparked her interest in mysteries.

Rose's work in distance education led her to take creative writing courses, where she discovered her passion for writing mysteries featuring strong, smart women protagonists.

Rose and her husband recently moved to Southern Ontario. When she isn't writing, Rose and her husband enjoy exploring the new region.

Rose is a member of Sisters in Crime and the Guppy Chapter of SinC.

Rose is most active on Facebook, Instagram, and Pinterest.

SOCIAL MEDIA HANDLES:

Facebook page: https://www.facebook.com/RoseKerrAuthor
Instagram: https://www.instagram.com/r.m.kerr/
Pinterest: https://www.pinterest.ca/RoseKerrauthor/
Goodreads: https://www.goodreads.com/rosekerr

AUTHOR WEBSITE:

www.rosekerr.com

Also by Rose Kerr

The Secret Ingredient: The Mystery Writers' Cookbook

Death on the Set, A Brenna Flynn Mystery

www.ingramcontent.com/pod-product-compliance
Lightning Source LLC
Chambersburg PA
CBHW020614110726
47899CB00002B/505